ATOMIC REX

BALLAD OF BRAVURA

BY: MATTHEW DENNION AND ANDRES PEREZ

COVER ART BY ALAN OW BARNES

SEVERED PRESS

ATOMIC REX: BALLAD OF BRAVURA

WWW.SEVEREDPRESS.COM

ISBN: 978-1-922861-16-0

This novel is dedicated to Christ Martinez. Your friendship made this story possible. We hope as you look down on us you enjoy this story as much as we enjoyed all the tales you created.

PROLOGUE

30 Years Ago

Thunderous booms echoed across the midnight sky as bright flashes of light illuminated the land. However, these were not the products of a lightning storm, but those of war, a war on a remote island currently invaded by man and machines. One year prior, a long-lost island was discovered somewhere in the middle of the Pacific Ocean between the western and eastern hemispheres, a microcontinent thought to have been the remnants of a lost world that may have inspired the legend of Mu.

In the ensuing months, foreign countries struggled to lay claim to the untold riches the new island may hold. They had hoped that such natural resources could give them an edge over the global economy. With so many political factions arriving on one destination, each under the public guise of a scientific expedition, war was bound to break out. Little did humanity know, what lay within this hidden Garden of Eden was a hellscape for anyone foolish enough to enter. Massive fauna from numerous bygone eras thrived on the lost continent. If the nations of the world were to seize their grip over the island, they would have to innovate and innovate they did. Each country began research on experimental twenty-meter-tall exosuits for their soldiers to brave the same harsh conditions of the island as their international rivals.

Initially, the United States started development on experimental man-piloted humanoid machines called Colossi to aid them in battle. After several successful attempts at capturing and reengineering these technical marvels, countries over the world began developing their own Colossi, resulting in a robotic arms race. Wave after wave of these mechanical warriors entered the prehistoric landscape, and Armageddon came to the natives and wildlife of the lost island. On this day, the US unleashed their latest Colossus model after numerous trials and errors, the Atlus. A small squad of ten made landfall on the isle and had already successfully slaughtered a pack of gargantuan animals that attempted to hunt them. At a record twenty-five meters tall, their machines, clad in black and white armor, proved more than a match for whatever wildlife the jungles could throw at them. These metal combat weapons were far stronger and faster than the pilots' previous units. They were lean, lightly armored save for their shoulders, chest, forearms, and shins. Their faces were adorned with a black helmet and a cyan visor that gave each pilot a wide view of the area. Leading the team were Captain Garcia and her lieutenant.

"Captain," the lieutenant called out as he executed the killing shot on a sharp-toothed theropod-like creature with his machine's giant rifle.

"I told you to remember the new codenames, Bravura," sounded Garcia as her voice came through on his cockpit's speakers.

"Apologies, uh, Alpha One. These things, they're a lot bigger than the reports said they'd be. Not only that, I'm picking up large quantities of radiation coming from them on my scanners."

"That's to be expected," the commanding officer explained in an assured manner. "Just last week a nuke was dropped on the island and wiped out a whole battalion of enemy soldiers. These animals are the result of the nuclear fallout."

"Nuclear fallout?" exclaimed the second-in-command, sweat dripping from his forehead. "Why weren't we alerted to this?"

"Calm yourself!" ordered Garcia. "I was told in advance but didn't tell our men to avoid panicking them any more than they already are. Besides, our new Atluses are more than capable of taking down anything this island can dish out and they can withstand any of the residual radiation. Now, keep this between us and tell our men to move out!"

"Ma'am! Yes, Ma'am!"

With that, the lieutenant ordered his men to follow Garcia's lead as they trekked through the jungles, encountering enemy mechs the deeper they went. Their enemies had unveiled a brand-new model of Colossus they had never seen before, more heavily armored than the last version and equipped with miniguns in their forearms. Due to the unfamiliarity he had with these weapons, the pilot had no means of identifying their country of origin, but their red coloring narrowed down the field of potential suspects.

"Men, split into groups of five. Bravura, you take the left flank. The rest of you, follow me."

"Ma'am. Yes, Ma'am!" all nine of them said in unison.

The lieutenant had his men maneuver through the terrain, utilizing the jungle's massive trees for cover.

"You three, stay here and cover us. Shadow Strike, with me. We're gonna test these babies out."

As he issued his orders, he placed his rifle on his mech's back holster and removed one of two identical devices attached to his Atlus's right forearm. It was a cylindrical device that when gripped in the center, extended outwards to form a lightweight metal staff. At that moment, each soldier activated a shield that folded out from their machine's left forearm module.

Immediately, their team sprang into action as the lieutenant and his partner snaked their way through the crossfire, moving steadily closer to their targets. For all the armor their opponents carried, they could not keep up with the Atluses' superior speed and agility. Mobility was further increased by the placement of rocket thrusters on their legs and backpacks for quick bursts of speed in any direction. As the acting leader got closer to the target, he began to use his shield to take the brunt of the damage as it folded out of the mech's left forearm. Thankfully, his arm-mounted shield held up as it displayed the name "Bravura," the very codename bestowed upon his machine by Captain Garcia from his successful performances in both the simulations and prior missions.

"Now!" With a push of a button, each end of Bravura and Shadow Strike's staffs crackled with electricity. Both soldiers wedged their weapons in between the visible joints of their foes, disabling their mech's limbs upon contact. A few well-timed swings to the chest and head were all that was needed to bring three of them down. Of the remaining three enemies, only one approached the two of them as the others fell back to start firing at the rest of the lieutenant's men. This unit was uniquely adorned with black and red-colored armor and carried an iron blade stored on its hip armor. Its bulky frame was adorned with shoulders built like massive pillars that carried odd rotating attachments with three harpoon spears each. In its hand was a massive laser rifle.

No doubt this was the squad's leader, Bravura's pilot thought; the machine's appearance set off major alarms in his head. During his Atlus training, he had heard rumors of a certain enemy soldier who was said to pilot a red mech. Official reports on this mysterious foe were few and far between as none had ever encountered him and lived to tell the tale. The only reason anyone knew of his existence was due to the captured enemies who left cryptic warnings detailing their ally's horrendous reputation. Could this pilot be him, the so-called "Red Menace?"

Without warning, his subordinate launched his mech at the enemy.

"You're going down!" he said with an arrogant attitude.

"Shadow Strike, wait!"

However, it was too late, the rookie pilot ran toward his foe like a loose cannon. Shadow Strike swung its staff towards the enemy, only for the crimson mech to have countered the attack with reflexes that belied its hulking appearance. As it gripped the part of the weapon that was not surging with energy, the enemy unit's emerald green visor stared into the face of the struggling Atlus.

The lieutenant's ally abandoned his weapon and attempted to back away when suddenly, three spiked protrusions shot out from the crimson machine's left shoulder and punctured his Atlus's torso and leg, preventing him from escaping. The second-in-command immediately moved in to rescue his teammate. However, before he could intervene, their foe drew in his prey by retracting the cables before unloading round after round into the cockpit, located within the mech's chest, at point blank range. All the lieutenant could hear were the man's screams over the radio until there was nothing but silence as the machine exploded.

Frustrated over his inability to keep his teammate safe, he decided then and there to finish the job his fallen brother in arms had started. He could hear laughing over his radio. It was coming from the enemy, who allowed communications to be shared between the two of them.

"Foolish American," chuckled what sounded like a young man with a thick Eastern European accent.

The black and red mech walked out of the smoke billowing from his fallen victim. The machine dropped its gun in an arrogant fashion and pulled from its hip a massive blade shaped like a hunting knife. The squad leader kept his eyes fixed on his enemy as he considered if the mysterious pilot was toying with him. Whoever this pilot was, he was more than ready for hand-to-hand combat. The lieutenant screamed as he clashed with his rival. Both combatants were seemingly of equal skill. Despite the machine's excess bulk, the pilot knew how to use its size and strength. Any attack the lieutenant threw, his opponent blocked. With every swipe of his adversary's weapon, the young leader dodged. In seconds, Bravura widened the gap between them and proceeded to take out his rifle, firing multiple shots at his enemy.

"All units, come in. I've initiated combat with their leader. Shadow Strike is down. I need backup!"

"Coward," he heard once more from the blood-red unit. He swore he was mocking him.

"All units, to Bravura," ordered Captain Garcia on the radio.

"Ma'am! Yes, Ma'am," responded the seven remaining lower-ranked soldiers.

As the lieutenant regrouped with his men, bullets, missiles, and bombs rained down from both sides of the conflict. The jungle quickly turned into a massive inferno of fire and brimstone. As the wildfire expanded, hundreds of small to mid-range animals ran for their lives. Some were crushed under the metal feet of the titanic soldiers, while others were caught in the crossfires.

"Bravura, where's the leader?" the captain asked as she covered him behind a stone hill.

Scanning the area, the young man found the black and red target in the distance.

"He's about a hundred meters away."

"Good. Since you got a lock on him, you have the go-ahead to use the Eagle Eye. I'll cover you."

"B-but, Captain-"

"It's Alpha One, dammit!" his superior interrupted.

"Alpha One, are you sure? What if news of the tech gets leaked?"

"Trust me, it won't. Now go get 'im."

With no other choice, the pilot grabbed two levers from his control console and slid them toward him. This activated a special mechanism made just for the Atlus model, the Eagle Eye. The cyan visor shut off for a brief second before both halves of the mech's helmet slid down over its entire face, combining into the semblance of a mask. Two individual burning red eyes sparked to life within the robot's new visage. Within the cockpit, a helmet lowered down and fit over the man's head. His vision was now limited to these new pairs of eyes that allowed him to zero in on a single target at the cost of a limited range of vision.

The lieutenant moved Bravura in for the kill as he ran across the battlefield. Mechs attacked his blind spots as they flanked towards his right and left, only to be shot in the head by Captain Garcia's massive sniper rifle. A few seconds later and the Atlus was closing in on his target. The leader's machine immediately noticed and began firing on his enemy. Bravura's enhanced vision picked up on the incoming projectiles, flashing warnings within milliseconds of their firing. Its pilot responded as he manipulated his mech to duck and weave around the spray of bullets with almost superhuman precision. At last, he was within striking distance of the crimson foe. He swung his staff harder and faster than ever before. Bravura destroyed his rival's right arm, causing the pieces of the decimated limb to scatter across the field.

"Nice toy," grunted the mysterious pilot as he pulled out his massive knife once more. "But you'll fall like all the rest!"

The two soldiers resumed their battle once again, weapons clashing amidst a bombardment of explosions and missiles firing all around them. The lieutenant could see that the pilot of the red machine was unfazed by his missing limb. Even with his mech's trump card, his foe still kept in tune with his own moves. Slowly, as the conflict raged on, he began to notice his enemy having a harder time blocking his quickening moves. Exhaustion was finally getting the best of him. Yet, at the same time, so too was the lieutenant succumbing to his own limitations. The Eagle Eye took a lot of endurance to maintain. The human body could only process so much information at a time and act upon it. This was why he was given access to the mechanism, for he had managed to last the longest in the simulations.

Ever since his early youth, the pilot was unusually adept at hand-to-hand combat. Whether it was the high school wrestling team, amateur boxing leagues, or the military's krav maga, the lieutenant was always a dominant competitor. When the time came to test out the latest Colossus model, his extraordinary physical and mental acuity allowed him to wield the machine's strength to its fullest capacity. It was through these trials that he and his mech received the moniker of "Bravura."

Just then, the very ground they stood on shook vigorously. The soil began to split between the two warring soldiers and before long, the two were separated by a widening fracture in the Earth. The lieutenant noticed warning signs flashing before his eyes.

"Alpha One, what's going on?" asked the alarmed soldier. "Radiation levels are through the roof! It's way past what our armaments can protect us from!"

"I-I don't know," replied Captain Garcia. "Tell everyone to pull back and regroup-"

Before the captain could reply, an explosive wave of atomic energy burst from the ground, sending all of the combatants tumbling in multiple directions. Bravura was thrown back hundreds of yards as the pilot inside rocked about in his cramped cockpit. The screams of his squad blared through his speakers while he felt his mech tumble into the ground. As the mech was pushed along by the mysterious blast, it was thrashed along the trees and boulders like a rag doll.

When the soldier regained consciousness, he proceeded to check his condition. He was bleeding over the left side of his face and could not see out of his left eye. What he could see out of his right eye was his cockpit and portions of his mech damaged. He called out to his superior.

"Alpha One, are you there?" He was met with no reply. "Captain?"

He proceeded to call out to his other squadmates, only to receive nothing but radio silence. His mind started racing. Just then, he received a barely audible reply obscured in static.

"H-here..." It was the captain's voice. She sounded as if every word she uttered was pain-inducing. "I-I'm 500 feet south of you."

The soldier checked his radar, only to find no signal coming from that location. Her Atlus must be on the fritz, he thought. He struggled to get his barely functioning weapon to stand. Once he found that his robot was stable, he rushed over in search of her, only to find her unit among the wreckage of several destroyed mechs, both enemies and allies. At last, he found Garcia's unit, missing the bottom half of its body and with a bladed weapon shoved into its cockpit.

"Captain!" the trooper cried out. He heard a faint chuckle from his superior.

"Heh, I-I thought I told you..." Garcia attempted to speak.

"Save your strength! Help will come soon. Just hold on!" the soldier said in a panic.

"It's alright." The superior coughed, sounding as if she was spitting up blood. "Just do something for me, will ya?"

"What is it?"

"Never stop fighting." Garcia gasped for air before coughing one last time. She was struggling to breathe. A few moments later, she was silent.

"Captain?" He received nothing but silence on the other end. "Captain!" the soldier cried out, but he knew what had already happened. Tears poured from his eyes as he mourned for his comrade.

Just as he thought of calling out for his team or any other survivors, an ear-shattering sound blasted across the entire land. It was guttural, uncannily like it was from a living being. The soldier scrambled to reactivate Bravura's normal vision. Once he managed to get his mech working, he caught a glimpse of a creature larger than anything he had ever seen. The being towered over the largest of Colossi. It was a reptile-like beast resembling the theropods he had encountered earlier, only mutated into the stuff of nightmares. As it arose from its resting spot deep within what must have been the inner catacombs of the island, the creature bellowed in defiance at all those that disturbed its slumber.

Its body illuminated a light blue glow with the remnants of the Atomic Wave it emitted mere moments ago. The beast surveyed the landscape, bearing witness to a smoldering land that once was the jungle that housed most life on the island. Scattered about were bizarre metal objects it was unfamiliar with. Though one, in particular, stood tall. It was Bravura.

The trooper grabbed his captain's rifle and fired multiple rounds at the monstrosity that killed his men until he finally ran out of ammunition. The bullets had zero effect on the still leviathan. It grew tired, having lost most of its energy from its previous attack. It roared one last time with a reverberation that caused an ear-splitting headache for the scarred pilot. He could do nothing to avenge his fallen friends. All he could do was watch as the beast took back his land from the foolish humans who thought they could covet it.

CHAPTER 1

The Settlement, California
Present Day

Emily McDuffy was fast asleep in the arms of her husband, Sean, when she was suddenly awakened by a loud *baaing* sound coming in through her window. She sighed as Sean woke up as well.

The burly farmer smiled at his wife. "That freaking sheep is getting to be pretty darn spoiled. It's like he expects us to have breakfast in bed ready for him first thing every morning."

Emily yawned. "Ramrod has just become conditioned to having his food taken to him. As annoying as it is to have him call and wake up the entire settlement at the crack of dawn every day, it's a good thing. Him calling out means he's learning to *baa* when he wants food as opposed to wandering off to find it somewhere else."

Sean climbed out of bed. "Well, it's your day to feed him. I've got the fun job of mucking out all of the cow manure and then fertilizing the cornfields with it."

Emily kissed her husband. "Crap job, just take a quick dip in the stream before coming home and put on different clothes." She gave him a sly smile. "Once you're nice and clean, I'll be sure to reward my strong farmer for a hard day's work."

Sean grinned from ear to ear. "I like the sound of that." He started getting dressed. "Do you want me to help you load the cart for old Rammy before I head out?"

"No, that's okay. My dad's coming over today with Steel Samurai 2.0. We're going to load up the mech's cargo bay with Ramrod's food and then I'm going to be his co-pilot as we fly his majesty's breakfast out to him."

"A little daddy-daughter bonding time?"

Emily smiled. "Yes, but it's also a functional trip. When Ramrod saved us from those giant rats last year, it finally convinced my dad that keeping the mutant near the settlement and feeding him was a way to provide some protection for us. Though he still thinks Steel Samurai 2.0

9

should play a role in the protection of the settlement and he's right. He also thinks that other people besides just him and my mom should learn to pilot it. So, after I get a few lessons in, you and my brother Kyle are going to join in the rotation as well.'"

Sean smiled and nodded as he looked at his wife.

Emily laughed. "What's so funny?"

"It's just seeing you and your dad compromise. Him helping out with Ramrod and you learning how to fly Steel Samurai 2.0. It's nice to see daddy and daughter working together. All it took was you two learning to listen to each other."

Emily kicked her husband in the rear. "Alright, get out of here with your homespun country wisdom."

The smitten husband grabbed his wife and passionately kissed her. When he pulled his lips away from Emily, he looked into her eyes. "If it's that homespun country wisdom that got you to fall in love with me, I'll be spinning it all day." He shrugged. "Helps to take my mind off the smell when loading several tons of cow manure."

"Well, that ass of steel you have didn't hurt either." Emily reached down and rubbed her foot. "Part of my training with my dad today will involve taking the mech into the ocean. Dad's going to show me how to open the bay doors to take in water and capture fish. He said the cooks can clean the fish right in the bay and then we'll drop their remains over the wheat fields tomorrow to act as fertilizer."

Sean laughed. "So, when it's your day to scoop manure, you get to dodge it by just flying a mech over the field and dropping pre-cut fish guts over it?"

"Yeah. It's one of the perks of having a father who owns the world's only remaining mech."

Sean shook his head. "Only mech that we know of. I reckon if there's another mech out there, I'm gonna find it to help make my chores easier."

"There haven't been any new mechs made since years before my parents even met and the remains of the mechs that were still around were used to upgrade Steel Samurai to his current 2.0 version. I think Dad said there might be part of one left at the bottom of Lake Michigan, if you feel like going for a swim."

Sean pulled his wife in closer to him. "Lake Michigan. Still pretty devoid of people around there, right? How long has it been since your parents flew us to Japan for our honeymoon? I remember you and I havin' some fun in a few lakes over there."

Emily grinned. "Yes, because we knew that there were no kaiju or mutants left in Japan. The Great Lakes still have hungry mutant fish and flocks of giant seagulls looking to snatch up anything they can. I don't know how much fun we'd have there."

Another loud *baa* echoed across the sky as Ramrod continued to request his morning meal.

Sean shook his head. "When we do have kids, we'll already be used to havin' to wake up early for mornin' feedings, thanks to Ol' Horn Head."

Emily gave her husband a quick kiss on the cheek. "Remember, it was Ol' Horn Head that brought us together in the first place when we had to work together to stop him from running through the settlement, back when we were teenagers."

"I know, I know. And he saved our lives too. I haven't forgotten. It's just that if we're going to have kids, it would be nice if he could give us a little time in the mornin' to ourselves."

"Well on the bright side, we should have a little more time to ourselves tomorrow since using the mech to drop fish fertilizer will only take a few minutes as opposed to using a horse and carriage to move manure all day."

Sean shook his head. "Keep rubbing it in that you get the easy job, why doncha."

"Well, I'm going to use some of that extra time to meet with Kyle and the electricians to see how well the windmill construction and installation is coming along. If everything goes according to plan, we'll have more electricity for the settlement. If you'd rather do that, I can move some of the…"

Sean cut his wife off. "Nope. Stop right there. I'd rather move crap all day than set up all the stuff for the settlement like you do."

The handsome farmer turned and was walking out of the room when Emily fixed her eyes on her husband's backside again as Ramrod continued to request his breakfast. The young wife and community leader grabbed her husband's belt and pulled him back toward her. "I shouldn't have taken another look at your ass before you walked out."

She kissed him and pulled him on top of her as she fell back into their bed. "Ramrod is a giant mutant sheep, not a baby. We don't have to go running the minute he calls."

The young couple started kissing each other and taking their clothes off when there was a knock on the door, followed by Chris Myers's voice. "Emily, sweetheart. I heard Ramrod *baaing*. So, I got dressed and ran over as quickly as I could. Are you ready to go? He sounds hungry."

Emily sighed. "Of course, my dad's here to do exactly what I asked him to do first thing in the morning." She looked her husband in the eye. "My dad can wait a little bit too, right?"

Sean stood up. "Nope. Standing up to Atomic Rex is one thing, but making your dad wait so we can have sex? No thanks. I'm off to work. I'll see you tonight after I'm all showered up."

Emily watched as her husband walked to the front door and greeted her father. She was genuinely happy to see her father smiling at Sean. The young woman knew that at first, her father felt Sean was not good enough for her. Thankfully, as he aged, Chris Myers continued to grow and become more aware of his own faults.

Once he realized he had set a standard in his head that no man could reach, Chris re-evaluated his criteria for what he considered a suitable match for his daughter. Once he realized that Sean was a caring person, a skilled farmer, a hard worker, and most of all really loved Emily, the hardened mech pilot happily accepted Sean as a member of his family.

After a few pleasantries, Sean and Chris shook hands.

As Sean exited the house, Emily's father walked over to her. "Morning, Emily." Chris had a strange grin on his face.

"Dad, what are you smiling like that for? You look like a giddy kid or something."

Chris shrugged. "It's just when I was younger, one of the scariest and exciting things a parent got to do with his son or daughter was to teach them to drive a car. It's kinda like a rite of passage thing for kids and parents. Cars aren't a thing anymore, so no one gets to do that. But in a world where cars don't exist, I get to at least teach my daughter to fly a giant mech."

He smiled. "It's just I'm excited. I mean you and your mom work on the stuff for the settlement together, but this is something I can do with you." Chris shrugged again as the grin stuck to his face continued to grow. "I know how corny it sounds, but I'm just glad I get to spend time with you passing on a skill. It just feels right for me as a dad, even though you're a full-grown adult."

Emily hugged her dad. "It's fun for me too, Dad. Every little girl sees their dad as a hero growing up. But my dad actually is a hero, and now he's going to show me how to be one too. Now come on, show me how to fly that old girl outside."

Chris and Emily walked out of the house to see the majestic form of Steel Samurai 2.0 standing before them. The samurai-themed mech still had the majority of its original gray color scheme with splashes of gold and red on the arms and legs. These were the result of parts salvaged from other mechs over the years that were used to repair the machine.

As Chris looked up at the mech, he felt a kinship with it. For more than thirty years, he and Steel Samurai had fought as one against creatures of unimaginable power. The metallic warrior had brought him to his wife and helped him start his family.

Chris's smile changed from one of excitement to pride as he looked upon the robot that helped give humanity a fighting chance at survival.

Emily could see her dad's right hand shaking. She reached over and grabbed it.

Chris turned his head toward his daughter. "Sorry, honey, it's just…"

"I know, Dad. I still get chills when I see her first thing in the morning too." She smiled. "I can only imagine what it's like to actually take her up."

"It's time for you to stop imagining and start learning. Climb on up there and we'll get this old girl into the air and under the water."

After scaling the ladder up the back of the robot, Chris and Emily settled into the pilot and co-pilot seats. Emily had seen her mother work from the co-pilot's seat enough times to know exactly what to do when preparing the mech for takeoff.

Chris silently watched his daughter as he beamed with pride over how well she was doing.

Emily looked to her dad. "Did I miss anything?"

He laughed. "Only to check your rearview." Emily gave her dad a confused look that he quickly waved off. "Never mind, car joke. You did great. It's time to take this old lady into the sky."

Emily felt a tinge of excitement as the colossus lifted into the air. She was grinning from ear to ear as she looked over at her father. "I think I get what you said about a parent teaching their kid how to drive. This is really cool, Dad. I mean, I know you use Steel Samurai 2.0 to fight monsters and stuff, but we're flying! We're the only people on the planet who can do that."

"It's about time for you to fly on your own now. I'm going to let go of my controls and she'll be in your hands. Are you ready?"

Emily nodded and grabbed the controls. She steadied the mech without any further instruction from her father. As she flew the majestic machine through the sky, a sense of power and freedom the young woman had never known coursed through her mind.

She shook her head. "Dad, I've been in the mech dozens of times when you've flown it, but to control it myself, it's...it's...it's just a feeling I can't explain."

Chris smiled. "I know, sweetheart. You're literally on top of the world and there are no words that can do the feeling you have justice." He tapped the interior of the mech. "She's a weapon we use to protect the people we love and those under our care. But she's also an escape. Like when we took you and Sean to Japan. With all that you do with your mom to help run the settlement, with all that Sean does to feed everyone, you guys are going to need some time to yourselves, and since you've helped teach Ramrod to protect the settlement, as long as nothing big is near us, you can use this old girl as your escape."

"Even more than that, we can see the world! If there are no kaiju or giant mutants sighted, we can expand past the sweep zone you cover. We can explore the rest of the planet. We can search for other survivors, other human settlements."

Chris smiled. "That's why you're so much smarter than me. You can see things beyond just protection, battle, and escape. You can see the world for the good things it might still be able to offer. It's not cliche to say this world will soon be yours, Sean's, and Kyle's. The people of the settlement already look to you three as leaders. Once you master operating the mech it will be one more thing they look to you for."

"Dad, I'm not smarter than you. We just see things differently."

"Okay then, let my escapist mind show you something different then." He took the controls back and flew Steel Samurai 2.0 over the Pacific Ocean.

Once they were several miles over the water, the more experienced mech pilot gave the novice instructions. "I'm going to lower us into the water. As we're going down, you need to open the external bay doors. That will let water in and help the mech stay close to the ocean floor. We only want the bays about half full for now. Once we are at the bottom of the ocean, I'll let you get some work moving Steel Samurai 2.0 underwater. She functions the same way she does on land, just obviously a little slower because we're underwater. After you move around a bit, we'll settle in on a spot so some fish will come near us. Once fish large enough to serve as food swim by, you can open the bay doors again to take in a bit more water and the fish."

Chris executed the plan just as he had described. As the mech was being lowered into the water, Emily was amazed at the beauty of the ocean as the sunlight danced through it. She watched in awe as a large manta ray swam past the mech's eye ports.

"Dad, it's amazing down here. It's so beautiful. It's like looking at another world, and it's so peaceful. I can see why you and mom spend so much time down here, to take in this incredible scenery."

"Yeah, that's exactly what your mom and I do when we're down here."

Emily shook her head. "Just stop right there, Dad. Don't ruin this for me. I'm going to keep the idea in my head that you and mom only look at the scenery down here."

Chris laughed. "Okay, that's probably a good idea." He gestured towards the controls. "Why don't you move us around a little bit. If it's the scenery you want there are a couple of old shipwrecks down here that are amazing to look at." He gestured to the sonar display between them. "See that object pinging there? That's one of the wrecks. There's always a ton of fish swimming around it. Why don't you take us there and we can settle down until we attract some schools worth catching?"

Emily gently grabbed the controls to the mech and started moving in the direction of the sunken ship. As she moved through the water, her father instructed her on matters such as moving with the current when possible, avoiding large beds of seaweed, and stepping over debris.

They had almost reached the wreckage when a second large target appeared on the sonar. When Emily noticed it was moving closer toward them, she turned to her father. "What is that thing?"

"It's either a whale, a mutant, or an undiscovered kaiju." He took his daughter's hand. "Part of piloting Steel Samurai 2.0 is knowing how to investigate something like this. You're going to take us to whatever that is, then we'll determine its threat level, and how to approach it. Don't worry, honey. I'm right here with you. We can do this."

Emily tightened her grip on the controls. "Alright, if I'm really going to learn to operate this thing, checking on monsters is going to be a part of the job. Let's do this." She then guided the robot towards the possible threat.

CHAPTER 2

The Ruins of Guadalajara

Guadalajara, once one of the largest metropolitan cities in Mexico, is now reduced to a land devoid of human life, a deserted wasteland where beasts run rampant. Among the various wildlife that survived the nuclear hellscape, brought on by the advent of the True Kaiju and mutants, the canines fared better than any other animal, having already adjusted to a life suppressed by mankind. With their former masters and oppressors gone, the city was theirs for the taking.

However, it was only a matter of time before their distant relatives entered the fray. Several years into their reign, the coyotes had not only invaded the dogs' territory through sheer brute force but had developed a stronghold around the largest sources of food from the pre-apocalypse days. As these mammals thrived, their exposure to radioactivity increased their size, as it did with all the dominant life forms over the past three decades.

However, their mutation did not end there as one more species found a means of survival, the mites. As the canines increased in size and population, so too did their parasites. Their mutual growth led to cases of mange more severe and out of control than before. The smaller animals, such as the previously domesticated dogs, kept themselves far away from the coyotes so as to avoid contracting the vicious arachnids. Despite having their skin feasted on by these unkillable creatures, this newfound isolation did allow the largest of the hounds access to what few sources of nourishment existed within the desolate metropolis.

Currently, one family of mutant coyotes, each the size of a grizzly bear, laid claim to a supermarket the week prior. Within the last surviving superstore, beyond the rotten meat, spoiled liquids, and other expired products laid a hidden treasure, canned food. With their enhanced senses, the coyotes tracked down the untainted sustenance that remained long neglected by the outside world as it was buried by layers of dilapidated rubble and concrete. Over the last several days they dug their way through the mall that held the superstore within its concrete walls. They tore down each layer of the shopping center as quickly as their two-meter-long mange-ridden bodies could. At last, this was the day when they finally enjoyed the fruits of their labor.

During this period of cooperation, the largest of the coyotes asserted its dominance over the makeshift pack. Their species originally never hunted together the way wolves did. Yet, this particular male maintained a pecking order as more of his kind gathered around the supercenter. He aggressively challenged anyone who came too close to the mall at night, only allowing himself the privilege to sleep near the food supply. On their fifth day of excavation, the male watched on as his anxious allies dug ever so closer to their holy grail. All the while, the leader chewed at its left paw, which was covered with rough, scabbed skin from months of scraping at the resilient mites.

As soon as the last of the walls fell, the alpha coyote ferociously howled at the rest of his kin to back off from the plethora of newfound nutriments. He squeezed through the portion of the shopping center that housed the hypermarket. The beast shoved past the aisles of dust-covered toys, sporting equipment, and clothing for he had no concern for such frivolous items. His nose picked up the ungodly order of spoiled goods. Yet, among the putrid stenches, he could pick up the scent of chicken, tuna and beef, among other delectables. This was no carcass roasting in the middle of the desert, it was man's food.

At last, he had found what he was looking for. However, the scents came from small, shiny containers. With one swipe of his paw, he knocked over an entire shelf of the cylinders. The mangy canine sniffed at them and determined they were made of a material similar to the fallen structure that housed the sanctuary he was in. The Alpha knew he could not digest them, but was aware of how his enlarged snout was more than capable of squeezing out their hidden delectables. He snatched up a handful of the aluminum cans in his mouth and immediately began chewing them. He could sense the food pouring out of these shells and sliding into his gullet.

The cans did not have the same exact taste as a fresh kill or a scavenged carcass, but it was more than enough to satiate his hunger. For the next few minutes, the coyote proceeded to scour through as many cans as he could find before he would leave the rest to his pack. At last, he had gone through a quarter of the supply. Just then, his ears picked up a series of loud barks, growls, and yelps. Something was going on outside, something bad. He sprang into action and headed his way back through the various layers of broken concrete. Once outside, he was met with a grizzly sight.

Each of his followers was either slain or fighting for their lives against five massive intruders. They outnumbered these foreigners two-to-one, but their size and ferocity clearly gave them an advantage. They were wolves, though far larger and menacing than any other creature in the surrounding area. Standing at an intimidating three meters at shoulder height, they were the size of elephants. Like their coyote counterparts, they too suffered from various degrees of mange. The portions of their bodies that lacked fur had grown thick and scaly, appearing more reptilian than mammalian. This skin gave them the perfect protection against the coyotes' numerous bites and scratches. For the wolves with less damaged skin, they relied on their unrelenting savagery.

The Alpha witnessed another gathering of creatures off in the distance. While he could not make them out, he could still pick up their scent. The canine recognized it as one he had not smelled in ages, humans. The pack leader knew that the humans were responsible for these wolves. Among the humans were massive metal boxes on wheels. The Alpha recalled seeing these contraptions around ruins of his abode but never were they that massive.

The coyote knew he must aid his pack and singled out one lone wolf that stood out from the rest. She remained distant from the others as she oversaw the carnage. Her body contained very little mange, with only streaks of hardened skin across her front shoulders and back legs. Her maw was accented with massive canine teeth that jutted out from her snout. The humans referred to her as Elise, something the coyote would never find out, nor did he need to as he confronted his enemy. Elise noticed the Alpha approaching her and, in response, she called out to one of her subordinates. He stood on three legs with his front left paw missing. In its place was a leg bone sharpened to a point. This wolf's face contained his most disturbing feature, an empty left eye socket. Like its paw, it too was missing, with the entire area of his face stripped of its flesh and muscle, leaving only a portion of its skull exposed. His name was Tucker.

Held in Tucker's maw was the neck of the second-largest member of the Alpha's pack. The defeated male's body was torn to shreds. Skin and fur were ripped apart and blood splattered all over the broken asphalt of what was formerly a parking lot. Upon hearing his leader, Tucker dropped his barely living victim and stood between the Alpha and Elise. With no choice but to face this mega wolf, the Alpha leaped at the wolf's mane. The intruder thrashed its body until the Alpha was forced off. Once the coyote made impact with the ground, he instinctively got back up. He knew he had to protect his clan, for if they were to fall, he would have no chance at survival.

The one-eyed lupin eyed the Alpha, waiting for it to make its next move. The coyote snarled at his enemy and then moved in to attack. The mono-eyed wolf lunged forward with its shive-like boney appendage. The Alpha dodged to the right and aimed for the wolf's neck while in its blind spot. At the same time, the bloodied ally he rescued earlier went for the wolf's only front paw, preventing it from swiping at the Alpha.

As both canines held onto their enemy for dear life, the Alpha attempted to suffocate its opponent while clawing at the wolf's remaining eye. Just then, something gripped the Alpha's back and tore him loose from Tucker before he was thrown back to the ground. The one-eyed wolf then bit onto another coyote before stabbing him with his bone spike, piercing right through his ribs multiple times. In a few short moments, the Alpha's ally was nothing but a lifeless husk.

The coyote got back up and saw Elise, who had come to Tucker's aid at the last minute. The Alpha then witnessed his comrades fall one by one all around him. Either their skulls were crushed, their throats were torn, or their lungs had been crushed by their adversaries.

With his entire pack gone and no options left, the Alpha made a run for it. He evaded the other mega wolves as he abandoned all hope of maintaining his rule over his newfound food source. All of a sudden, a sharp pain erupted from the coyote's back and he found himself tumbling over. The perplexed canine looked toward the source of the pain and noticed a sharpened rib bone stuck in its body. He reached toward the projectile in an attempt to remove it.

As the injured canine struggled to remove the weapon from his back, he noticed a tall elongated figure walking toward him. The coyote was too tired to make out what it was, other than it appeared to be a human.

Yet, at thirty meters tall, this human was far larger than any of the mutated wolves and coyotes and it seemed to be carrying something massive on its back. This human's scent was also unlike any he had smelled before. It was the same irradiated odor that he and the wolves gave off. As the figure approached, the coyote could make out more of the human's bizarre and frightening appearance. Its pale, almost yellowish skin, was covered in ragged clothes consisting of a shirt, shorts, and a wide brim that concealed his head from the sun. The Alpha tried desperately to escape, limping across the scorching desert landscape until his legs gave out from stress and blood loss. He felt a massive shadow envelop his body as the figure blocked out the sun.

In one last desperate move, the coyote barked as loud as it could, baring his teeth as he made his last stand against the enemy. He could finally make out something the figure had been carrying on his back the entire time. It was an enormous leather sack that made a rattling sound with each step the figure took. The tall one reached into his back and pulled out what appeared to be a humerus. It held the club-like weapon high into the air, and with one quick strike, made short work of the injured animal.

A short time later the figure returned to the pack of wolves, who were all feasting on the remains of the smaller canines. The man was now carrying the last of the coyote's corpse in its bag, a macabre collection of its former enemies, man and beast alike. It was tradition for the creature that was neither man nor beast. He was a ghoul-like figure who had sought to dominate all life before him using his intellect as a former human being, and the strength of his irradiated body. This was the figure known simply as "El Silbón."

The mutant giant whistled at his wolves, who all approached him on command. In the short time he had known these fellow mutants, he had come to view them as kin. Approaching him were three of the beasts. First came the most approachable of the wolves, one completely covered head-to-toe in scabs, blistered, and scaly skin, Ada. She was an outcast among the enlarged canines due to her scarred appearance, yet El Silbón loved her as much as the rest and punished any of the wolves if they ever treated her with hostility. For this, she became the most loyal of the pack.

Next came Baldwyn, a beast with a line of mangy skin running from his left eye all the way to his hip. He was thin and appeared almost anorexic as a result of an unstable metabolism that burned energy faster than he could eat. Despite his handicap, his lightweight appearance belied a frighteningly nimble creature capable of outrunning any target. Following Baldwyn was Thor. The largest of the pack, Thor was a brute who used his immense size to overpower all of his enemies. If it were not for a scarred and blinded left eye and a back paw riddled in painfully scabbed skin, he may have been the leader of his team.

El Silbón noticed that two of the wolves were absent. He heard growling nearby and turned to find Elise growling at Tucker, who had refused to respond to his call, rather preferring to enjoy his most recent kill. The three-legged lupid was always the most troublesome of the bunch. His ferocious temper and uncontrollable appetite meant that he needed some "convincing" in order to get him to obey any order that did not involve killing. El Silbón then began to reach for his bag of bones. The clattering of the contents inside was enough to start Tucker, to which he quickly fell in line, whimpering apologetically. Despite being his least favorite of the lupins, Tucker's tenacity certainly made him a valuable asset for the towering man.

Last, but certainly not least was Elise, who approached El Silbón with a dismembered leg of one of the slaughtered coyotes. El Silbón reached out his hand for the wolf to place the limb in his palm. It was a sign of respect between the mutants as Elise knew the humanoid collected bones and had aided her and her family on many occasions. El Silbón knew this and accepted the offering. As he placed the tool back in his bag, he performed a loud whistle that reached across the entire valley.

After a few minutes, a caravan of fifty humans arrived on the scene. This was the small empire he helped build over the course of ten years, the Hounds of Hell. Originally a small band of thieves from the former United States of America, the amoral nomads found an ally in the mutants they hunted across the land, specifically the very wolves that currently surrounded their colossal ally. It was decades ago that they traveled down south in search of new opportunities that they discovered El Silbón, starving and on the verge of passing out under the desert sun. They had sent their wolves after him, only to find that the dying giant's will to live far exceeded the strength of their hounds. After he knocked all five dogs out, El Silbón too fell unconscious. That was when the marauders knew they had discovered a new opportunity for their survival.

Using the few Spanish speakers they had and along with food and shelter, the raiders welcomed the giant into their ranks. From there he not only came to befriend the wolves, more so than any of the humans, but would eventually share his story with the curious men.

Once, he was a normal human in Venezuela, who like anyone thirty years ago had struggled to survive the dawn of the age of monsters and the collapse of civilization. After discovering a small outpost in Peru, he learned they were looking for volunteers for an experimental procedure to utilize the properties of radiation-based mutations to potentially elevate humanity to a level on par with the True Kaiju.

Having lost all of his friends and family, the man jumped at the chance to enact vengeance on the titans who took everything from him. Yet, as fate would have it, he was the failed result of such experiments. As his body grew in size and strength, he experienced pain and trauma unlike anyone could fathom. His body could not seemingly handle the procedure and his pulse went silent. He was declared dead from what appeared to be a heart attack and his body was disposed of miles away as the local scientists prepared their next subject.

Little did they know, the former man was simply under a form of hibernation. Once he had awoken, untold amounts of months later, he found himself buried by the corpses of hundreds of men, women, and children, all of whom died of various forms of radiation poisoning. He fought through the various bodies of the deceased until he, at last, reached the surface. From there he discovered he was surrounded by numerous mutated wildlife who had discovered this pit of ripe meat. With no weapons at his disposal, the enlarged man used the bodies of the dead as makeshift tools to fend off the beasts.

After successfully defending himself from the ravenous beasts, he began collecting as many corpses as he could, inspiring him to abandon whatever name he once held in favor of the title, "El Silbón." Back home, El Silbón was an urban legend of a nightmarish figure of conflicting origins who hunted drunkards and womanizers and carried their bones with him wherever he went, all while whistling to each of his victims.

The raiders, each decked out in full police riot gear, swarmed past El Silbón and the wolves as they made their way towards the supermarket. Their commander, Sebastián Lopez, approached the titan.

"Congrats on a job well done," he said as he addressed El Silbón in his native Spanish tongue. The mutant turned his head in response to his associate, whom he had known since his first meeting with the bandits. He nodded in acknowledgment.

"Once we're done assessing the building, we'll be sure to get you your share."

"Good," El Silbón uttered in a raspy baritone voice. It would have sent chills down Lopez's spine had he not been accustomed to his partner over the past decade. *"It's been some time since I've had canned meat,"* he spoke as he leered at the remains of the coyotes that surrounded him.

Then suddenly, he began to hear an unfamiliar sound. It sounded like a jet quickly approaching their location. He veered off and saw in the horizon a reddish object approaching them.

"Get the men ready," the giant ordered Lopez. In no time, Lopez called everyone on his radio and within seconds, everyone came out guns in hand. Meanwhile, El Silbón grabbed the largest bone he had, a massive elongated fang from a mutant jaguar. The five wolves all aggressively howled at the new arrival.

The object landed before everyone with an earth-shattering thud. It stood nearly a head taller than El Silbón himself. Most shockingly was that it was humanoid and appeared to be composed entirely out of metal. This was something no one had seen before, a mech. Beyond the legendary Steel Samurai, the very machine that took down the True Kaiju of the Americas and drove thieves like them out of the US and Canada. Beyond the exploits of Chris Myers, no one else had ever reported sightings of another humanoid machine after the apocalypse. Yet strangely, this mech was much smaller than that of the Meyer's. Though, even at only twenty-five meters, it was still a grave threat to the Hounds of Hell with who knows what it was capable of.

However, this machine did not attack. It did not approach them, nor did it move. It simply stood in place. That was until its chest opened up, revealing a lone man. The man stepped out from his cockpit and held out a device connected to his machine. He wore a helmet that covered his entire face save for his exposed mouth and chin. In English, with a hoarse European accent, he cheekily asked one single inquiry that blared from his mech's external speakers.

"Are you guys recruiting?"

CHAPTER 3

El Tigre, Panama

The temperature was a scorching one-hundred-one degree Fahrenheit and the humidity was well over ninety percent as the sounder of wild mutant pigs rooted up the marshland that bordered the ocean. Each of the mutants stood about forty meters tall at the shoulder and was over seventy-five meters long.

The drift of female pigs had been led by their matriarch from Mexico through most of Central America. The monstrous swines had left a path of destruction in their wake as they rooted through the east coast of Mexico and made their way into the strip of land that connected the two continents. Along the way, the mainly female group of mutants had met with several males of their species. By the time the creatures had entered northern Panama, many of the sows were pregnant. Knowing they were soon to give birth, the matriarch led the sounder down toward the marshlands of the west coast where they knew they could find ample plant life to root out as well as food in the estuaries created by the ocean and freshwater sources.

When the sows had originally made their way to Panama's shoreline, they encountered other mutants in the form of giant ocelots and margays. Like the sows themselves, the typically small predatory cats had been mutated by the radiation of passing kaiju and grown to a height of roughly thirty meters tall.

The solitary gargantuan felines had at first tried to hunt the mutant pigs, but they soon found out that they were no match for the swines' superior size, weight, and numbers. The group of mutant pigs had slain and eaten nearly a half dozen giant cats before the former apex predators surrendered the territory to the sounder and moved out of the area.

The pigs had taken control of the entire western coast of Panama and were able to raise their piglets as the unchallenged masters of the lush coastal region. Despite the sweltering heat, the matriarch of the titanic swines marched up and down the beach in front of those under her protection. She would periodically look at the ocean, kick up large piles of sand, and snort, all while shaking her prodigious tusks back and forth in a threatening motion.

The matriarch knew that something in the ocean was watching her sounder and preparing to attack. The aggravated swine had no idea of what was lurking in the depths and stalking her family, but she was determined that whatever the creature was, it would soon perish and serve as food for her and her family.

She was in the process of turning around to pace back in the opposite direction when a swell of water started moving toward the shoreline. At the sight of the oncoming intruder, the matriarch squealed, alerting her sounder to the approaching threat. In response to the matriarch's call, four more females who had no piglets to care for, rushed to her side and mirrored her actions of scratching the sand with their hooves, snorting, and swinging their tusks from side to side.

The gathered sows watched the approaching bulge of water, ready to charge whatever emerged from it, as it continued to move closer to shore. When the mound of displaced water was roughly fifty meters from the shore, one of the four pigs gathered at the water's edge made her way out to meet it. She had nearly reached the mysterious swell when a dome of bright blue energy exploded from it, expanding out a full three-hundred-and-sixty degrees from its origin point.

The four giant pigs that were gathered at the water's edge were struck by the dome of radioactive energy and sent tumbling backward. As the blast washed over the mutant animals, the explosion burned their skin to a crisp. For one of the mammals, the intense heat completely seared her eyes, blinding the struggling creature. The blast continued past the four guardians and the shoreline and washed over the mother sows and their oversized piglets, causing both parents and offspring to squeal in pain from the heat scorching their bodies.

As the dome of energy faded, the nightmarish form of Atomic Rex was standing in its wake. The nuclear theropod unleashed a roar that shook both the surface of the water and the beach. The four sows who had been nearest to the water were still trying to return to a standing position as the kaiju approached them. Once he saw the bloody eye sockets of the monster who was closest to him and had caught the brunt of his Atomic Wave, the irradiated dinosaur moved in to kill the blinded beast.

The disabled mutant's legs were flailing as it rocked back and forth in pain from its burnt-out eyes and scorched skin. When he reached the downed beast, Atomic Rex lifted his right claw into the air, and with a single swipe, he eviscerated his prey. The giant swine let loose one last pitiful squeal as the contents of her stomach spilled onto the beach while her intestines were yanked from her body by Atomic Rex's claw.

The reptilian horror opened his powerful jaws and tore the dangling viscera from his claws as the other three guardian hogs finally managed to return to a standing position. The matriarch grunted and then charged the saurian demon while the other two she-pigs followed her lead.

When Atomic Rex saw the trio of pigs charging him, the kaiju roared at them with pieces of their slain sister's entrails hanging from his teeth and claws. Just before the matriarch reached him, Atomic Rex spun around and struck the head of the sounder in her shoulder with his thick tail. The blow knocked the matriarch on her side and sent her tumbling across the beach. After knocking down the lead sow, the nuclear theropod turned around in a full circle just in time to see the other two mutants slam into his thighs.

The combined strength of the mammalian mammoths knocked Atomic Rex backward and sent him falling on his back into the surf. With Atomic Rex down, the two mutants who had knocked him down rushed into the surf and began goring the True Kaiju. As their leader stood up to join them, the sows back on the beach formed a protective circle around the piglets.

A cloud of blood appeared around the reptilian horror as the two pigs drove their long tusks into Atomic Rex's arms and torso. The matriarch snorted in anger at the invader who dared to threaten her family as she joined her sisters and buried her right tusk into the nuclear theropod's tail.

Atomic Rex's body was wracked with a level of pain that would have paralyzed most creatures, but the True Kaiju was like no other beast in the world. The saurian monster's mind had no room in it for pain because it was filled with anger, solely focused on the beasts who thought they could usurp his territory and slay him. Atomic Rex closed his powerful jaws on the sow goring his torso, while also using his right arm to push aside the pig that was attacking it. At the same time, he swiped his clawed toes across the face of the matriarch who was biting into his tail.

The matriarch's face was covered in a crimson mask from the multiple cuts running across it, causing her to back away as the sow Atomic Rex had pushed over struggled to stand in the slippery sand beneath the waves of the coast. The mutant that the nuclear theropod had closed his jaws on felt only the briefest sensation of pain before the kaiju's jaws crushed her skull and his dagger-like death sliced into her brain.

Atomic Rex tore the head and part of the spine out of the pig whose skull he had just crushed. As he attempted to swallow it whole, the matriarch slammed her head into his stomach. The blow caused the saurian nightmare to first fall onto the matriarch, then roll off and crash back into the water. Atomic Rex was on his back, looking up through the crashing waves when the matriarch and her sister once more attacked him.

As the voracious beasts used their tusks to slice into Atomic Rex's scales, the kaiju tried to roar only to have his mouth filled with a mixture of blood, sand, and seawater. The reptilian beast was choking on the sand and water, while simultaneously, his taste buds were sent into overdrive by the taste of blood sliding across them.

With the two mutant pigs ripping his torso to shreds, Atomic Rex reached deep into the power stored within his cells. The radioactive dinosaur's body began to take on a light blue glow as he drew the nuclear energy stored within him from countless power stations and the phoenix he once slew on a distant world.

The two enraged mammals were unable to understand the connection between the glow of their prey and the blast of blue energy that had struck them only moments ago. The Atomic Wave erupted from the saurian horror's body and struck the pigs who had him pinned to the ground. The quickly expanding dome of radiation lifted the two attacking sows off Atomic Rex and sent them flying backward once again.

As the swines were trying to recover from the blast, Atomic Rex rose out of the surf and expelled the saltwater and sand that had gathered in his lungs. After taking several deep breaths of air, he roared and turned his attention to his opponents.

The skin on the entire front half of the matriarch's body was burned down to the muscle tissue in the fraction of a second that she was in the air. When the queen of the swine crashed down into the warm ocean, she squealed in unimaginable pain as her exposed muscles were suddenly submerged in the stinging saltwater. The matriarch opened her mouth to cry out in pain only to have it filled with the same water that was assaulting her body. The queen of the swine fought her way back to her feet and vomited up the water she had swallowed. What remained of the skin on the front half of her body sloughed off into the sea. The pig's eyesight was only saved by the fact she was attacking Atomic Rex below the water which had forced her to close her eyes.

The other pig that had been goring Atomic Rex had the lower section of her jaw completely destroyed by the monster's blast. The swine was in such pain and so badly injured that when she caught the scent of Atomic Rex coming toward her, she panicked and tried to escape the approaching death by making her way out to sea. The fleeing sow was struggling to swim when the reptilian monster closed his jaws on her spine and crippled her. The paralyzed mutant hog was still alive as Atomic Rex let her sink to the bottom of the ocean.

The True Kaiju intended to eat the drowning creature, but he knew full well the majority of her corpse would be there for him to devour at a later time. With this enemy defeated and her meat relatively secure beneath the waves, Atomic Rex turned his attention to the gathered sows on the beach and the piglets they were protecting. With each step that he took, the nuclear power surging through the monster's body worked to heal his wounds. The True Kaiju had walked less than halfway back to the beach by the time his amazing healing abilities had closed off the majority of wounds inflicted on him by the colossal hogs.

When the circled sows saw the reptilian predator wading through the surf and approaching their piglets they squealed in unison. The group squeal was not only a warning to Atomic Rex but a call to their leader to help them.

The badly injured matriarch heard her sounder and she grunted as adrenaline raced through her body in response to the call to protect the newborn piglets. The matriarch grunted and then charged through the hip-deep water toward the juggernaut that was going to kill her family.

Atomic Rex had just stepped onto the beach when the matriarch slammed into his hip and knocked him on his side. The matriarch's body was in nearly intolerable pain from the wounds already inflicted on her, but with the lives of her entire sounder in the balance, she bravely tried to fight off the beast that threatened them. The matriarch swung her head from side to side, using her tusks to rip into Atomic Rex while also biting the nuclear theropod and tearing out a mouthful of his scales whenever she could.

Despite her best efforts, the matriarch was no match for the True Kaiju. Without her sisters helping her and with her own strength depleted from the damage done to her body, the matriarch was unable to keep Atomic Rex down. The immensely more powerful monster simply stood up as the matriarch continued to gore him. Atomic Rex roared at the blur of exposed muscles and tusks that were attacking him. He then reached down, dug his claws into the matriarch's rib cage, lifted her into the air, and then slammed her head-first into the beach. There was a loud crack when the matriarch's neck broke as Atomic Rex drove the former queen of the swine into the sand.

The saurian horror roared at his defeated foe, proclaiming his dominance of the territory to any other invaders that sought to intrude upon his domain. He then turned his attention to the circle of swines and the tender piglets they were surrounding. As he approached the encircled hogs, the adults began swinging their tusks back and forth. The mother sows were in such a fervor to protect their young that they had no concern for the damage their movements were causing towards each other or any wounds that were inadvertently being inflicted on them. All that mattered to the gathered sows was protecting their young.

As Atomic Rex stared at the wall of tusks and fur, he quickly understood clawing and biting his way through the gathered mutants would be a time-consuming and painful endeavor. The nuclear theropod walked as close as he could to the gathered animals while still staying out of their reach. The monster then lifted his leg off the ground as his body once more took on a light blue glow. When Atomic Rex brought his leg crashing back down to earth the Atomic Wave exploded out of his body.

The blast immediately killed the three hogs who were directly in front of him while badly injuring the piglets behind them and the rest of the encircled mutants. The monster stepped over the three dead sows so that he was standing above the badly burned and slowly dying giant piglets. With the infants below him and what remained of the injured adults around the dinosaur, the kaiju unleashed another Atomic Wave that killed what remained of the sounder of mutant pigs.

With the smell of burnt pork wafting through the air around him and the sun beating down on the freshly killed meat, Atomic Rex once again roared in triumph. With his pick of dead pigs to gorge himself on, the nuclear theropod turned his head toward the deceased matriarch. The ruler of the Americas decided his first meal of the day would come from the corpse of the creature that thought to challenge his supremacy.

Atomic Rex crushed several dead piglets beneath his clawed feet as he walked over to ingest their defeated queen.

A set of cold eyes watched from a distance as Atomic Rex feasted on his meal. Having studied the radioactive dinosaur for years, this new predator was certain that Atomic Rex would return to the water after eating. He spoke aloud as if he were addressing some imaginary audience of his brilliant scheme. "Finally, the pieces are all in place. Soon, this land will be cleansed of all my enemies. Neither beast nor machine will be left standing. All who have wronged me shall perish, and any who stand in my way will fall."

The mastermind knew that victory over Atomic Rex would not come in one fell swoop. What he needed was a strategy that had only been utilized once decades prior. It was one composed of a series of strategic moves that would lead to the monster's downfall. The predator had already made preparations for his master plan and the time to place his first piece into play was at hand.

In the years that he had been developing his scheme, a key aspect to it was studying the various kaiju and giant mutants that roamed this savage world to determine what creatures would be of use to him.

He had located several such beasts off the coast of Hawaii that were exposed to the radiation given off by the True Kaiju, Kolong. The mutant crocodilian's energy had transformed an entire bloom of box jellyfish into colossal versions of their former selves. With the cnidarian's already long tentacles, extended to a length of nearly a kilometer, they proved to be deadly predators.

Like most of the True Kaiju, Kolong both created mutants and hunted them. The kaiju served to develop his own food web and ecosystem with himself in the center as its apex predator. A year ago, when the invading Hagan had slain Kolong, the Japanese kaiju had taken away the predator that controlled the giant box jellyfish population he had created. Without Kolong hunting them, the mutant jellyfish population had exploded. The creatures quickly wiped out the oceanic life around the Hawaiian Islands and were moving into new territories.

Knowing that one of these creatures could be a weapon he could utilize against Atomic Rex, the predator flew to the Hawaiian Islands. From there he scouted the waters around the islands until he located one of the massive invertebrates. Wielding mechanically enhanced strength, the predator punctured the gelatinous mutant with two enormous metal cables, each tipped with harpoon-like spears. The being then towed the creature away from the coastal waters of Hawaii, and left it off the coast of Central America.

Once the mutant was in the waters he needed it in, the kidnapper fired a tracker into it so that he could retrieve the leviathan and use it to initiate his plan when the time was right. That time was now, and the vengeance-seeking manipulator was ready to take full advantage of his opportunity. He flew once more out over the ocean to the location of the giant box jellyfish he had brought across the sea. Upon locating the mindless creature, he once more ensnared the soft mass as he did before and pulled it towards Atomic Rex.

CHAPTER 4

Zambia, Africa

Wind and rain pelted the two deformed and overgrown pachyderms as they challenged each other for the right to breed with the female who stood on the opposite side of the river from them. The creatures were the descendants of what had once been African elephants. When several of the True Kaiju escaped from the island that had formerly been their home, the radiation given off by their bodies caused some of the flora and fauna they came into contact with to change in drastic and often grotesque ways.

Like most animals that were contaminated by the radiation of the True Kaiju, the elephants grew to a massive size of fifty-five meters at the shoulder. In addition to their dramatic increase in size, the elephants also grew two additional sets of long tusks that curved out from the sides of their faces.

The behemoths also developed elongated spines from their backs similar to the long-deceased Amargasaurus. These additional spikes, along with their immense size and strength, left the elephants with few challenges to their dominance of the continent with the expectation of the True Kaiju who had settled there.

The two males trumpeted, pawed at the ground, and swung their huge tusks back and forth in an attempt to scare off each other. Twin trails of liquid seeped down the sides of both of their faces, indicating that they were in a state of must. The liquid was a relic trait from their unmutated ancestors. It indicated that the bulls were ready to mate and that testosterone coursing through their bodies was at six times its normal level. After a few minutes of the obligatory display of power, it was clear that neither of the beasts was going to back away from the opportunity to mate with the female.

One of the males was young and this was his first mating season. The young bull was anxious to mate and he was determined to vanquish his fellow suitor and claim his prize.

The second bull was older and covered with the scars of past battles. The older monster had mated many times over the course of his life, but he was far from prepared to back away from a challenge.

The two males each lowered their heads and charged at each other while the female stood by, watching to see which of the two males would prove himself worthy of her. The two males met head-on, crashing their heads into one another and interlocking their three sets of tusks, and wrapping their trunks around each other's faces.

The two behemoths each tried to turn their opponent and throw them to the ground, allowing them the chance to gore or stomp their adversary to death. For nearly two hours, the enraged and enhanced pachyderms struggled to assert their dominance over the other. The storm that was at its inception when the two males first locked horns continued to increase its ferocity as the struggle escalated. It was almost as if the storm was mirroring the battle below, increasing in ferocity and strength as the battle between the unrelenting bulls raged on beneath it.

As the two bulls fought for the right to create new life, they had no idea that certain death was circling them in the storm clouds above. Rain pelted the wings of a hellish creature as it soared through the skies, lightning streaking around its body. The beast had the head, rear legs, and body of a Smilodon. Instead of front legs the monster had bat wings that, when on land, allowed it to walk in the same 4-legged manner as the wyverns of legend. The beast's tail was thick and armed with a stinger at the end similar to that of a scorpion.

The people of Africa had named the kaiju Manticore due to its uncanny resemblance to the mythological creature. Like the True Kaiju Hagan that had ruled Japan for numerous years, Manticore was a combination of multiple creatures fused together into a single demonic being by the nuclear blast that had occurred on the island. A Smilodon was resting in a cave with bats and scorpions crawling over it when the nuclear bomb was dropped on its home.

The Smilodon that had been sleeping in the cave saw a brief flash of light that caused it to close its eyes. When the beast opened its eyes again it was no longer a Smilodon but a True Kaiju. As the monster emerged from the cave it was nearly sixty-meters long and stood forty meters at the shoulder. The saber-toothed monster looked to the sky, reared up on its hind legs, spread its bat-like wings and then leapt into the air.

The monster would come to land on the southern part of the African continent. The mammalian horror would establish the country of South Africa as its territory. The South African military had attempted to slay Manticore, but the beast easily crushed all human resistance. The creature would roam the country, spreading its radiation and mutating the wildlife there, thus creating its own food supply of giant mutants.

For several decades, Manticore was content to stay in his own territory. That changed when his food supply slowly started to dwindle. The reduction in Manticore's food supply was partially a result of his own nearly insatiable appetite and partly due to a recent invader to his lands. A metal giant had started appearing in Manticore's territory slightly over a year ago. On several occasions, the True Kaiju had seen the invader slay some of the mutants that were his prey and then fly off with their remains. The winged monster challenged the stranger whenever he saw it, but each time the pillager chose the option of flight over fight. The feline-esque monster had tried to chase down the thief but to Manticore's surprise, the assailant was fast and agile enough to evade him every time. Over the course of a year, the stranger's impact on Manticore's food supply had been significant. The monster's available prey within his territory had been reduced to the point that it was no longer able to sustain him.

In order to survive, Manticore needed to head north into the realm of the kaiju known as Gol-Drill. Gol-Drill was a mandrill that had been mutated to gargantuan size. When humans first saw him, they combined the words Goliath and Mandrill to form his name. While not a True Kaiju from the original island, Gol-Drill's already intelligent primate mind was further enhanced by his increase in size.

Gol-Drill had learned to fashion weapons like clubs and spears which helped him dominate his territory. One of the simian's favorite forms of prey were the herds of mutant elephants that roamed across his lands. The very same mutant elephants that were fighting for breeding rights and were currently being stalked by Manticore.

Manticore had no desire to engage Gol-Drill in direct combat. The flying monster preferred to fly across the Atlantic in search of new hunting grounds, but in order to traverse the ocean the kaiju first had to feed, and Gol-Drill's elephants were the only organisms on the continent that would give him enough food from a single kill to make the flight.

As Manticore circled his prey from above in the cover of the storm clouds the two mutated elephants continued to battle. As the battle approached its third hour, the older male finally succeeded in using the rain-soaked terrain to shift the younger bull's weight, causing him to lose his footing and fall to the ground. With his opponent flailing in the mud before him, the older male reared up and brought his tremendous weight crashing down on the younger bull. There was a loud cracking sound as the downed mutant's ribs splintered into pieces under the assault of his adversary.

The injured bull trumpeted in pain as his rival kept his weight pressed down on him, forcing his body deeper into the thick mud that accumulated around them during their battle. The older pachyderm could feel the young challenger still moving beneath his feet. The victorious monster looked over at the female who was to be his prize. After a quick glance at the cow he was about to mate with, the older bull decided he would make sure there was no chance the younger bull would rise up to challenge him again. The bull reared up with the intent of bringing his feet down on the young challenger one final time to end his life.

When Manticore saw the victorious mutant rise into the air he knew it was time to strike. The True Kaiju folded its wings to its sides and dove from the sky in the same manner as a peregrine falcon. As the hunter closed in on his prey the intensity of the rain increased and lightning streaked across the sky behind him, illuminating his descent with an unearthly glow.

The feline-esque horror fell from the skies with both the shape and speed of a living missile. Just before he reached the reared-up pachyderm, the winged demon shifted the back half of his body in front of him, so that his lion-like claws and scorpion tail would strike his target with the full force of his dive behind him.

The older bull had reached the apex of his stance when Manticore slammed into him with the force of a falling meteor. The predatory creature's claws and spiked tail were driven deep into the left side of the multi-tusked beast. As Manticore's telson entered the mutant it instantly injected his prey with a dose of paralyzing venom. The pachyderm was sent tumbling across the muddy savannah with two sets of deep cuts along its side from the flying horror's claws and a deep wound in its gut that was spreading scorpion venom throughout its body.

As the victorious elephant struggled to get back to his feet from Manticore's attack, the invasive chimera turned its attention to the injured elephant at its feet. The young bull with the crushed ribs was rolling back and forth as it tried to stand and defend itself. Manticore roared at the beast and then drove his long, twin, saber-like fangs into the mutant's throat. After biting the beast, Manticore did not tear his prey's throat out. Rather, he backed away from his prey, knowing that the wound he inflicted on the beast would cause it to drown in its own blood.

Manticore turned his attention to the female elephant who had decided to turn and run away from the slaughter wrought upon her would-be suitors. The hybrid sprang into the air, flew over the female, and finally landed in front of her. Manticore's bat-like wings touched down in front of him to function as his front legs and his scorpion tail swayed back and forth behind his head, ready to strike his victim.

With the option to flee taken away from her, the female lowered her head and charged at the nightmare that was hunting her. When the female was only a few steps away from him, Manticore leapt to the side to avoid the pachyderm's attack. As the behemoth was moving past him, the kaiju's telson shot in her front right leg, injecting it with a dose of venom just as he had done to the cow's intended mate.

The female ignored the puncture and when Manticore was no longer in front of her she once more attempted to flee. Unsure if a single strike from his telson was enough to bring down his prey, Manticore again leaped into the sky. This time when he was flying over the female, he used his rear claws to slash deep cuts above the female's eyes. The cuts were not serious wounds to the cow, but they did have the effect of causing blood to pour into the cow's eyes, obscuring her already poor vision.

The disoriented cow came to a stop and was shaking her head to clear the blood from her eyes when Manticore landed to her left and delivered two more quick strikes from his stinger to her stomach and leg. The female trumpeted in a mixture of pain, frustration, and fear. As Manticore was waiting for his venom to take effect on his victim, he felt the ground rumbling beneath his feet. The saber-toothed creature turned to see the older male, whom he had stung and maimed, charging towards him.

As he did with the female's charge, Manticore leaped out of the way and delivered a quick sting to the male's right side. The male charged past his target, slid to a stop in the wet mud, and then turned to charge the predator once again. With two stinger wounds sending venom throughout his system and blood pouring out of a series of gashes on his side, the older male wobbled on his feet and then collapsed on the ground.

Manticore watched as the old bull struggled to get up, and once he was sure that the beast would not be returning to his feet, he pounced on it. Manticore drove his canines into the beast's throat, severing its arteries just as it had done with the younger bull. While the older bull died in the same manner as his younger counterpart, Manticore looked back at the female who was still trying to escape her inevitable fate.

With blood seeping into her eyes and poison wrecking her body, the confused female staggered around the mud in an awkward circle before she too fell to the ground. Manticore slew the female in the same manner as he did the bulls. Then, with all three of his targets dead, Manticore unleashed a victorious roar that caught the attention of another apex predator roughly eight kilometers away.

With all three of his targets slain, Manticore walked up to the nearest corpse, unsheathed his back claws, and then sliced the beast open. The kaiju began to salivate as it looked down at the blood and muscle spilling into the mud. As tempting as the muscle and fat of the beast were, Manticore knew he needed to prioritize energy over taste. The beast pushed his face deeper into the mutant's carcass and quickly ingested the creature's liver and heart before moving onto its kidneys.

Before devouring the rest of the slain mammal, he moved on to his other kills and repeated the same process on them, eating the organs that would supply him with the most amount of energy in the shortest period of time. Manticore had just finished eating the organs of the female when he heard a crashing sound coming through the trees. As the sound of the crushed vegetation grew louder, the chimeric monster tried sniffing the air to identify what was coming toward him, but the steady rain lessened the smell. To further complicate the situation, the wind was blowing towards the source of the sound, carrying its scent away from the predator.

A high-pitched howl boomed across the sky, to which Manticore replied by shaking his body and snarling at whatever had produced the sound. The response to the winged kaiju's roar came in the form of a giant spear flying through the air at him. The hybrid creature leaped backward just in time to avoid being skewered by the massive projectile.

The spear was followed by the imposing sight of Gol-Drill leaping out from behind the trees and landing in the open savanna. The kaiju had the look of a mandrill with a brightly colored, red, and blue elongated mouth. The ape's thick gray fur wreathed his head in a mane that not only made him look more imposing but also protected his neck and throat from attacks. In his hand was a large tree that he had fashioned into a club, and slung across his back was another spear made from a tree, a sharpened boulder, and thick vines.

Unlike typical mandrills, the radiation that had affected Gol-Drill had changed his body to the point that he was able to operate in a standing position for long periods of time. The simian kaiju was equally adept at both locomotion and offense on two legs as he was on four. When the best stood fully erect, Manticore could see the rippling muscles beneath his rival's thick fur.

Gol-Drill beat his chest and leaped from side to side showing off his strength and agility. Despite all of Gol-Drill's physical attributes, it was not his agility or strength that made him such a formidable opponent. The danger presented by Gol-Drill truly came from the attributes that were not immediately visible.

Manticore looked at the strange objects in Gol-Drill's possession, then he looked at the gargantuan ape and roared a challenge. Manticore knew that Gol-Drill's weapons could hurt him, but he felt that as long as Gol-Drill did not have his most powerful asset at hand he could defeat the beast and claim the ape's land as his own.

The winged demon was about to pounce when Gol-Drill responded not with a roar, but with a series of deep guttural sounds. As Gol-Drill's call echoed across the stormy sky, more trees began to fall as multiple shapes began to exit the jungle and walk out onto the savanna.

Mutated apes and monkeys of various species including baboons, gorillas, chimpanzees, bonobos, samangos, and vervents began to congregate around their master. The gathered primates ranged from ten meters in height to fifty meters, roughly the size of their master. Despite being smaller than most mutants, Gol-Drill's army was legion, and not to be trifled with. As primates, evolution had predisposed them to social behavior and to look to an alpha male for guidance. Gol-Drill had taken advantage of these traits with the mutant primates of Africa and had unified them into a single force under his complete command.

Manticore took a step back and snarled at Gol-Drill. Meanwhile, the two dozen mutant apes gathered around him. The flying monster had thought that in an individual battle he could defeat Gol-Drill and claim the primate's home as his own. However, with Gol-Drill's army facing him on all fronts, Manticore knew he would be crushed in a head-on attack. Were it not for the storm masking the smell of the giant mandrill and his followers' approach, Manticore would have sensed them coming from several kilometers away and would have taken to the sky long ago.

As things stood now, Manticore knew he would have to get a running start in the thick mud that was covering his paws and wings if he wanted to attain flight. The hybrid monster roared once at Gol-Drill and his masses, then turned and began running in the opposite direction.

At the sight of Manticore fleeing, Gol-Drill pointed his club at the feline-esque predator and roared, signaling his troops to catch the trespasser to their land and tear it apart for its transgressions.

Manticore's paws and wing joints kept slipping beneath him as he ran. With each step, he could feel Gol-Drill's minions closing in on him. He felt the tip of Gol-Drill's spear graze his right rear leg, slicing open a shallow wound. The minor injury forced Manticore to push himself even harder. The chimeric kaiju thrust his body forward, opened his wings, and leaped into the sky.

Manticore flew into the storm clouds above him and circled around Gol-Drill and his gathered forces several times to take in their full measure. Once he was sure that even with the added advantage of attacking from the sky he would be unable to defeat the ape's forces, Manticore turned towards the coast and flew out over the Atlantic Ocean in search of new hunting grounds.

Gol-Drill watched as Manticore fled. When the bat-winged beast was out of sight, Gol-Drill lifted his club over his head and beat his chest. In response to their master's victory cry, the rest of Gol-Drill's army followed suit. As the shrieks died down, Gol-Drill looked to the south. With Manticore heading out to sea, the territory that had been his now belonged to the apes.

Gol-Drill had the lower two-fifths of the African continent in his possession. As the intelligent ape pondered what the acquisition of this new land meant, he also began to consider if he should set his sights on conquering the rest of the continent as well.

CHAPTER 5

Fortuna Village, Guerrero, Mexico

A new day dawned on a settlement, hidden within the sunbaked mountains of what was once called Sierra Madre del Sur. Men and women of various ages exited their makeshift homes made of bricks, clay, wood, metal, or any other material they had managed to salvage since the establishment of their new home fifteen years ago. It was that time of the week when the village would split in two. Half of the men would travel down the hills and towards the ocean in search of resources, both natural and artificial. The rest would stay behind to look after the children, the first generation to have been born since the founding of Fortuna, and continue their farming of vegetables.

Leading the expedition was Joaquín Muñoz, a thirty-five-year-old father of two, who had recently volunteered to be his team's guide since he took over for his father, who had died the previous year due to illness. Prior to his death, the senior Muñoz taught his son everything he knew about the surrounding land, having once lived in the beautiful beach resort town of Acapulco. When the True Kaiju and their smaller mutant spawn began their invasion of North America, countless men, women, and children sought refuge within the mountainous ranges in an attempt to stave off their demise. Eventually, their journey brought the Muñoz clan and many others to the archeological site of Tehuacalco, an ancient Mesoamerican city originally founded by the Yope people.

Joaquín's father, a man who prided himself on his farming as he sold his homegrown produce to tourists back home, found the untainted soil of the area to be sufficient enough to establish a new village. For over half a decade he would make several trips to the nearby decimated cities to scavenge with his party members for any usable items that could aid them, be it electronics, weapons, or medicine. Now that his father was no longer there to guide the people of Fortuna, the role had been passed down to Joaquín, who until recently was content to live the peaceful life of a farmer with his wife and twin sons, Nicholás and Carlos. He had hoped that some other person would volunteer to fill his shoes, yet no one was more equipped nor knew the land as well as he did. The former leader made sure his son knew the land he sought to cultivate up until his dying breath.

As unsure as he was, Joaquín knew the truth. If Fortuna was to continue thriving, they needed to expand, especially as their population grew. To accomplish this, they needed the assets necessary for survival. Their first stop was the remains of Chilpancingo, a city devastated by a True Kaiju that had long since abandoned its territory. Half of Fortuna's settlement hailed from the former capital of Guerrero, Mexico, as did a good portion of Joaquín's men. By mid-afternoon, they reached the outskirts of the city. To none of their surprise, they were greeted by a landscape of crushed concrete and destroyed dreams. It was a sight that Joaquín was all too familiar with. So began his team's excavation through the ruins of a lost civilization from a slightly less chaotic time.

Joaquín and his fifty-person team traveled deeper than they had ever gone into the city in hopes of searching for new materials. They passed by the familiar broken roads and collapsed neighborhoods. This time, they were in search of the downtown region, the heart of the city, where they hoped to find a treasure trove of new materials to help build their territory. At last, they arrived at the unfamiliar locale, marked by the fallen Chilpancingo Cathedral.

As his men began combing the surrounding rubble of lost banks, supermarkets, and shops, Joaquín decided to rest within what was left of the destroyed church. Having lost everything he knew at a young age, his faith in the Lord was what kept him, along with the rest of his family, going during their darkest hours. The man approached the building, though he could not enter through its collapsed doors. Surrounding the structure were skeletons of those who had sought sanctuary in their final moments of life. If Joaquín were to find his way into the hallowed halls, would he find more gruesome remains in there as well? For the moment, he found it best to pray outside in the presence of the Lord's home.

His prayers were interrupted, however, as one of his teammates and longest known friends, Pancho, called out to him. He turned to see his companion running frantically towards him.

"*Joaquín! You gotta come quick!*" he spoke ecstatically in their village's local native tongue, Spanish.

"What is it? You found something good?"

"Did I find something good? Come see for yourself!"

Joaquín signaled for everyone else to follow suit as they encountered an electronics shop, wedged between two knocked over buildings. To Joaquín's surprise, the majority of the shop was intact as the majority of the equipment was undamaged.

"This is amazing, Pancho!" commented the stunned leader.

"That's not even the best part. Check this out!"

Pancho scurried to one particular shelf and took down one of many radio devices. Joaquín was in sheer astonishment. For the longest time, his father hoped to find a workable communication device to contact the outside world for help. Sadly, no such item was found. By the time his son took over, he had abandoned any and all thought of ever possibly finding such a device. Yet, here it was, right in front of him.

"God has blessed us today, my friend," said Pancho as he gave a wide grin.

"Absolutely, now we can get our best men to work out the machinery and send a signal!"

The men rejoiced in celebration of their most recent accomplishment. However, their cheers simmered as the ground beneath them shook. Joaquín called to his men.

"It's an earthquake, get out of the building!"

"But what about the shop?" asked his friend.

"Forget it! None of it matters if we're dead."

Joaquín and his squad ran out of the building as his friend lagged behind as he still hung on to the emergency radio device. The head of the expedition felt the tremors increase in ferocity as he heard a massive shift in the rubble. His morbid curiosity got the better of him as he turned to see what had caused the disruption. There he laid eyes on a gargantuan arachnid, which stood over forty meters in height with each leg adorned with red stripes. The creature resembled a mutated Mexican redknee tarantula. Not only had its size increased over the years, but the hairs covering its body had grown into spike-like protrusions that scraped the surface of anything its legs brushed up against as it crawled out of its burrow.

All eight of its eyes leered at the men fleeing for their lives. It decided to make its first meal out of the nearest prey as it toppled over the electronics store, destroying once usable equipment housed within the structure.

"*Pancho, hurry!*"

The panicked man did not need to look back to realize something massive was heading his way. Joaquín noticed his men heading into a pile of concrete for shelter. Once he secured himself within the small crevices, he saw his friend attempting to pick up the pace while still holding on to what was now the last of the radios.

"*Let go of the damn radio already!*" he shouted. "*It's not worth it!*"

"*Yes, it is! It's our only hope!*" replied Pancho as the spider outran the minuscule appetizer.

As soon as he was near the entrance, the man tossed the device into his lifelong friend's arms. The moment Joaquín caught the radio, Pancho took a hard left turn away from the rubble.

"*Hey, freak. I'm right here!*" he shouted to the arachnid as he waved his arms.

Joaquín was about to scream at his friend, pleading him to come back, before his compatriots restrained him.

"*Shh, don't speak,*" one of them whispered.

"*You want his sacrifice to be in vain?!*"

"*Sacrifice?*" he muffled through his teammate's hand.

The situation finally sunk in. Joaquín realized what his most trusted confidant was attempting to do. He was going to drive the behemoth bug off as far as he could to give the rest of the crew time to escape. He saw Pancho climb over a small pile of bricks before he disappeared out of sight. The tarantula followed suit before diving its spiked limb at the ground where a short cry was heard, followed by silence. The head of the journeymen looked away while the mutant fed. He could not risk shouting in pain. All he could do was weep for his fellow man.

Frustrated, Joaquín pounded on the wall in front of him. The structure rang like a bell. This was not any ordinary building, thought Joaquín. It was made entirely out of metal. He felt the rough, filthy plating that did not seem to match any of the debris surrounding them. Before he could investigate further, one party member called out to him.

"*Joaquín, the spider's gone!*"

He peered outside and noticed that indeed, his associate was right. The multi-legged beast had marched off. Joaquín then looked down at the machine in his arms, given to him by his now deceased friend. His father spent the remaining years of his life in search of a device like this, and Pancho willingly sacrificed himself for it. Joaquín felt obligated to see his friend's dying wish fulfilled and accomplish what his father could not.

"Let's move quickly, but don't make any sudden noise," he told his men.

The squad quietly moved out into the open from the entrance of the cement cave. They hurried along back the way they came. As Joaquín led the group to safety, his eyes were blinded by an intense glimmer. He found that everyone else was blinded by a light emanating from the ground. He saw that the sun was at the highest point of its daily cycle, but what exactly was causing the ground to reflect its rays was unknown. He kneeled down and felt the ground. It appeared to be dirt and broken asphalt, but there was a thin layer of smoothness he never noticed when they entered Chilpancingo.

"What do you think it is?" someone asked over his shoulder.

"Webbing," he whispered.

Just then the rumblings of the titanic invertebrate returned. Joaquín suspected that the creature must have adapted its webbing to convert the surface of its territory into one giant invisible web. Only it did not capture its prey, it merely picked up its vibrations and signaled the predator. It must not have attacked when they first entered its domain as it was likely resting in its burrow.

"Run!" he shouted to the rest of his entourage.

The beast picked up speed and recklessly smashed through the humans' hiding spot, exposing more of a strange metallic structure shrouded in a massive tarp. If Joaquín did not know any better he could have sworn he saw a giant hand. Yet, he had no time to process the revelation as he joined his men in their escape from the spider's lair.

The arachnid slammed its spiked appendages and slew five more men. It did not stop to consume its kills, however, as it continued its pursuit of the intruders. It moved ahead of the squad, sealing off the exit to the city. Joaquín instructed his men to move right into another passageway, only for it to lead them to a dead end. He and several of the escapees attempted to climb up the heaps of debris that surrounded them. Yet, every hand or foot they laid on the mound slipped off the surface and they slid back down.

"*We can't climb up. Everything's covered in webs!*"

"*Damn it!*" shouted Joaquín.

There was no chance of escape and certainly no means of fighting back against the mutant. Joaquín had been taught every possible means of avoiding mutants and kaiju since he was a teenager, yet all of it was for naught. He continued to curse himself for failing to live up to his father's expectations, failing his men, failing his family, and failing all of Fortuna.

Just then an explosion erupted from the tarantula's abdomen. The creature squealed in pain and spun around to find the source of the attack. Everyone could see that the creature's armor was singed off as its bodily fluids leaked. Both Joaquín and the spider followed the trail of smoke to a lone figure standing more than two hundred meters away. The chief explorer recognized the tarp that covered the metal structure from before. It stood roughly half the height of the arthropod, beside it was a large cylindrical object. A gust of wind ruffled the massive piece of cloth, revealing a pair of legs, arms, and a head with a glowing blue visor. Its humanoid shape told Joaquín that this was no beast at all, it was a mech, the first he had ever laid eyes on.

This machine however was surprisingly smaller than the ones his family watched on television during the eve of the apocalypse. Most were around sixty meters in height. How could this thing take on a mutant twice its size? There was no way it would leave its abdomen vulnerable after being blindsided the first time around with that projectile if it was even capable of firing another round.

The spider blindingly scurried towards its new target. The automaton placed its massive weapon away and pulled out a gargantuan blade from its shawl. The tool appeared as though it was forged from various pieces of metal. The creature made the first move as it attempted to stomp on the minuscule challenger. With absurd agility, the mech managed to dodge each strike from the arachnid's spine-filled appendage. Then, with one swing of its crooked saber, the mech lobbed off the left front limb.

The monster shrieked in pain before the metal giant ran underneath the creature's body and sliced off another leg. Now the beast had four limbs on its right side, with two on its left. Joaquín could see what the warrior was trying to do. It was attempting to knock off the animal's balance by hacking away at its limbs. With no limbs to support the left half of its body, eliminating it would be significantly less difficult.

Just as the mech aimed for a third limb, the spider spun its body and aimed its massive fangs at its mutilator. The artificial fighter held its sword and blocked the attack, only for its weapon to break in half. With the remaining portion of its blade, the mech flung the shard into the creature's face. The saber was embedded in the mutant's face, causing the titanic tarantula to throw itself into a furious barrage of strikes with its remaining legs.

That was when Joaquín noticed a red glow emanating from the robot's head. He noticed its face morph into something that appeared to have two red eyes. The machine now moved gracefully, almost as if it was effortlessly evading each attack with grace. The machine pulled out its projectile weapon from before, now clearly revealed to be a bazooka. The machine aimed the cylinder right underneath the center of its target and shot one more round into the arachnid's body, blasting the bug in an awful display of its outer shell, organs, and fluids.

The men cheered all around Joaquín as he too was stunned at the robot's victory. Like David and Goliath, the diminutive mech had gone toe to toe with its gargantuan opponent and came out victorious with a strike to the cranium. If only the savior was active to save poor Pancho and the rest of his fallen brethren.

The victorious shouts lightened as the humanoid frame marched closer towards them, its face converting back into its previous visor arrangement. Several members of the group began to move towards the exit.

"*Stop! We are no threat to the mech,*" Joaquín ordered his men.

While two-thirds followed their leader's order, the rest ran for their lives, having already had enough of giant-killers for one lifetime. The chief addressed his followers once more.

"*If the pilot wishes to address us, let him. We all owe this person our lives.*"

Perhaps it was a sign that his fate led him to this rare weapon. With enough luck, this pilot could be just what Fortuna needed. To do this, Joaquín had to be on his best behavior.

The mech stopped before the expeditionary force. At last, Joaquín got a good look at the machine in its full glory. The machine dropped the now ammo-less rocket-launching weapon behind it. What other devices did the machine have in its arsenal? Whatever it was capable of, the mech had certainly seen better days as its armor had been scarred and discolored from what must have been decades of survival. Still, it was a technological thing of beauty. The cockpit in its chest opened up, and out of it stepped a man who appeared to be in his mid-to-late forties. He had a grizzled mug, wore a pair of sunglasses, and a distinctly American military uniform, though lacking any sleeves. The pilot leered at the group in disapproval.

"One of you owes me a new sword," the man bluntly spoke in a grizzled voice.

The mech operated its arm as it carried the pilot down to ground level. On its forearm was a shield that had a name written across it: "Bravura."

CHAPTER 6

The Pacific Ocean off the Coast of California

Emily moved Steel Samurai 2.0 slowly through the water toward the oncoming object. At the depth they were at, visibility extended only about twenty meters in front of the mech's eye ports. She was tightly clutching the controls and sweat was pouring down her brow. The young woman tried to calm herself down as her mind raced with scenarios she could encounter.

Her father could see how stressed she was and he did his best to scaffold her through the situation. Chris offered suggestions, but let Emily figure out as much on her own as she could.

"Emily, look again at the sonar. What are the two biggest things you see?"

"The object moving toward us and the other stationary object."

"Right, the stationary object is the wreck I was telling you about. It's a nineteenth-century steamship. I can tell you from past experience it's roughly thirty meters in length. How does the object moving toward us compare to the wreck? Is it bigger or smaller?"

Emily studied the sonar display for a moment. "The object moving toward us is a bit larger than the wreck."

Chris spoke softly. "The largest whales are roughly the length of the wreck, so the creature moving toward us is either a mutant or a kaiju."

He saw Emily's grip on the controls tighten. The father and veteran mech pilot reached over and put his hand over his daughter's.

"Try your best to relax. There are plenty of mutants, whales, and rays for instance, that are just as harmless with their bigger size as they were before they were mutated. That thing could be one of them. In case it is something dangerous, however, let's start taking precautions. Take a minute and think what should we do?"

Emily took a deep breath and then evaluated her situation. She began turning off the exterior and interior lights to the mech. "First, we need to not make ourselves stand out as much. If we turn the lights off, we'll be less likely to draw attention to ourselves."

Chris nodded. "Good. What else should we do?"

Emily looked at the controls in front of her. "Activate Steel Samurai 2.0's sword. We'll want to be able to defend ourselves as quickly as possible if needed."

She looked at her father to see him nod in approval. She then used her controls to open the compartment on the mech's leg and activate its close-quarters weapon.

She looked down at the control stick in front of her, like it was Excalibur itself. She was fully aware of the countless legendary battles her parents had fought using the control stick to guide the mechanical arm and the sword it wielded. She grabbed the controls and took a deep breath.

"It's really simple, Emily. The arm will follow the control stick. You can use it to move the arm in any direction. If you want the sword to go up, just move up. If you want to go at an angle, move at an angle. If you want to change the direction at the wrist, click the button on the top of the control once to shift your grip horizontally, twice to shift it back to vertical."

Emily took a few practice swings with the sword and when she felt comfortable with it, she got the mech moving again. She was slowly moving the mech forward as she saw the object getting closer to them.

She shook her head. "Dad, I'm not sure what else to do."

"You're scared because something you're unsure of is moving towards us. Whatever is out there is likely either scared or angry that there's something large it can't identify moving toward it. We're here to provide for our people and serve as protectors, not exterminators. Unless that thing poses a direct threat to the settlement, our best course of action is to avoid confrontation. What can we do to deescalate the situation?"

Emily's eyes went wide and she pulled back on the controls. "We can stop moving. If we stop moving, it won't look like we're aggressively heading toward whatever that thing is!"

Chris smiled. "Right, keep your hands on the controls though, and keep our sword in front of us. If we're attacked, we want to be in a position where we can quickly react."

The father and daughter waited quietly in the hull of the colossal automaton. Emily kept her eyes fixed on the sonar display as the creature continued to move toward them.

Right before the approaching beast was going to be visible to her, Emily looked up from the display and out into the dark ocean. She gasped when she saw the form of a bulbous brown creature with a round body and four sets of flippers moving toward her. The creature had the appearance of a seal with the exception of what looked to be an extremely long nose covering up the majority of its mouth.

Emily shook her head. "What is that? Some kind of mutated sea lion?"

Chris shook his head. "No, it's an elephant seal. They used to be all up and down the coast of North and South America before the world ended. I came across a mutant pack of them off the coast of southern Canada a few years ago. I was trying to use the mech to gather there just like we are now, and when I started taking in fish it attacked me."

"When I was stationed in California the other pilots used to point them out when we were on the beach. The damned things are highly territorial and can be pretty aggressive, even before they were mutated." He shrugged. "I guess they're even more aggressive now."

Chris pointed at the mutant as it swam closer to them before circling Steel Samurai 2.0.

"It uses its weight to slam into enemies and its teeth are also pretty sharp. The one I ran into a few years ago knocked your mom and I around in here pretty good before we finally used the sword to kill it."

The giant elephant seal circled the unmoving robot two times before it turned and made its way back to the shipwreck and the fish that swarmed around it. Chris grabbed the controls and moved the mech forward. When they were close enough for the mech's exterior lights to reach the sunken vessel, he turned them on.

The ocean floor lit up to reveal a cloud of red from the fish the elephant seal had torn asunder and eaten.

The old pilot shook his head. "The moment we start trying to take in fish, that damned thing is gonna attack us." He shrugged. "I hate to say it, but we better kill that thing while it still thinks we're not a threat. If he realizes there's food at this location, he could go back to his pod and lead them back here. Like I said, they used to be pretty widespread across the entire Pacific Coast. Once they were mutated, they seemed to have settled

52

in Canada. I guess their food is starting to run out, so they're looking for new hunting grounds."

He looked at Emily whom he could tell was both studying the animal and felt sorry for it. He grabbed his daughter's hand. "I'm sorry, babe. I know right now that thing's not currently a threat. If it brings the rest of its herd down here though, we could be facing two issues. First, they could wipe out our fish supply. In addition to that, if we're fishing when they're hunting, they'll attack the mech."

He tapped the interior of Steel Samurai's 2.0 cockpit. "This old girl still has a lotta fight left in her, but we gotta pick our battles. Better to take out one giant elephant seal now than a dozen of them later. At least you'll get some combat experience today."

Emily nodded as she continued to look at the ravenous elephant seal devouring fish in front of them. "You might be right, Dad, but we may not have to."

She turned her head to her father. "The robot still has pretty extensive databases, doesn't it?"

He shrugged. "Yeah, it's got a lot of internal information on all kinds of things. At home, Kyle's even been able to run a cord to it to access the internet as well."

Emily called out to the mech. "Computer, pull up information on elephant seals' diet and put it on frontal display." Steel Samurai 2.0's eyes suddenly displayed information on the various diets of elephant seals across them.

Chris looked at the first few lines. "It says they eat a lot of fish, which is why they could be a problem."

Emily pointed to a line farther down the information displayed. "They could be a problem, but they could also be the answer to numerous problems we have."

"Are you thinking these things could be like Ramrod?" Chris shook his head. "Baby, I was wrong about Ramrod, but these things are a different story. Even if they were to settle here, they eat mainly fish, the same ones we rely on, elephant seals are territorial. They may inadvertently protect the settlement from any kaiju attacking from the water, but they pose a bigger problem than they're worth. Those fish provide food and fertilizer for us. Losing access to the fish here could cost human lives."

"Dad, look here." She pointed to the line of text lower in the information Steel Samurai 2.0 had displayed. "It says that elephant seals eat mollusks, like slugs. How often do you and mom have to kill the giant leeches that form in the rivers north of the settlement?"

Chris shrugged. "About once a month we go up there. We found out before you were born that if we didn't cull those bastards on a regular basis, they would start to make their way into our river. The giant leeches would not only attack people, believe me, I know from past experience, but they would also contaminate the water."

"Right, that's why you and mom bury the dead leeches, because even if you leave them in the water, giant mutant birds like seagulls and vultures come and eat their bodies, right?"

"Yes, mutant seagulls are not something you want to try to use to protect us. They're as likely to eat live humans as they are dead monsters."

Emily shook her head. "I know, but we may be able to use the leeches to have the elephant seals protect our shoreline! Follow me here. Elephant seals eat slugs, right?"

Chris shrugged. "I guess so."

"Well, it says here they do. Anyway, while leeches are technically worms, they're kind of like slugs. So, if we kill a giant leech and leave it here for the mutant seals, they'll eat it. If it survives on leeches, we won't have to bury them anymore. We can fly them out here for the seals. You already said that they seemed to stay in one spot until the food supply starts to dwindle. If we can give them a steady food supply, they'll settle here, and then their territorial nature will serve as another natural deterrent. Also, if we keep them well fed enough, they won't need to go after our fish supply."

Chris was silent as he looked at his daughter while she explained her plan. Fearing that she had not convinced her father, Emily continued to bring up points in favor of her plan. "Think of it this way as well. You just said we have to pick our battles with Steel Samurai 2.0. We have to fight the leeches anyway, but if this plan works, we won't have to fight the elephant seal, its pod, or whatever threats they can divert away from us."

Chris sighed and nodded. "Okay. I was wrong about Ramrod, So, I'll give you the benefit of the doubt on this one." He gestured to the controls. "Let's take her up. You'll have to start by letting out some of the water so we only surface about halfway. We have to go up slowly so that we decompress."

Emily guided the mech to the depth her father had suggested, then allowed the robot to float there for a few minutes. As the father and daughter were suspended in the water, Emily noticed that her dad had a downtrodden look on his face.

She looked over at her father. "What's wrong, Dad? You look like you've just gotten some terrible news or something."

He did his best to smile. "Honey, this is something I was hoping to explain to you before we went to do a sweep for leeches. However, since we are going to do this now, it's something you're going to have to learn about now. Long before you figured out how to use Ramrod to help protect our settlement, your mom and I found another way to use mutants to help protect our loved ones, but it's not as pleasant or mutually beneficial for the mutants, as is your relationship with Ramrod."

Emily shook her head. "What are you talking about?"

"We already discussed the problems the mutant leeches pose to our settlement in terms of direct attacks and water contamination." He gestured to the interior of Steel Samurai 2.0. "Leeches aren't going to come out of hiding to latch onto all of this metal. They're not overly fond of dead things either."

"A long time ago, before I met your mother when our settlement was a dying wasteland in the middle of the country, I still had to fight off giant leeches. Back then, I would pretty much have to wait until they attacked a group of people who would call for help. By the time I heard that people were in danger, they were mostly dead. I would only show up in Steel Samurai to kill the leeches and prevent the next attack. I couldn't figure out how to get ahead of them because leeches prefer to attack live targets."

Chris shrugged. "As always, it was your mom who came up with a better way to draw them out with things that, while not a direct threat to us, are also still dangerous." He gestured to the controls. "Take us out of the water and head for Los Angeles."

"Los Angeles? Dad, you destroyed the Colony out there long before I was even born."

"I know I did, and something else took their place. Do you know how many feral cats were in LA even before the kaiju took over?"

Emily shook her head. "I have no concept of what the world was like before the kaiju. I only know the stories that you and mom have told me."

"Well, suffice to say, it was a lot. After the Colony was gone, there was still enough radiation from other mutant animals to turn some of the cat population into giant mutants. Before I intervened, the Colony more or less kept them under control. But when I took out those ants, the cats inherited the city. The one blessing about those animals is they fight over territory so much they seem to have implemented their own population control."

"Okay, so let me get this straight. There's a population of mutant cats in LA that you and mom have been using as bait to draw out leeches from nearby water supplies?"

Chris nodded again.

"I can buy that, and even see why you and mom are using the mutant cats for bait, but my main question is what's the food supply that's sustaining the cats there?"

Chris shook his head. "Anything, and everything. I know you've seen a lot of terrible things in your life, but you've never seen something like this. I just want you to be ready for the carnage you're going to see, and the horror that'll follow when we bring a mutant cat back to feed the leeches."

Emily nodded. "Okay. I'm not thrilled about this course of action, but I can see why you and mom have implemented it for so many years. Obviously, the lives of those mutants, even if they don't attack us, aren't worth putting the lives of our people at risk."

The daughter and father then flew towards the City of Angels where they would face a nightmare that neither one of them was prepared for.

CHAPTER 7

The Pacific Ocean off the coast of El Salvador

The cool ocean water slid across Atomic Rex's massive body as he glided through his aquatic kingdom. With his terrestrial domain successfully defended from the encroaching hogs, and his stomach full from those same invaders, the nuclear theropod had taken to the water.

While the mutated dinosaur's body no longer required him to absorb radiation, his colossal body still quickly burned through calories provided by food. The mammoth reptile had learned that by spending the majority of his time in the water, as opposed to on land, he could decrease the amount of food he needed to ingest.

The energy needed to move Atomic Rex's gargantuan frame through the ocean was roughly half of what was required to move the same distance over land. The majority of Atomic Rex's existence was focused on defending his territory and hunting for food. While there were few experiences that could be described as pleasurable in regards to the saurian monster's existence, swimming through the ocean was one which gave the kaiju a sense of calmness.

As the saurian moved through the water his heightened senses were fully aware of everything around him. The nuclear theropod's large nasal cavity allowed him to smell everything in the water for hundreds of kilometers. The nuclear energy coursing through his body gave him a sense akin to a shark's electroreception capabilities. The cells in Atomic Rex's body could detect the small amount of electrical energy given off by fauna as it swam.

Atomic Rex was fully aware of every living creature in his domain. While the kaiju was not currently hunting, he was searching for any potential threats to his dominance of the waters off the coast of the Americas. As he moved through the ocean, Atomic Rex could sense the presence of a group of minke whales, several sharks, numerous schools of fish, and several octopi.

He could also sense the presence of several mutants, none of which posed a threat to him but several that could later provide an abundant amount of food. Several gigantic lobsters were mating roughly thirty kilometers west of the reptile's current position. Nearly twenty kilometers ahead of him, the True Kaiju was able to detect a colossal Sperm Whale heading north.

Atomic Rex's electroreceptive abilities informed him that the creature dwarfed him in size. The beast was well over one hundred meters in length, making it more than twice as large as the nuclear theropod. In addition to the anger the saurian creature felt toward the whale for moving through his territory, the beast's scent also reminded Atomic Rex of a hated rival he had not seen for several years, but still yearned to destroy.

Currently, the gigantic whale was moving away from Atomic Rex and the nuclear theropod was content to let the beast flee his domain. In his decades of ruling the western Pacific, he had learned that whales, both natural and mutated, migrated through his kingdom. On rare occasions, some of the beasts would attempt to challenge his rulership, but mostly, the mammals only hoped to move through his waters without being hunted down by him.

Due to its sheer size, Atomic Rex had wanted to chase the mutant whale out of his territory, but with his stomach full he decided against directly attacking the creature. Food was becoming more difficult to find with each passing year. If Atomic Rex was able to slay the mutant whale its body would provide him enough meat to sustain him for a month. The nuclear theropod knew the whale's migratory pattern would bring him back down along the coast at some point in the future. The reptilian horror would simply chase the leviathan away until it either directly challenged him or he was in need of a large supply of food.

As he continued his slow pursuit of the mutant cetacean, the kaiju continued to track any other potential threats. There was only one creature within a hundred kilometers that was large enough to pose a threat to him. The organism was some manner of mutant jellyfish. Atomic Rex's past interactions with similar life forms had led him to conclude that the spineless mass of cells were both not a threat to him nor were they a viable food source. For the most part, Atomic Rex simply ignored the cnidarians as they drifted past him.

Atomic Rex could sense that the jellyfish moving toward him was different from others he had encountered. In this instance, the invertebrate had a different scent than most of the creatures of its kind he had encountered. The strange thing about the beast was that it seemed to be propelling itself through the water toward him. To the kaiju's limited mind, however, those differences posed no reason for him to be concerned with the creature. Atomic Rex's past experiences had taught him that if he avoided the jellyfish, it would pose no threat to him.

In this instance, Atomic Rex's indifference to the massive cnidaria would prove a grave mistake. The monstrous jellyfish that was moving toward Atomic Rex was a mutant box jellyfish. Unbeknownst to Atomic Rex, the mutant box jellyfish had the deadliest sting of any creature in the world. The True Kaiju was also unaware that the creature was being pulled toward him by an unknown newcomer for the express purpose of engaging him in battle.

The saurian kaiju continued to his pursuit of the mutant whale as the titanic cnidarian drew ever closer to him. With each passing second, the mindless horror inched closer to its prey with unnatural levels of sentience. When the two monsters were off the coast of El Salvador, the coelenterate's tentacles were finally within reach of his prey. The giant creature was directly on top of Atomic Rex. Upon sensing that danger was imminent, the theropod peered upwards and noticed a bizarre sight. Not only was the jellyfish dangerously close, but hovering above the water's surface over the sea native was a tiny metallic figure. It was similar if not smaller in stature to his old rival. However, the waters were too dark and murky to make out any details of the foreigner. Before the dinosaur could further process what was happening, the humanoid figure dove into the water and forced the invertebrate down onto the reptile. The assailant watched as the tentacled creature ensnared Atomic Rex upon contact. The figure then took off towards the sky at blinding speed and left the True Kaiju to his fate.

Atomic Rex was about to surface and refill his lungs with oxygen when the tentacles of the colossal jellyfish wrapped around his torso, tail, and limbs. The moment that the tentacles touched the kaiju, millions of microscopic stingers entered his body and injected it with venom. The saurian monster was in excruciating pain that caused him to roar despite still being underwater.

The venom coursing through the True Kaiju's body attacked his central nervous system. Between the lack of oxygen and poison attacking every nerve in his body, Atomic Rex was severely disoriented. The reptilian horror tried to break free of the giant cnidarian's grip by pulling free from it. This action only had the effect of the mutant jellyfish wrapping even more of its seemingly endless tentacles around its prey.

With an increased amount of the deadly appendages attached to his body, Atomic Rex was experiencing a level of pain he had never felt before. Every nerve in the reptile was on fire while his lungs were bursting from a lack of oxygen. As his vision started to fade, Atomic Rex's mind focused on the nuclear power stored within his cells. The nuclear theropod attempted to access that power and unleash his Atomic Wave on his attacker. To his surprise, when the saurian beast tried to utilize his most powerful attack, he discovered that his radioactive power would not heed his command.

The neurotoxin that the box jellyfish was injecting into Atomic Rex had blocked off the nerve endings that typically received the command from his mind to unleash his Atomic Wave. Atomic Rex looked up to the quickly dimming sunlight above his head as his vision continued to fade. The combination of pain and lack of oxygen had finally caused the mighty creature to lose consciousness.

The gargantuan cnidarian could feel its prey stop struggling beneath him. The mindless invertebrate gave no victory cry or display of dominance. It simply pulled its defeated prey closer to its body in order to better digest it.

When Atomic Rex's back touched the underbelly of the mutant coelenterate, his eyes suddenly snapped open. Despite being in desperate need of air, and being wracked with pain, Atomic Rex's fighting spirit pushed through those obstacles to force him back to consciousness.

With his very life force ebbing away, Atomic Rex spun around in the water and turned his powerful jaws toward his opponent's body. As Atomic Rex turned, the colossal cnidarian wrapped itself even tighter around his body. The act caused countless millions more of its tiny stingers to embed themselves further into its prey.

The nuclear theropod pushed past the pain and used his jaws to tear a massive section out of the box jellyfish's body. Due to its lack of organs or nerves, losing nearly a third of its body had no effect on the deadly coelenterate. Atomic Rex's eyes were beginning to dim again as his chest felt like it would collapse in on itself. The pain the monster was feeling was quickly overtaken by anger at the thought that a barely living collection of cells could defeat him.

The saurian demon opened his mouth as wide as he could and then slammed his jaws shut with enough force to crush a battleship. The moment the underside of the spineless horror made contact with the reptile's mouth, the microscopic stingers in the creature's body attacked. Atomic Rex's gums, tongue, and throat immediately experienced the same debilitating pain that the rest of his anatomy was experiencing. The saurian monster fought against the reflex to pull his mouth away from the source of his pain. The True Kaiju forced his jaws to open and slam shut on his attacker once again.

Atomic Rex's second bite tore the enlarged box jellyfish in half. The reptilian horror looked up through the vivisected body of his adversary and saw sunlight. With the tentacles of the colossal invertebrate still attached to him and pumping venom into his system, Atomic Rex swam toward the surface.

Each stroke of his feet and tail caused the tentacles to work themselves deeper into his body. A lesser kaiju would have given into the pain and would have succumbed to a lack of oxygen. This however was no lesser creature. This was Atomic Rex! The nuclear theropod's will to live and refusal to be defeated were without equal.

Even as his eyes were forcing themselves closed one final time, the monster's indomitable spirit forced him upward. Just as he lost consciousness again, Atomic Rex's jaws broke the surface of the water and his body instinctively inhaled the air it direly needed. As oxygen filled the monster's lungs he slipped back beneath the waterline. The gargantuan reptile was sinking to the ocean floor when his eyes suddenly snapped open. With oxygen in his lungs, he could feel his uncanny healing power fighting against the tentacles still attached to his body and the poison they were injecting into him.

Atomic Rex once more forced himself to the surface where he exhaled and then took in another deep breath of air. The exhausted monster looked to the shoreline roughly a mile to his left and he began swimming toward it. With each movement of his body, Atomic Rex could feel the horrible pain that was surging through him lessen as his healing factor continued to force the titanic jellyfish's stingers out of his scales.

When he was close enough to shore that he could lay in the surf and keep his mouth and nostrils above water, Atomic Rex finally allowed himself to pass out. As the beast rested, his body continued to heal him from the neurotoxins that were ravaging his body.

Dozens of kilometers ahead of Atomic Rex, the leviathan-like mutant sperm whale that the giant dinosaur had been chasing sensed the struggle which had occurred in his wake. The intelligent mammal was also able to discern that the kaiju who ruled these waters, the very waters that he and his kind needed to traverse to mate, was severely injured. Knowing that the main predatory threat to himself and the females he mated with was weakened, the enlarged cetacean turned around and began swimming back toward the unconscious form of Atomic Rex.

Atomic Rex had slept for over an hour as his body worked to force the innumerable stingers attached to his torso, arms, legs, mouth, and tail out of his body. When he finally awoke, the nuclear theropod took a look around him to see long pieces of tentacles floating in the water. The beast could see the tentacles squirming in the surf as each individual piece of the giant box jellyfish attempted to regenerate into an entirely new version of itself.

While the reptilian monster's mind could not fathom the concept of regeneration, he fully understood when a foe was vanquished and when it still presented a threat. As he stared at the still moving tentacle remains, Atomic Rex decided that the pieces of his attacker represented a danger to him. The lord of the ocean lifted his foot into the air as his body started to take on its familiar light blue glow. He then slammed his foot to the ground sending out an Atomic Wave that disrupted the water all around him as the dome of pure radiation expanded out from his body.

As the dome's blast radius increased, it flowed over the pieces of tentacle that had been attached to Atomic Rex, incinerating them. With the threat of the tentacles addressed, the saurian horror looked back out at the ocean where the bisected massive box jellyfish was still floating. Atomic Rex was still in dire need of rest, but his desire to rid his waters of the foe who had so direly injured him outweighed his lethargy. The kaiju roared and then swam back out into the water to finish his battle with the creature that dared to attack him.

Atomic Rex's keen senses were still damped by the neurotoxins in his body as he made his way back out into the water. Both his sense of smell and his electroreceptive capabilities were barely functional. The only sense that had recovered part of its functionality was Atomic Rex's sense of taste. By leaving his mouth open and letting the ocean water flow over it, the radioactive dinosaur was able to follow the taste of his own blood back to his attacker.

The True Kaiju's journey was shorter than he had expected as the tide was coming in toward land and had carried his prey closer to him rather than deeper out to sea. When he came across the first half of the now binary coelenterate, the reptilian monster stopped several meters short of the reach of the beast's tentacles. He glared at the bisected horror in anger before blasting it with his Atomic Wave. The underwater explosion incinerated every cell of the half of the jellyfish within its blast zone.

With half of the threat destroyed, the remnant of a prehistoric age repeated the process of following the taste of his own blood to the second half of the creature. Atomic Rex followed the path for roughly fifteen minutes before he found the other half of the deadly cnidarian. Once again, the nuclear theropod stopped short of the halved monster's tentacles. This time he did not take a moment to stare at his opponent. The saurian nightmare's body was still fighting off the neurotoxins, and aside from his senses being severely diminished, Atomic Rex was nearly exhausted.

He called forth the radiation stored within his cells and unleashed another blast of his Atomic Wave. The weary kaiju watched from the epicenter of his blast as the last vestiges of the giant box jellyfish were wiped away. With his foe finally vanquished, Atomic Rex turned to head back to shore where he could rest and his body could finish healing itself.

Atomic Rex had only taken two strokes toward land when the colossal mutant sperm whale he had been chasing crashed into him and sent the saurian monster tumbling through the water.

CHAPTER 8

Fortuna Village

After several hours, Joaquín and his party were only several miles away from their sanctuary. Among his men were various cases and backpacks with an assortment of food, electronics, medicine, and farming equipment. With the massive spider vanquished, the team was free to extract what they needed before the arachnid's death attracted the attention of any more dangerous wildlife.

Trailing behind them ever so gently was the mysterious pilot of the equally enigmatic machine labeled "Bravura." Back when the excavation crew was directly addressed by the Hunter, demanding for them to pay him back for the loss of his vital weapons, Joaquín had stepped forward and offered him shelter at Fortuna. Many of his compatriots were dubious that harboring such a dangerous machine could benefit their home in any way. Yet, their leader convinced them that without him, they surely would not have survived their encounter with the mutant arachnid. Allowing him the chance to rest for a while in Fortuna was the least they could do.

Once Joaquín proposed the idea, in English as it appeared to be the man's native language, the disgruntled mech pilot sighed and only responded with, "Alright, lead the way."

Despite their begrudging gratitude towards the man, Joaquín's men could not help but wonder why he did not assist them using his mech. Surely, they thought, this machine could have made transporting their supplies significantly easier, if not having it carry more of their bounty. The father of the Muñoz family did his best to keep tensions down, telling them that perhaps he could convince the pilot to stay and protect the village for a while.

"*You know that's impossible!*" one of his men angrily protested. "*You and I know what'll happen if they come back and see this thing.*"

"*Carlos is right,*" another journeyman chimed in. "*We know he saved our lives, but he can't stay for more than one night!*"

Joaquín was deep in thought as he had not considered the significant dangers that lay beyond the former borders of Gerrero, Mexico. He turned to look back at the tall machine. Was he making the right call by bringing this man along? Should he have given his findings to the pilot instead? What would his father do at a time like this?

Soon, more questions began to fill his mind. Where did this mech come from? Was the name "Bravura" some kind of name or designation? Why was it significantly smaller than any of the robots he heard about on the news as a child? He could have sworn that all but one of mankind's mechs were destroyed in the war against the True Kaiju. Though he hesitated to call it a war, but rather a slaughter as by the time the mutants and kaiju took over the planet, only one lone American machine survived. From the rumors he had heard from fellow travelers and newcomers to Fortuna, the American machine, dubbed "Steel Samurai," still protected most of North and South America to this day. This would explain the lack of any True Kaiju living nearby, though, without any sort of wireless communication, Fortuna was still vulnerable to the various mutants that still thrived in the area. He hoped the emergency radio his now-deceased friend had discovered, held tightly in his arms, would change all of that.

At long last, they arrived at their humble abode. Everyone left their homes and gasped in awe at the gigantic figure tall enough to block out the sun from view. The automaton's massive cloak covered the gathering crowd in a blanket of shadow. Its pilot still remained in the machine. Meanwhile, down below, various men, women, and children embraced the returning men, while others desperately searched for their loved ones.

After embracing his wife and sons, Joaquín took it upon himself to break the news of their tragic deaths. It pained him and his father whenever either of them lost anyone in their journeys. Much like his predecessor, Joaquín attempted to console each widowed wife, orphaned child, or mourning sibling with a solemn and sincere attitude. He also tried to provide for them as best he could in the absence of a lost loved one. This was the hardest part of his role as leader of Fortuna, carrying the burden of responsibility for any deaths that occurred as a result of his actions. This one proved the most painful of all as he informed Pancho's wife of her husband's selfless sacrifice.

"He died a hero, Bianca. Without him, we would not be here today, with the hope of a greater future. Because of him, we found what could be

our salvation." He pointed to his radio and gestured to the mech. However, neither praise nor optimism could ever bring back his lost friend. As Bianca collapsed in tears, Joaquín's own wife, Lupe, took it upon herself to attend to her weeping friend.

"*I'll take care of her and the others. You do something about that thing,*" she said as she eyed the giant robot. She trusted that whatever it was, her husband had good reason to bring it to their village.

"*Right, dear.*"

Joaquín faced the audience and raised his voice in an encouraging and positive tone to instill hope in his people.

"*Today, we came face-to-face with certain death when we encountered a mutant in Chilpancingo. Many brave souls lost their lives, and we all would have died ourselves if it weren't for this great machine and its amazing pilot you see before you.*"

Joaquín then raised his radio in the air. "*Through the actions of our brave brothers and the skills of this selfless pilot, we now have a chance to reconnect with the rest of the world!*"

As the crowd cheered, the mech began moving its head, catching everyone by surprise. Was the pilot getting impatient? Joaquín thought. It appeared that the man was surveying the area before his mech's armored right arm raised and pointed to a nearby mountainside. The village leader knew he wanted to head in that direction. He quickly told everyone to move away from the machine, allowing it to stomp its way towards the mountainside, narrowly missing a house along the way. Once it reached the mountain, the robot proceeded to turn around, bend down, and lay against the rocky mountain, its cloak camouflaging most of its metal exterior within the brown boulders and vegetation. A hissing sound was heard coming from the mech's chest underneath its massive tattered shawl. Joaquín knew that he must not let the villagers disturb the stranger or risk upsetting him. He ordered everyone to head back to their homes and for his team to leave their findings in the warehouse.

Finally, the man who had successfully slain the arachnid and followed them all the way back to Fortuna revealed himself as he stepped out from the machine's makeshift tarp. He looked no less relaxed than when he first came face to face with Joaquín back in Chilpancingo. Now that the village leader could see the pilot at eye level, he was able to pick up more information about the mysterious man. The man was lightly tanned and had dark brown hair that started to gray. He appeared to be Latino if not mixed-race.

Clothing-wise, the pilot wore a ragged US army aviator uniform with its sleeves torn off. On his chest were two embroidered army patches, one of which read "Air Force." His fingerless gloves and combat boots however did not appear to be army-issued and appeared mismatched compared to the rest of his attire.

Looking up at the man's worn and stoic visage, he noticed a gash down the left side of his face. As he approached him, he noticed his left eye was discolored, most likely blind. It was perhaps the reason he wore his sunglasses. Lastly, Joaquín was perplexed by the tattoo on the monster hunter's right shoulder, which appeared to be a cross between the Greek letters alpha and omega.

Whoever this man was, he had come from a trained military background and may have lived through decades of combat. At last, the Hunter spoke up.

"Where will I be staying?"

"O-oh, this way," Joaquín responded in his rusty English as he pointed at a guest house for the rare passerby. "Just follow me."

They made their way to a small shack no bigger than a shed, built with wood like the other buildings. Inside was a small rickety old bed frame with nothing more than a mattress.

"I'll get a blanket and pillow."

"None needed," the Hunter interrupted. "This is all I need."

"Oh, okay, Señor. Then I'll have my wife make your dinner. You'll love Lupe's cooking!"

The man sat on the bed and seemed to be deep in thought. What he was thinking, Joaquín could never guess.

"W-well, I'll be back soon." As he faced the door the visitor spoke once more.

"Who were you and your men talking about on the way here?"

"What?" a startled Joaquín said in shock.

"Back there, one of them said something about someone coming here."

"Y-you could hear us?"

"I can hear everything from Bravura." Joaquín could hear a light chuckle coming from the man as if he took pride in his machine's capabilities.

"Bravura. Is that your machine's name?"

"Yup," the pilot confirmed, without divulging anything else about his humanoid weapon.

"And yours?"

"Don't have one, not anymore. Now, who were you guys talking about? If they're a problem, I'm out of here." The tone in the man grew more aggressive. Joaquín could tell his guest was dead serious.

"This village," he paused as he struggled to choose his words carefully. Suddenly an animalistic howl echoed across the village. Both men stood and ran outside. They saw several of the villagers running for their lives towards the back of the settlement. One of the men sprinted towards the pair.

"*They're here!*"

"*Damn it, not now!*"

"What's going on?" demanded the pilot. "Is it mutants?"

"Y-yes," but before he could say anything else the Hunter was already heading to his mech at lightning speed.

"W-wait, Señor!" Unfortunately, it was too late as in a short amount of time, the pilot was already in the cockpit of his mechanical frame.

Its blue visor illuminated and stood tall once more. The pilot scanned the area and found two large masses were slowly approaching. They were four-legged mammalian animals. Judging by their stocky muscular builds, short coats of fur, and wide flat heads, they were most likely Pitbulls. The hunter had seen various dogs, wolves, and coyotes over the years, but never before had he encountered a purebred species. He was curious if their notorious reputation as aggressive dog-fighters would stand a chance against his old yet reliable machine.

With a press of a button from its pilot, Bravura reached out with its left hand to dismount one of two metal cylinders from a compartment attached to its right forearm. The mech held out the object and tightened its grip around the middle section. The applied pressure caused the cylinder to extend to three times its length, resulting in a steel bo staff. Bravura entered a combative stance, with both hands on its newly formed weapon, and waited for the giant dogs to make their move. Inside, a small part of the Hunter was hoping for the animals to attack first. Struggles like these were the only times he truly felt alive. He could imagine if only for a moment, he was back on the battlefield with his brothers in arms.

The Pitbulls were left surprised by the sudden appearance of this giant that stood nearly as tall as them, yet their resilient instincts kicked in and their aggression heightened. One of the dogs lunged forth and attempted to bite down on the mech's leg, only for the terrier to be knocked back by a swift strike to the jaw before it crashed onto a nearby house. With its partner temporarily out of action, the second Pitbull went up next. Bravura slammed its staff down, only for the canine to dodge the attack, and pounced at the large metal mass.

What the dog did not know was that it bit down not on the mech, but its large cloak. With his enemy distracted, the pilot commanded his titanic avatar to remove its cloak, freeing the mech from the beast. Bravura immediately thrusted its pole into the terrier's torso and, with the press of another button, electrocuted the Pitbull as sparks crackled from each end of the staff. The mutant mammal yelped in agony and abandoned the cloth. With the mutant preoccupied by the searing pain in its chest, Bravura landed several electrifying hits with its staff, all precisely targeted at the creature's torso.

Both dogs were panting, with one wheezing and carrying broken ribs, the other reeling from a dislocated jaw. Yet, both refused to back down as the two barked and growled at their foe. The Hunter was impressed, yet was curious as to what drove these creatures to keep fighting when there was nothing to be gained from this battle. Regardless, it did not matter to him.

He looked around and noticed all manner of destruction from their clash. All around him he could see villagers continuing to flee for their lives. He witnessed collapsed houses and dead bodies. Then, he began to notice the dead bodies of several men, women, and children. Memories began to flash before the pilot's mind. These were memories of flames, beasts, destruction, and death. Even after so many years, he still could not purge himself of the trauma that had haunted him for three decades. His breath began to shorten, sweat rolled down his forehead, and his heart rate increased rapidly.

"No more," he muttered to himself in a quivering voice. "No more!"

Primal screams erupted from the cockpit as Bravura ran toward the Pitbulls. The dogs kept their distance from the random swings of the taser-like staff. The Pitbull with a working jaw found the opportunity to latch its teeth on the weapon the moment the mech moved towards it. As it tried prying the staff away from Bravura's tight grip, the second dog came to aid its ally. The beast leaped with its claws aimed at the struggling machine but was abruptly halted when the robot countered with a forceful kick. The Hunter had perfectly aimed for the terrier's already weakened jaw, snapping it in two. With one of the dogs down, the pilot revealed his second hidden piece of equipment. One lever pull later and the bulky compartment on the mech's left forearm unfolded into a flat angular shield with razor-sharp edges. Bravura rammed the pointed front end of the shield into the mutant's throat before tearing it open with one swiping motion.

He left the dog to its morbid fate to bleed to death on the ground as he heard the remaining dog beginning to whimper. It quickly turned tail and escaped from the arena as fast as it could. As much as he wanted to chase after the canine, the Hunter was reeling back from his kill. His pulse slowed down as he finally came back to his senses. He told himself that he was no longer in the war and that the badly wounded animal was sure to die from its injuries anyway. He was in a small village in the middle of nowhere, and he needed to leave soon. However, he was too tired and needed to rest after two consecutive battles. On top of his deteriorating endurance, he still had yet to eat.

He managed to place the tattered cloak back on Bravura's frame before parking his machine in his previously selected resting place. Normally, he would wait until virtually no one was around before he stepped out of his cockpit. However, in his condition, he needed that comforting bed in the shack. He figured he would be treated as a monster no less dangerous than the Pitbulls that attacked, but what he found was a crowd of mostly children and young adults. Never before had he been received so positively. Yet, beyond the applause he noticed several individuals glaring at him with various looks of concern, rage, and fear. He had to know what was going on. Luckily for him, the person he needed to see came right up to him.

"*Ladies, gentlemen, please! Let our hero rest. He badly needs it!*" Joaquín stated in his native language.

"I'm sorry," the host said as he grabbed the pilot's arm. "I need to talk to you, now!"

The pilot was too exhausted to protest and allowed the man to drag him away from the crowd of grateful villagers. Yet, they were not going to the shack from before.

"Where are we going?" he wearily asked.

"To my house, it'll be much quieter there. No one bothers my family."

Once they reached his abode, Joaquín signaled to his wife to take the kids out back as he placed the man on a seat next to the dinner table within their makeshift living room.

"You have no idea what you did just now!" a trembling Joaquín stated.

"Yeah," said the pilot as he started putting the pieces together. "How about you start getting me up to speed. Between the secret visitors you guys mentioned, the random mutants showing up, and half the town in terror, something's going on around here and I don't want to stick around long enough to find out."

"H-hold on, Señor!" a panicked Joaquín yelled out. "Before you decide anything, let me explain."

Just then, Lupe came in from the kitchen with a coffee mug and handed it to her guest. The pilot drank it, expecting it to be coffee, only to be caught off guard by the taste of cinnamon.

"It's champurrado, an old family recipe. I was saving it for a special occasion."

Surprised by the act of kindness, the guest was at a loss for words.

"Uh, thanks."

Lupe whispered to her husband.

"*You need to tell him everything, for our children's sake.*"

"*Understood, my love.*"

A now calmed Joaquín sat in front of the former soldier as his wife sat beside him for support.

"For the last several years, the majority of this area has been under the control of a band of thieves. They call themselves the Hounds of Hades. Any settlement they come across, the Hounds expect them to feed their smaller mutants with whatever food they have cultivated or found, otherwise, they'll face certain death. Over the years we've been visited by the Hounds and it always ended with us losing everything we had."

"Figures," the guest said. "You want me to be your muscle and get rid of all those guys, right? Forget it. If what you're saying is true, and these were their 'smaller mutants,' then you can bet those guys are coming back with more than what Bravura can handle. I already used up the last of my ammunition on that spider and I ain't gonna risk my life and my mech on a suicide mission!"

Joaquín shook his head. "No Señor, you misunderstand. Those mutants you fought aren't with the Hounds. They're wild animals that came from the south. When we first came across their pack, we lost several people. However, we found that unlike the Hounds of Hades, the Pitbulls don't actively hunt us. Their leader, and on occasion his hunting partner, patrol their territory which we live on the outskirts of. If they find us outside, they will attack us, but if we stay inside our houses, they will likely pass us by. So, while they are dangerous, the Pitbulls provide us some protection from two other much deadlier threats."

The Hunter sighed. "One of which is the Hounds of Hades, right? These bandits and their mutants would have to move through the Pitbulls' territory to get to you. I'm guessing those mutts wouldn't let a bunch of intruders just go through their land like that."

"Indeed, Señor. The Pitbulls do keep away the Hounds of Hades. They also serve to satisfy the larger threat, Atomic Rex."

While he maintained his stoic demeanor, a shiver went down the Hunter's spine at the mention of the True Kaiju. The wanderer and his military squad were the first humans to encounter Atomic Rex. He recalled how, in a matter of seconds, the monster had destroyed the majority of his unit.

Joaquín saw the look in the Hunter's eyes. "I can tell that you have come across Atomic Rex before. Then you know that he is a true bringer of death. If the monster was to make his way inland, he would utterly destroy this village and kill everyone in it. Luckily for us, he has learned that if he simply approaches our land and sends out a challenge, the current pack leader will arrive at the beach to fight him."

Joaquín walked over to his window and looked in the direction of the ocean. "I've seen it happen a couple of times whenever my team and I venture far beyond the mountains. The alpha male always goes and puts up a good fight. In the end though, he is slain and eaten by the demon.

While the dog dies, he provides Atomic Rex with the food he needs and the monster moves on and avoids our village.

"Typically, the alpha's second-in-command will take his place and rule the pack. This allows the balance of the pack to keep the Hounds at bay and the feeding of Atomic Rex to continue. Today, however, you slew their leader and crippled his partner. This will throw the pack into disarray. They will fight on the outskirts of town to determine a new leader. Some of them will die and those who survive the chaos will be too injured to lead the rest. This will lead to two things. First, the Hounds of Hades will notice this and move past the pack unchallenged and attack our village.

"The second thing that happens, is the next time Atomic Rex comes here for food, he will not find it when he sends out his challenge. The Pitbulls' fight for a new alpha will leave their new leader too injured to fight the demon. Usually, if the dogs have to fight to determine a new leader, it's right after Atomic Rex has killed the previous one. Since Atomic Rex has just fed on his predecessor, the new alpha has time to recover from his battle to lead the pack. It has been many weeks since Atomic Rex slew the last alpha. He will soon come here and challenge the leader. When that challenge is not answered, he will move right through this town as he hunts. Either way, Señor, your actions to save our people may have doomed us all."

The Hunter cursed under his breath. He had seen the destruction the beast had brought on first hand. Everyone he ever knew or cared for was lost in a single instant. It was something he never wanted anyone to ever experience. After taking a moment to regain his composure, he focused on the matter at hand.

"Look, I didn't know killing those mutants would screw everything up, but the fact still remains. Bravura and I can't fight a whole gang of mutants and we sure as hell can't fight off Atomic Rex. I'm sorry, but there's nothing I can do for you or your people. I suggest that you flee while you can."

"But Señor, there is a way we could solve all this! Wait here." Joaquín entered an unknown room and came back with the emergency radio from before.

"Do you know how to work this thing?" he asked.

"Yeah," said the veteran. "Who do you think's been keeping Bravura operational all these years? I can fix a radio."

"Great, then with your help we can finally get in contact with those people up in the US. Maybe send an SOS call to get Steel Samurai here. With Steel Samurai and Bravura working together, the Hounds of Hades will be no more!"

"Woah, hold on there, pal!" interrupted the man. He stood silent for a moment. Deep down, his mind kept telling him to run away as far as he could. He had already caused enough trouble by facing the mutants. Doing anything more would only cause further pain and suffering. He failed to protect his team. What could he do for this defenseless village? Yet, part of him wanted to aid these people. He was the one who had endangered their lives, his responsibility to bear. He owed them that much. Still, self-doubt plagued his mind. Was he still capable of fulfilling his duties as a soldier? he thought.

"I'll admit I caused this mess. So, I'm willing to help you fix your radio, but I still ain't fighting no battles. That part of my life is over. Occasionally, I'll hunt a stray mutant for food and a place to stay, but nothing more than that. These Hounds of Hades sound like bad news. No reward is worth that kind of trouble!"

"Please, Señor!" Lupe cried out as she stood up. "It's not just the Hounds of Hades, there's something else I haven't even told my husband about."

"What?" a shocked Joaquín asked. "Mi Amor, why didn't you say anything?"

"You already had enough to worry about." Lupe then began to cry. "I prayed to God I was seeing things, but I'm sure of it. Several days ago, I saw a robot up in the mountains while I was tending the garden. I thought I imagined it until I saw it again today!"

She then faced the pilot. "I don't know what it was doing here, but I think it was spying on us. It was just as big as yours, only red."

Just then, the old war vet dropped his mug. It shattered upon impact with the cold hard cement ground. He stood up with a faint twinge of something he had never shown anyone before, distress. His sudden shift in attitude scared the married couple as he met Lupe's gaze.

"Did you say you saw a... red... robot?"

CHAPTER 9

The Atlantic Ocean.

Manticore's muscles ached as he continued to fly over the seemingly endless Atlantic Ocean. The True Kaiju flew through both raging storms and scorching heat on his nearly ten-hour flight across the sea. As the hybrid creature was soaring over the water, he observed all manner of creatures swimming below him. He saw numerous schools of fish in the Atlantic but none of them had individual members large enough for him to feed on.

The winged horror was roughly six hours into his flight when his incredible metabolism had burned through the mutant elephants he had eaten. As the beast made his way to his new hunting grounds, he kept his eyes fixed on the vast blue waters beneath him. The predator's keen eyes were constantly scanning the depths below him for something he could eat while in mid-flight.

As he searched for sustenance, Manticore saw several spiked creatures nearly as large as him swimming through the ocean. The winged beast knew these creatures must also be kaiju, as he had never beheld organisms like them when he hunted over the ocean of his former kingdom. As he stared down at the spiked beasts, he saw a large dark shape coming up from the depths below them. The school of spiked monsters moved aside as the shadow surfaced.

The leviathan surfaced to reveal a huge sea lion-like body with four serpentine heads undulating from its shoulders. All four heads looked up to the sky at Manticore and then made a barking sound to challenge him. As the Scylla-like creature barked, the spiked creatures that were accompanying him lifted their pig-like faces out of the water and wailed a challenge as well.

Manticore growled back at the multi-headed behemoth and his followers, but he knew better than to accept the serpent's challenge. Not only was the serpent much larger than him, but it was also in its element.

While Manticore was hungry and his very nature urged him to fight the aquatic reptile, he knew that he was not adept at swimming or fighting in the water. Were he to attack the hydra below him, his fate would be sealed the moment its heads grabbed a hold of him and pulled him beneath the waves. Manticore roared once more at the monsters below him and then continued on his way toward the Americas.

With Manticore passing over him, the multi-headed horror slipped beneath the waves and continued to swim toward Africa and Gol-drill.

After flying for another two hours, Manticore finally found a viable food source when he came across a pod of unmutated orcas chasing a school of fish. The deadly mammals were swimming close to the surface and their large black fins constantly breached and then dove back down. At roughly twelve meters long, even the largest orca was less than a quarter of Manticore's considerable size.

The chimeric kaiju set his eyes on one of the smaller orcas at roughly nine meters long that he felt he could pluck from the ocean and kill with relative ease. The flying nightmare slowed his speed as he gradually decreased his altitude. He was nearly skimming the surface of the water when he flew above his targeted prey. The orca barely noticed the shadow of death flying above her when Manticore thrust his head down and drove his curved canines into the mammal's back.

The orca wailed in pain as her pod circled the water and sent out high-pitched cries begging for their lost member to return. Manticore tilted his back as he let the blood of his still-living victim slide down his throat. The orca thrashed violently trying to free herself, but her actions only served to further impale her on the True Kaiju's teeth.

After a few minutes of losing several liters of blood per minute, the orca finally expired. With the creature dead, Manticore bit down hard into her spine. The result of the monster closing his jaws was that the orca was sliced in two. The hungry kaiju quickly chewed and swallowed the back half of his prey that had fallen into his mouth. The front half of the orca fell back into the ocean directly in front of her pod members who were still pursuing their captured family member. The slain female's mate tried to nudge his partner back to life as her head slid past him, while in the skies above him Manticore ingested her torso and tail.

Eating the orca provided the feline-esque creature enough calories to complete his flight over the Atlantic. It was nearly midnight when the flying beast landed on the shores of what had once been Cancun. The exhausted kaiju sighed with relief when the tips of his overtaxed bat-like wings reached down and planted themselves in the sand. The former king of the southern part of the African continent took several steps away from the ocean before he laid down in the sand and drifted to sleep.

From Manticore's perspective, it seemed like he had just closed his eyes when a loud hiss echoed across the sky and awoke him from his slumber. The beast had to blink several times from the bright sun peeking out from the clouds above. The presence of the glowing orb indicated that Manticore's nap had been longer than it felt like.

The winged horror closed his eyes and focused on the information being directed to his brain by his olfactory senses to determine the location of the monster that had roared at him. The scent of scales and cold blood combined with ocean water wafted into the hybrid's lion-like nostrils.

The mammalian beast's sharp ears caught the sound of something moving through the sand as the scent of scales and cold blood drew closer to him. Not willing to have the creature that was approaching him attack first, Manticore bounded forward. After taking several steps, he planted the tips of his wings into the sand and then used them and his legs to launch himself into the air.

Manticore felt his attacker's claw scrape across his thick scorpion tail as he was taking off. The winged creature flew a tight circle over the beach as his eyes became accustomed to the sun's glaring rays. When Manticore opened his eyes, he saw the form of a colossal iguana hissing at him from below.

As the African monstrosity circled above the remains of Cancun, he saw several other mutant iguanas like the one below him scattered across the landscape. The beast's heart rate began to increase as he saw the supply of food the mutant iguanas could provide him. Hunting grounds like that which was displayed before him was the exact reason Manticore had left his home and made the treacherous journey over the Atlantic.

The mutant iguana kicked up sand and swung his whip-like tail back and forth as he continued to challenge this new invader to his beach. The reptile displayed his large razor-sharp teeth as he tried to draw the flying monster back down to earth where he could slay him.

The vastly more intelligent Manticore continued to circle the gigantic iguana knowing that each pass he made over the creature taunted and infuriated him. As the mutated lizard displayed his teeth, claws, and tail, Manticore was able to determine what weapons his adversary possessed. When he felt as if he had the full measure of his opponent, the flying demon rose into the air. He positioned himself directly beneath the sun, and then spread his wings wide, casting a dark shadow over his reptilian prey.

Manticore's heart was racing as he considered how slaying this creature would not only provide him with much-needed food, but it would also be his first step in asserting his dominance over this new world. With his opponent fully covered by his shadow, Manticore plunged down toward the mutant iguana. The instant that the flying kaiju folded his wings, the full light of the sun shone into the iguana's eyes, temporarily blinding him.

The reptile shut his eyes, shook his head, and took several steps backward in an attempt to regain his vision. Manticore took full advantage of his prey's disorientation by flying over him and using the Smilodon claws on his back legs to rake the giant lizard's back.

The colossal iguana hissed in pain and turned his head in the direction of the passing Manticore as blood from the newly inflicted wounds gushed out of his back and down his sides. In the sky to the left of the iguana, Manticore circled around and prepared for another attack. The mammalian kaiju made a tight turn and dove once more toward the scaled mammoth.

The invading monster had nearly reached the native beast when the colossal iguana suddenly leaped in the air toward the descending Manticore. The iguana's leap caught Manticore by surprise and caused him to rear back, thus slowing his descent and leaving his neck and chest open to attack. The mutated lizard slammed into Manticore with the force of a flying battleship.

As the impact from his attack caused Manticore to fall backward, the iguana clenched his powerful jaws around the cat creature's right shoulder. As the massive lizard's teeth were embedding themselves into his foe's shoulder, he also dug his front claws into Manticore's left hip and the right side of his ribs. With the flying monster trapped within the grasp of his teeth and claws, the iguana let the momentum of his jump carry him and his prey back to the ground.

Manticore crashed back first into the beach with the full weight of the mutant reptile on top of him. The ferocity of the impact not only forced the air out of the feline demon's lung, but it also caused the reptile's teeth and claws to tear even deeper into his flesh.

The iguana shook his head back and forth and raked his claws across his opponent, sending geysers of blood spraying over the beach. The reptile thought he was on the precipice of slaying the furry invader, but his small mind failed to grasp Manticore's capabilities.

Despite the damage being done to him, the flying beast's keen mind quickly generated and executed a plan to defeat his opponent. The lion-like horror opened his mouth, reared his head back, and then plunged his long canine teeth into the reptile's shoulder. He then pulled forward, forcing the native monster's mouth closer to him, limiting his ability to rend and tear with his teeth.

With his opponent trapped on top of him, Manticore lifted his scorpion tail into the air behind the lizard and plunged it into his back leg. The mammalian nightmare repeated the attack several times until the iguana's entire back half of his body was paralyzed.

As the back half of his body was failing, the iguana tried in vain to use his claws to kill his opponent. He continued to rake his claws against Manticore's ribs and hip, but with each slash from his claws, his attacks were slower and weaker.

Sensing that his opponent was slowly dying, Manticore jerked his head to the side, shifting his saber-like canines deeper into his opponent's torso. The action caused the tip of the lion-beast's teeth to scrape across the right lung of the mutant reptile. The wound caused blood to flow into the creature's organ and inhibited his ability to respirate.

Poison coursed through the iguana's body from Manticore's stings while simultaneously, his lung was filling with blood and drowning him. Manticore looked into the iguana's eyes and he stared at them to watch the life slipping out of his prey. The tenacious iguana struggled for several minutes to break free of Manticore's grip but his strength was unequal to the task at hand.

With the mutant reptile barely hanging onto life, Manticore pulled his teeth out of the beast's shoulder. He then shifted his head and drove his long canines through the back of the iguana's neck and into his spine. There was a loud crack as the iguana's cervical column was sliced in two. The giant reptile's body went rigid and shook for a moment before his eyes rolled into the back of his head, signifying his death.

Once Manticore was certain that he had vanquished his foe, he brought his legs up under the deceased giant and pushed him off of him. The chimeric creature then moved to a standing position and placed the edge of his right batwing onto the corpse of the dead lizard. With his ribs and hip still losing blood, and the front of his body covered in the crimson fluid of his rival, the nearly completely dyed red kaiju lifted his head and roared in victory.

The roar shook the beach and caused dozens of sea birds to take flight in fear of the beast that had produced the blood-curdling sound. After proclaiming his dominance, Manticore began to devour his prize. As he had done with the elephants he had slain before, the winged demon focused first on the mutant's organs, before moving on to eating its muscles and bone marrow.

After eating his fill, Manticore laid down in the sand to rest and let his body heal from the battle. The beast knew there were other mutated iguanas in the area and he looked forward to utilizing them as a food source. Now that he was aware of the iguanas' jumping abilities, he would be prepared for an attack the next time he went hunting. The cunning beast had internalized the iguana's fighting style and abilities and committed them to memory. The next time he came across an iguana it would not be a battle but rather a slaughter.

Aside from the iguanas, the True Kaiju could sense other mega-fauna in the area. Most of what he could detect seemed to be other giant mutant animals, like the creature he had just fed on. There was a faint scent however of something much more powerful than simply the mutants that currently surrounded him.

Like all True Kaiju, Manticore could sense that another True Kaiju had been in this area relatively recently. The scent he was picking up was reptilian but the scent carried within it a poisonous taint that the iguanas did not possess. Manticore was detecting the traces of Atomic Rex, the ruler of these lands, and the most powerful kaiju on this half of the planet.

The flying beast growled at the thought of the rival True Kaiju. His experience with Gol-Drill had taught him that if he wanted to claim these lands for his own, he would have to challenge this potentially dangerous horror and slay it. It was clear from the faintness of the scent that Atomic Rex had not been on this particular beach for several months.

Manticore decided that he would rest, let his wounds heal, and then find and destroy the beast who was currently the master of this continent. The feline-esque terror closed his eyes and fell asleep with thoughts of battling his foe flashing in his mind's eye.

As the True Kaiju drifted off to sleep, another predator watched him from a safe distance. When his artificial radar picked up a large object approaching from the ocean, the metal giant flew towards the object's landing spot to investigate what manner of beast had come to his shores.

When his cold eyes beheld the sleeping form of the demonic kaiju, the predator nodded with grim satisfaction as his plan continued to unfold.

CHAPTER 10

The Pacific Ocean off the coast of El Salvador

The mutant sperm whale slammed his spermaceti-filled head into Atomic Rex's body. The blow sent the reptilian creature tumbling through the water. Still disoriented from the after-effects of the neurotoxins in his body, Atomic Rex was having difficulty ascertaining his position in the ocean. The saurian beast had no idea if he was facing the surface of the water, the seafloor, or simply floating horizontally with the tide.

The question as to which direction the surface was in relation to the reptile, was answered when the colossal sperm whale attacked him from below. The whale was more than twice the size of Atomic Rex, and his mouth was large enough that he was able to close his jaws around the nuclear theropod 's torso. While the alligator-like carapace on Atomic Rex's back prevented the whale's bite from crushing his spine, the whale's bottom teeth cut deep into his chest and stomach.

The whale's teeth inflicted over a dozen puncture wounds into the True Kaiju's body, as it was pushing him to the surface of the water at the speed of over twenty knots per hour. The monstrous mammal breached with Atomic Rex still trapped in his powerful jaws. The mutant whale's momentum carried both creatures out of the water and sent them flying into the air.

As he was soaring above the waves, Atomic Rex had enough sense to expel the air in his lungs and inhale a fresh supply of oxygen. The nuclear theropod had no sooner taken a breath than the whale brought the full weight of his immense body crashing down onto Atomic Rex as he forced the reptile back underwater. As the whale pushed Atomic Rex back down toward the ocean floor, he shook his head. The movement created a sawing motion with his mouth that greatly expanded the damage his teeth were inflicting on the saurian monster.

Atomic Rex was in unbearable pain as the colossal cetacean tore his stomach to shreds. The ruler of the western Pacific knew that if he was to survive this encounter that he would have to end the battle quickly and decisively. With the whale still pushing him down and its teeth embedded in his stomach, Atomic Rex reached down into his cells to gather the nuclear energy stored there.

Atomic Rex's scales began to take on a light blue glow and the cetacean could feel his enemy's body temperature rising. The whale was intelligent enough to understand that the increase in temperature coming off his prey meant that an attack was coming. The mammalian monster immediately regurgitated the contents of his stomach and spat out Atomic Rex. The beast then swam past Atomic Rex putting as much distance between himself and the forthcoming attack as possible.

The reptilian horror found himself floating in a cloud of stomach lining and giant squid as the glow emanating from his body continued to increase. The vomited up remains of the whale's prey were pushed away from Atomic Rex when he unleashed his Atomic Wave. The bubble of radiation shot out in all directions from his body and boiled the ocean water around him.

The gargantuan whale was moving away from the saurian at top speed when he felt a dramatic increase in the water temperature behind him. The intelligent beast let his body go limp as the wave struck him. The mutant's forward momentum and his limp body allowed him to be pushed through the water by the blast rather than being obliterated. The Atomic Wave tossed the whale around like a piece of seaweed in the tide and it scorched its skin, but the attack did not kill the beast as the nuclear theropod had intended.

When the giant sperm whale finally stopped being thrust forward by the blast, his skin was covered in lesions and burns, but he was largely unharmed. The whale turned around, shook his mighty head, and then charged Atomic Rex once more. As the whale was moving through the water, he fired a sonar blast at his target.

The reptilian monster's senses were still dulled by the effects of his battle with the box jellyfish as he floated through the water in the aftermath of his radioactive attack. The monster was simply letting his body drift in the tide, in order to minimize movement. The beast had learned over time that his fantastic healing ability worked most effectively when he was resting. Currently, he was in dire need of healing the puncture wounds in his stomach and restoring his long-range senses.

The kaiju knew the most efficient way to accomplish these goals was to rest. With his lungs full of air, he would not need to surface for almost an hour. This afforded him the perfect opportunity to let the ocean bear his massive weight and for his body to heal.

As the nuclear theropod floated peacefully in the water, he was unaware of the whale's survival or desire to continue the battle until he saw the beast coming at him through murky depths. A second after Atomic Rex saw his foe charging toward him, he was hit with an overwhelming sense of vertigo.

The True Kaiju growled at his persistent foe and he was gathering the energy to unleash another Atomic Wave when his body was assaulted by an unseen force. Once again Atomic Rex lost all sense of direction and his hearing, sense of smell, and sight were all disoriented. The beast's central nervous system was disrupted by the whale's sonar blast. Atomic Rex's body convulsed in the water causing him to exhale the air from his lungs. The saurian monster was still shaking and drifting helplessly in the water when his opponent slammed into him.

The blow sent the defenseless beast tumbling through the water. When the effects of the sonar blast wore off, the nuclear theropod shook his head and tried to focus on how to reach the surface and replenish his supply of oxygen. The monster saw a thin ray of light by his tail and he immediately flipped the orientation of his body and began swimming toward it.

As he was swimming to the surface, Atomic Rex considered the attack the whale had just utilized. The green-scaled juggernaut had experienced a similar attack before from the extradimensional kaiju known as Chimera. From his encounter with Chimera, the reptilian nightmare knew the attack would disrupt his ability to control his own body. He was also aware that even his advanced healing abilities would not be enough to negate the effects of the blast. If the whale were to hit him with the sonar blast again, his body would essentially endure a seizure until its effects wore off.

Atomic Rex was less than three strokes of his tail and legs away from reaching the surface, and much-needed air, when the leviathan struck him with another sonar blast. Atomic Rex's body went rigid and began shaking, causing him to sink deep into the Pacific. The nuclear theropod 's life may have been spared when the mutant whale struck him from below and forced him closer to the surface.

It took several seconds for the True Kaiju's central nervous system to recover from the effects of the sonar blast. When he could feel his body return to his control, Atomic Rex quickly used his powerful tail to propel his face the final few meters to the surface. The saurian beast once more drew life-giving air into his lungs. After nearly drawing several times over the course of his consecutive battles, Atomic Rex was determined that this would be the last time he needed to surface for air before he destroyed his current opponent.

He looked back into the depths, through the cloud of blood still leaking out of the slowly healing wounds on his chest, to see the mutant whale rushing toward him from below. At this point, the nuclear theropod knew what the whale's attack plan would be. The mammal would first strike him with a sonar blast, then look to either ram him, or more likely bite, breach, and then slam him back down into the water.

In an attempt to disrupt the whale's attack plan, Atomic Rex stayed on the surface of the water and began swimming to his right as quickly as possible. He only managed to move roughly twenty meters when the mutant's sonic blast struck him. Atomic Rex's body was in the midst of a seizure as the whale struck him. Unlike the last time when the whale closed his teeth around the saurian's torso, Atomic Rex's slight movement to the right caused the cetacean to only grab the nuclear theropod's tail.

The monstrous aquatic creature soared into the air, with Atomic Rex dangling out of the side of his mouth by the tail. When the beast was at the apex of his breach, he turned his head to try and land on top of his enemy when entering the water. When the whale struck the water, Atomic Rex's body had slid to the side of his face allowing the reptilian kaiju to avoid being struck by the vast majority of the whale's weight.

The mutant whale's momentum caused his body to continue its downward trajectory sending him hurtling toward the seafloor. The whale's descent to the bottom of the ocean caused countless millions of gallons of water to rush past his face. As the wake of the whale's dive struck Atomic Rex, it forced his tail free from the whale's grip.

A moment after being released from his adversary's grip, Atomic Rex's body ceased convulsing. The whale's body had almost completely passed by the radioactive reptile when he plunged his claws into the right side of the beast's tail. The True Kaiju tried to open his mouth wide enough to tear out a section of the cetacean's hide, but the creature was so immense that even the jaws of Atomic Rex were unable to hurt the majority of its body.

With his claws still embedded in the whale as it finally stopped its descent and started swimming in a horizontal motion, Atomic Rex shifted his gaze to the creature's fluke. The nuclear theropod recalled how several times both this creature and the box jellyfish had used his need for oxygen against him. The True Kaiju pulled his claws halfway out of his opponent's flesh. He then let the wake of the whale's own movement push him back toward its fluke. As the water pushed Atomic Rex backward, he kept his claws in the whale's flesh cutting a gouge in its tail as he was pushed toward the fluke.

When the saurian monster finally reached the mutant's fluke, he dug his claws into its blubber as deeply as possible. The whale's fluke was not nearly as thick as the rest of his tail and presented both an easy and vital target. Atomic Rex opened his mighty jaws and clamped them shut on the web-like patch of skin that propelled the whale.

Atomic Rex violently shook his head back and forth, tearing the left lobe of the fluke to shreds, and causing the whale to significantly decrease its speed. In an attempt to fling his attacker off himself, the whale shook his body violently and moved his tail up and down as fast as he could. The whale's efforts were in vain as Atomic Rex's incredible strength allowed him to maintain his grip and continue his attack.

The nuclear theropod waited for the whale's motions to slow. Then when the injured and exhausted mammal stopped moving his tail, the reptile bit down onto its fluke again. With jaws clenched, Atomic Rex pulled back and ripped off another section of the fluke. As he swallowed the flesh, he looked down at the damage he had wrought. The entire right side of the whale's fluke was gone. The massive beast was reduced to swimming in a circle as his body slowly sank to the bottom of the ocean with Atomic Rex still latched onto his tail.

With his opponent crippled, the radiation-infused monster attacked the remainder of his opponent's means of propulsion. Atomic Rex bit into the left side of the whale's fluke and chewed on it until the mutated cetacean's tail was nothing but a bloody stump. The attack was extremely painful for the bull whale but it fought the urge to bellow in pain as it knew doing so would cause it to expel the precious oxygen in its lungs.

Atomic Rex continued to hold onto the end of the whale until it crashed into the bottom of the ocean. He then let go of the whale's bloody stump and climbed on top of his prey. The nuclear theropod used his own weight to pin the buoyant beast to the bottom of the ocean. He then moved toward the monster's back and dug his claws into the beast's blubber, anchoring himself to the rear section of its body.

The saurian monster knew that if he moved toward the front of the beast, it would hit him with another sonar blast and send him into convulsions. Atomic Rex was also aware that if he were sent into another seizure as deep as he was it was possible that he would drown. While it was possible that he would drown if hit by the whale's sonar blast, the mutant mammal's fate was not in question. Without its tail to provide locomotion the whale would never reach the surface again. No matter how hard he struggled, the mutant was going to drown on the ocean floor.

Atomic Rex laid on top of his opponent as his healing abilities slowly began to return to their normal capabilities. He dug his claws deeper into the mutant as the whale shifted his body from side to side in an attempt to throw him off its body.

At one point, the whale even tried to roll over in order to force Atomic Rex off of him and position himself at an angle where he could hit Atomic Rex with his sonar blast. While the mutated whale knew his own life was over, he at least hoped to not only take his opponent with him but to also rid the migratory path of his species from the threat of the reptilian predator.

With each slight turn the whale made, Atomic Rex shifted on top of him. The nuclear theropod made sure to keep himself directly on top of the mutant and out of the blast radius of its sonar attack. For half-an-hour, the whale struggled to move his body in a direction where he could fire one last blast at Atomic Rex, and for that entire time, the True Kaiju simply moved with him.

With his movements causing his body to use up the oxygen in his lungs at a more expeditious rate than it typically would, the whale stopped moving at the forty-minute mark. With his body in dire need of air, the mutant whale laid on the seafloor with Atomic Rex holding him down. In his mind, the whale longed for Atomic Rex to kill him. He hoped the predator would tear out his heart or unleash his Atomic Wave and end the long process of suffocating to death. To the whale's horror, Atomic Rex simply kept himself pinned to the mutant's body, waiting for it to expire.

As the colossal whale neared the extent of his ability to hold his breath he began to try and lift his body toward the surface. The now panicked animal slammed his bloody stump on the sandy ocean bed but his efforts were futile. The whale opened his mouth as air bubbles poured out of it and its blowhole. After a long-drawn-out battle, the giant mutant had finally expired.

With his opponent defeated, the now almost fully healed Atomic Rex swam back to the surface. Once the True Kaiju reached the surface, he expelled the fresh air from his lungs, not in the form of a gasp as he had done in the midst of battle, but rather as a victorious roar. As Atomic Rex's victory cry echoed across the ocean the whale's corpse drifted to the surface.

Having expended an enormous amount of energy fighting the colossal box jellyfish and mutant sperm whale, Atomic Rex was in dire need of food. The saurian monster swam over to the carcass of his defeated foe and then used his claws to tear a huge gash in the side of it. A large wad of the whale's blubber floated out of its body and Atomic Rex quickly devoured it. He fed off the leviathan for over thirty minutes until his body was fully healed and his senses had returned to normal. With his stomach full of whale blubber, Atomic Rex turned away from his defeated foe and swam toward shore. Once the kaiju had abandoned the body, countless sharks and seabirds descended on the dead whale to feast on it as well.

With each stroke that he took closer to shore, the True Kaiju could sense that some other kaiju had invaded his domain. The kaiju's eyes thinned as he prepared for yet another clash in the seemingly endless battles that comprised his life. He had successfully defended the pacific domain of his oceanic kingdom, and now it seemed as if he would need to defend his terrestrial holdings as well.

When he reached land, Atomic Rex sniffed the air and took in all the scents around him. The monster was able to detect the invading kaiju, but he knew it was several days' travel from his current position. The nuclear theropod also detected another familiar metallic scent. Atomic Rex had detected this scent on numerous occasions. The metallic scent would sporadically travel into his territory, but the owner of the scent seemed to pose no real threat to him. As such, the True Kaiju ignored the invader and laid down on the beach to rest so that he was ready to fight off the intruding kaiju when he caught up to it.

Hovering above the sky, a red machine watched the saurian creature lie down. Once Atomic Rex was fully asleep, the mechanical being landed near him and implanted a mysterious device as large as itself into the ground like a giant metal stake. Once it was fully set, the top portion of the contraption extended outwards, revealing two meters that read as "empty" before they started rising steadily with a blue electronic light.

Inside the humanoid contraption, a pair of eyes filled with anger and hatred gazed at the monster before him. Twice in his life, he had come across an adversary who he was unable to defeat. One was a fellow soldier with skills rivaling his own, the other the mutant dinosaur he currently beheld. While the pilot's ego urged him to attack Atomic Rex while he was sleeping, his keen mind kept his emotions in check. He knew full well that he was unable to slay the True Kaiju in one-on-one combat. To defeat the beast, he had to force him to relive a deadly trial of endurance he had once experienced. What seemed like a lifetime ago, this gauntlet of battles was what wiped out the first generation of True Kaiju, all but one. Now, the watchful predator was ready to finish what his predecessor started.

The pilot spoke not to himself, but rather his hated enemy as he drifted closer to the sleeping titan. "We're alike in many ways. We have both known far more victories than defeats. Additionally, neither one of us can abide an enemy challenging us and living. Of the two of us, I am the only one intelligent enough to use the past to my advantage. It is my superior and tactical wits and my knowledge of your battles that will allow me to finally best you. You may be resting now but you will go where I want you to, and I shall make sure you are sufficiently debilitated when you arrive at your final resting place!"

CHAPTER 11

The Ruins of Guadalajara

The sun had begun to set on the ruins of the former mall of Guadalajara. By now, the Hounds of Hades had established their campsite and base of operation around the perimeter of the location. Ten armored vans were parked there, each surrounded by vehicles and tents. Throughout the day, armed marauders infiltrated the various dilapidated buildings and raided each and every square inch of the destroyed shopping center for any and all items worth preserving, be they food, clothing, technology, or weapons.

Beyond the perimeter was El Silbón stationed alongside the band of wolves. The mutants had positioned themselves there to guard the area against possible intruders. To keep the wolves from getting too comfortable, El Silbón had decided to engage in light tussles between him and his furry companions. Each hound took turns fighting their humanoid caretaker as the rest stood by and watched. While each wolf had the strength to tear a man to shreds in seconds, their bites and scratches did little to pierce through El Silbón's thick leather-like skin, making him the perfect combatant to train this ragtag group of mutants.

First was Elise, the leader of the pack. She was the easiest to engage with as she enjoyed the chance to play with her master. Thor's strength proved difficult to take down due to him being the strongest and heaviest of the five. Baldwyn came the closest to tiring out the mutated human as his spry nature made him almost impossible for El Silbón to catch. Ada was a special case, however, as due to her blindness her master had trained her to use her ears to detect any sound he would make, such as clattering bones, in order for her to make up for her handicap.

The wolves' light bites and soft growls indicated that none of them would attack their superior with any murderous intent as they each took turns wrestling with him. The same could not be said for Tucker, who despised the giant with a passion. El Silbón knew to watch his back when engaging with the one-eyed wolf. He saved his fight for last, giving the canine a fair chance at potentially killing him, having tired himself out from the last four matches. At the same time though, he would use his full strength. A smile crept on his face as he grew excited at the thought of this long-awaited face-off.

The impatient Tucker jumped at the chance to tear apart the giant's throat. The force from his pounce pushed El Silbón and forced him onto his back. When the giant hit the ground, he latched his hands onto Tucker's jaws, preventing the wolf's teeth from biting down on his face. Ferociously, the half-blind wolf took his sharpened stump of a leg and repeatedly stabbed at his master's arm. As El Silbón's appendage began to bleed he rolled over, now being the one applying his weight onto the giant mammal. Catching Tucker by surprise, he got back up on his feet with his hands still clinging onto his opponent's face. Finally, he slammed the animal's face into the ground and proceeded to end the match with a pummeling his rival would not soon forget.

Around El Silbón the rest of the wolves were howling in excitement as Tucker, embarrassed by his loss, walked back to join his ranks. The wolf's violent disposition had subsided as a result of the tussle, though both master and wolf knew Tucker would surely try his luck again another day. Soon afterward, a military dune buggy headed their way. The giant stood back up, knowing well that it was Lopez, ready with another report. He waited silently for his ally to step out of his vehicle.

"We got word that Ivanov is heading this way," Lopez stated. *"Got a call from him several minutes ago on our radios."*

"Do you know where he's coming from...?" asked the giant in a slow, lingering tone. *"Or why he's returning?"*

"We don't at the moment, Silbón. We think it may have to do with the plan he told us about concerning Fortuna."

"Yes... the village in the mountains."

The giant stood in silence as he contemplated what had occurred since they acquired their latest plot of land. A massive machine appeared before them with a pilot who never took off his helmet. What portion of his face could be seen through the mask revealed a horribly burned visage that he preferred to keep hidden. He claimed his name was Alexander Ivanov, a former soldier from the war between mankind and the kaiju thirty years ago. Five years prior he had abandoned his home in Eastern Europe and journeyed over to North America where he surveyed the land since coming here. Having found a village with rare materials, he decided to join forces with the Hounds of Hades.

"*Don't you think it's strange…*" the giant commented, "*that he is after the exact same village as we are?*"

"*It is an odd coincidence,*" Lopez replied. "*Maybe he heard of our efforts to take over the village.*"

"*And what of his story… Do you believe any of it?*"

Lopez paused, thinking over what several of his men had been saying.

"*He definitely had to have come from Europe going by his accent, plus there's never been any record of that machine of his.*"

"*Right… the 'Red Menace' as he calls it,*" said El Silbón, amused by the name that reflected a previous conflict in human history in a time before mutants and True Kaiju.

"*As for the rest of his story?*" the mutant continued to ask.

"*To be perfectly honest, Silbón, I don't believe a word of it. And what kind of name is 'Alexander Ivanov'? It almost sounds made up. On top of that, it's suspicious that he'd have a mech that well-kept if he really was in the war against the True Kaiju.*"

"*Well… what do you suppose we do when he returns?*"

"*I say let's hear him out. Where he came from doesn't matter, it's what he aims for that's important. If his goals align with ours, then we may find this a mutually beneficial alliance.*"

"*Very well,*" said El Silbón, still wary of the mech pilot's true intentions. Normally, he never cared for who they allied with and who they attacked, just as long as he was guaranteed safety. However, something about this man, Ivanov, was off. Though, he trusted his ally as he was merely the Hounds' muscle at the end of the day.

"*I'll leave the decision-making to you and your men.*"

Just then, a familiar jet-like sound echoed across the sky. It was the Red Menace, making its promised return. Lopez, El Silbón, and the wolves regrouped and got ready to confront Ivanov and confirm whether or not they could trust the individual.

"What do you got for us, Ivanov?" Lopez addressed the visitor in English as El Silbón stood by his side.

"I came to let you and the rest of the Hounds of Hades know that all preparations are complete; within twenty-four hours Fortuna will be ours."

"First off," Lopez interrupted, having his giant partner's words still ringing in his ear. "Did you know we were after that village when you first approached us?"

Ivanov paused for a second before responding. "Yes, I did. I had overheard your conversations over the course of several years and had pieced together a list of locations you've been wishing to expand into. I knew that if I wanted to earn your trust, I needed to help you acquire one of these places."

"And why Fortuna exactly?" Lopez eyed the helmeted man. "There's gotta be something in it for you, so spill it!"

As he finished his statement, El Silbón let out an aggressive grumble to intimidate the stranger. While he did not comprehend a word of English beyond certain commands from the Hounds of Hades, he did understand when to use intimidation tactics by the sound of Lopez's voice. It was this partnership that helped his human companion rise up through the ranks, becoming one of the top men in the organization.

Yet, the stranger did not show any signs of fear. Rather, he chuckled and raised his hands.

"Very well. You caught me red-handed. I knew you were all after Fortuna, and it just so happened that there's something else in that area that I want for myself."

"Enough with the cryptic nonsense," Lopez angrily replied. "What exactly are you after?"

The pilot dug into his pants and took out a small tablet. After a few seconds of fiddling with the options, he presented the device to Lopez. The commander of the Hounds cautiously grabbed ahold of the device and peered at the screen's contents. It was recorded footage of a large mechanical humanoid, similar to both Steel Samurai and Red Menace, fighting off a giant mutant spider.

"There's another mech?" gasped Lopez.

"Indeed, there is. Its designation: 'Bravura,'" answered Ivanov as he wore an enormous grin. "As I was surveying North America I came across an old rival of mine from the war, he's responsible for taking my face, and I intend to return the favor by taking his life! I kept tracking him without being seen due to my machine's stealth capabilities until he eventually found himself around Fortuna. You help me take care of him and his machine is yours. It's quite valuable from what I've gathered, even among mechs."

"Hold on," Lopez once more interrupted, making sure no questions were left unanswered. "First off, where exactly did your mechs come from? Second, there's never been any mech-on-mech combat during the kaiju war."

"That's because our war came before," Ivanov hinted. "Indeed, I lied about my involvement in fighting against the kaiju. There's much you clearly don't know about what occurred before the rise of the kaiju."

Lopez was in shock. Was there truly some kind of secret war between machines that was unknown to the public? If so, how had this gone under everyone's radar? Before he could ask the details pertaining to this lost conflict, Ivanov had already begun to brush past the details.

"But that's not important right now! What is important are two factors, both of which concern us dealing with certain monsters. What's the one thing keeping you from attacking Fortuna?"

"It's a pack of mutant Pitbulls that have claimed the area around the western mountains where Fortuna's hidden. Not even our wolves can take them down."

"Lucky for you, that's already taken care of." Ivanov swiped the tablet away from Lopez only to show him new footage of the same machine fighting off two of the dogs.

"My old rival killed the pack's alpha and incapacitated the second-in-command when they entered the village." Ivanov proceeded to show another digital recording, this time showcasing several more Pitbulls attacking one another. In the background there was a dead Pitbull with a visibly broken jaw. "Without their two strongest members, the pack has since gone into disarray as they all fight for supremacy."

"Then... if what you're saying is true, we can finish off the Pitbulls and invade Fortuna!"

"But why do that..." interrupted the masked man, "...when you can have someone, or dare I say, something, do it instead?"

"Explain."

"While I was away, I've taken the liberty of acquiring some 'help,' shall we say."

With a fleck of his finger on the tablet, he showcased one last video, this time depicting a winged lion battling a giant iguana. Lopez let out a gasp as El Silbón's eyes widened.

"This, my friends, is the most powerful True Kaiju I could find. Hailing from Africa, I call it 'Manticore!' This beast will no doubt take care of those Pitbulls and that mech."

"You maniac!" shouted Lopez. "Do you have any idea what you've done? You can't control a True Kaiju!"

His raised volume alerted every one of his men to raise their weapons and aim squarely at Ivanov and his mech.

"That's certainly true. This is why I purposefully aggravated it, making sure it follows me and confusing the Red Menace with my rival's mech. Meanwhile, we'll avoid involving ourselves until we know for certain who the victor is. Whoever comes out on top at Fortuna won't stand a chance from our combined forces!"

Lopez paused for a moment. This plan made sense. Surely, no beast nor machine could last a battle as heavy as that and survive a full-on assault from the Hounds of Hades.

"So, the destruction of my rival and permanent membership into your organization, in exchange for the acquisition of both Fortuna and Bravura," said Ivanov as he extended his hand out to his potential ally. "Do we have ourselves a deal?"

Lopez thought it over. He looked up to El Silbón, who remained stone-faced. He was clearly leaving this decision up to him. Lopez looked over his options. If there truly was a True Kaiju involved, Ivanov would have kept it a secret if he was planning to eliminate them. This was a situation that would only benefit both parties.

"Deal," he answered as he shook Ivanov's hand.

"Excellent. I've been tracking Manticore's location all this time and he should be here within an hour. I'll get his attention and lure him towards the Pitbulls and Fortuna. I suggest you get your men moving so that the Manticore can pass without detecting any of you. In the meanwhile, I'll keep in touch via radio."

Lopez quickly faced his men. *"You heard the man. Pack everything and let's move out!"*

As the Hounds of Hades began their evacuation of the mall, the man who went by the name Alexander Ivanov stepped into his machine and made preparations for take-off. He laughed to himself at the sheer gullibility of what were supposedly the most ruthless armed forces in the south.

It was true that he had brought Manticore to North America in order to take care of Bravura and his rival, whose name continued to elude him all these years later. Yet, he consciously neglected to inform his "allies" of the involvement of Atomic Rex, his only other rival left alive on this planet. He was only partially true in that his rival left his face scarred, but not which one. He could still feel the stinging sensation of the burns left on his skin to this very day. While he miraculously avoided radiation poisoning following his initial encounter with the titanic theropod, the ability that came to be known as the Atomic Wave left a severe imprint that left the former soldier with nothing but seething hatred of the beast, matched only by the only other pilot he had failed to kill during the war. It was the very same rage that kept him going for three long decades, long after the end of the war and the collapse of civilization. Within that time, he had searched for his enemies and planned out his revenge. Now, all those years of waiting were about to pay off.

As his machine took off into the air, he detected both True Kaiju were on their course towards Guadalajara. The pilot would have to get Manticore's attention and divert its path towards the village, with the Hounds of Hades following right afterward, and Atomic Rex in the back of this hellish caravan of destruction.

Ivanov's wish was to see the extermination of both his longtime nemeses through the combined efforts of Manticore, the Hounds of Hades, and his Red Menace. Regardless of who eliminated who, he would see to it that he remained the last one alive.

CHAPTER 12

Los Angeles

Both father and daughter were silent as they made the flight to the City of Angels. Chris felt that Emily seemed to understand the reasoning behind using mutant cats to draw out the giant leeches. He could tell, however, she was not pleased with the concept. Chris thought that if she had been born before the end of the world, Emily would have been the type of girl who would feel sad for the worms he would put on her hook to go fishing.

As the dilapidated skyline of Los Angeles came into view, Emily gasped. Chris looked at the numerous half-wrecked buildings that dotted the skyline as a part of him wept. When he was younger, he had made several trips to the majestic city. In his mind's eye, he could see the grandeur of downtown Los Angeles. Now, all that stood in the place of that grandeur were dilapidated buildings with their roofs falling off, several of which he had caused himself years prior when he attacked the Colony and baited them into chasing him to their deaths within Amebos's gelatinous body.

Emily started to tear up and Chris brought Steel Samurai 2.0 to a halt to take a moment to comfort his daughter. This was her first time seeing the ruins of what was once the second-largest city in the US. The pilot guessed that his daughter was feeling the crushing weight of what had occurred here and the horror that had been wrought upon the millions of people who lived in the once great metropolis.

Chris leaned over to hug his daughter when through the tears in her eyes, he saw a sense of wonder and a smile on her face.

She shook her head in disbelief and then looked over at her father. "Dad, I've seen the remains of the towns near us, and many pictures of buildings from the archives, but to see them with my own eyes. It's...it's amazing what people were able to do before the kaiju."

She pointed to several of the buildings. "I mean, just one of them could fit our entire settlement in it. Not only that, it would have plumbing for showers and toilets. A constant supply of gas and electricity." She waved her hand across the breadth of the skyline. "And ways for everyone to get around. I mean look at how big the city is! Could you even walk across it in a day if you wanted to? If so, there must've been like hundreds of people walking through these streets every day?"

Chris himself was almost overcome with joy at the wonder his adult daughter was experiencing. He shook his head. "Thousands, sweetheart. Thousands of people on each block every day. In some areas, tens of thousands, if not more."

She whispered to herself in disbelief. "Tens of thousands of people on a single block." She pointed to a solitary building. "It must have been crazy when you were a kid. I mean, just seeing that many people on any given day. I mean, you must have seen people you didn't know all the time."

Chris shrugged. "When you were in the city that's pretty much all there was around you. Strangers you didn't know."

Emily shrugged. "I can't imagine it. Seeing these buildings in person is astounding enough, but to think of what went into running a city, creating structures like that, keeping everything running. I mean, I'm flying a giant mech, so I know there was technology before that we don't have now but to see all of this in person and to imagine what went into it. It's...it's really incredible that humans were able to achieve so much."

He smiled at his daughter. "You know, your mom and I never brought you and your brother to a large city because of the devastation that has been wrought upon them both by giant monsters and time. We didn't want it to depress you. I'd never considered that it might inspire you." He shrugged. "I guess from your perspective it's like when I first saw the Coliseum in Rome or the pyramids in Mexico. When I first saw those ancient structures, I didn't think about what they used to be like or how the people who had used them were all gone. I was just taken in by the fact that ancient people had such wondrous structures and how creative those people were. I guess it's the same thing for you when you look at LA."

"Like I said, I've seen the photos but again, in person it's breathtaking. We have to bring Sean back here, heck even Kyle. They have to see a city like this in person, pictures don't do it justice."

"Sweetheart, once again you've helped me to find beauty in destruction. I know I've told you this a thousand times, but when you were born, you gave me the first real reason to hope again. Then, each day when you go out there and help the people of our settlement, you show me how we can live in a world where humans and mutants can co-exist."

He gestured toward the LA skyline. "You helped me open my eyes to a brand-new world of amazement and beauty, whereas before I only saw sadness."

Emily grabbed her dad's hand. "Well, Dad, thank you for bringing me here. The first time seeing a city is something I'll never forget, and I'm glad I got to experience it with you."

Chris smiled. "Well, honey. This is where things are going to get darker. We're going to go into the city. It's beautiful from afar and I'm immensely glad you got to have that experience. Now though, you'll see how hungry animals live. Hungry mutant animals. I doubt we'll run into anything that can hurt us inside Steel Samurai 2.0, but what they do to each other," he shook his head. "That's another matter altogether. So, brace yourself mentally. For the animals that have taken over LA, it's survival of the fittest, and the first things we're going to see are the remains of the unfit. We're also going to have to walk the mech through the city to find what we're looking for. With those buildings, we won't be able to just swoop down from the sky and grab a mutant cat."

Emily took a deep breath and looked at her father. "Okay. I'll bring her to the edge of the city, then maybe you should take the controls to maneuver through it. I don't want to accidentally walk the mech into one of those buildings and have it crumble on top of us."

"Okay, sounds like a plan, but you should be ready to work the mech's weapons systems. Also, make a note for us to practice having you walk the mech through smaller cities so you get the hang of piloting her on the ground around obstacles."

"Noted, now let's enter the city." Emily pushed forward gently on the controls causing Steel Samurai 2.0 to drift toward the crumbling metropolis.

As the mech floated toward the abandoned city, the clouds parted and the sun shone down brightly on the decimated concrete jungle. The bodies of lesser non-mutated animals such as dogs and raccoons were spread across the city. Each of the bodies near the entrances to the city were in varying states of decay. Most of the dead mammals were not entire corpses but simply scattered body parts.

Chris grabbed the controls and started flying the mech down toward the bones. "We're going to need a handful of those. We need bones that still have some meat on them. They're sort of the bait for our bait."

As Steel Samurai 2.0 was picking up a handful of remains, Emily stared at the carnage below her. "Dad, the cats that we're looking for, did they do this to those dogs?"

"The cats mainly hunt in the middle of the city. The dogs down there mainly hunted each other and the other animals scattered around them." Chris shrugged. "Trust me, if those dogs were killed by the mutant cats, there wouldn't be that much of their bodies left."

Emily winced. "The dogs cannibalized each other?"

"Hungry and desperate animals will do pretty much anything to stay alive, including turning on each other. Part of the reason why I used Steel Samurai all those years ago to draw the True Kaiju into each other's territory was because if what remained of the human race stayed where we were, that would have been us."

Emily's body shook. "You mean, people would've started eating each other?"

"It would have taken a while for things to get that bad. We were pretty close to turning on each other though. I think more than eating, fighting, and eventually killing for resources would have started."

"The people wouldn't have been much better than kaiju battling each other for territory. I always knew what you did was brave and a great thing, but I always saw it as just you clearing out monsters. I never considered that you were preventing humans from becoming monsters."

He shrugged. "When you've been in as many battles as I have you realize pretty much anything has the potential to become a monster. The question is what can you do to stop that from happening in the first place." Chris smiled at his daughter. "When I started to think about your work with Ramrod, or what you're trying to do with the elephant seals right now, I realized that's part of what you're trying to do. You're trying to prevent them from becoming monsters. You're helping to make them beneficial to humans and vice versa. You're doing the same thing I tried to do. You're just going about it your own way and even I can see it has some benefits over mine."

Emily smiled. "You're always saying I'm just like mom, but maybe a lot of my better traits came from you too."

Chris was almost blushing with pride when Emily gasped at the sight she now beheld through the mech's eyes. Scattered around the streets closer to the heart of the city were the bodies of nearly a dozen mutant cats. Each stood roughly fifteen meters high and thirty meters from face to tail. Each of the felines had its chest and stomach torn open and their organs removed. Several of the cats were completely ripped to shreds with their body parts all in relatively small groups.

Emily gestured down toward the dead felines. "Did the other cats do this to them?"

"I don't think so. Your mother and I have been coming here for over a decade now and I've never seen the cats' bodies strewn across the streets like that. Sure, they fight once in a while but it usually ends with one cat chasing away the other. Whatever killed those cats was something bigger and stronger than they were. From everything we've seen, the cats have been the apex predators for a while here, so this is something new and pretty damn powerful.

"I'll keep piloting the mech, because if we run across whatever did this, we don't want to crash into a building." Chris gestured toward the controls in front of his daughter. "You arm the sword and keep it in front of us. I've seen those mutant cats move and they are pretty darn fast. Obviously, whatever killed them is even faster. We need to be ready to defend ourselves as quickly as possible."

Emily took hold of the controls in front of her and used them to open the compartment in the robot's leg which held its legendary sword. When Steel Samurai 2.0 gripped its weapon, and held it in a defensive position, the sun glistened off it and reflected onto nearby buildings. The reflecting sun caused a shadow effect that gave the brief illusion of something large moving toward the mech.

Emily quickly turned the weapon in the direction of the mirage and then released a deep breath when she saw there was nothing attacking them.

Chris spoke in a calm voice. "Easy, Emily. The way light bounces off these buildings can be tricky. Stay focused but loose. As tense as you are you'll be swinging at every shadow or glare we see. Remember, we don't need to play exterminator for a dead city. We don't need to engage with whatever is eating the cats. All we need to do is catch one of the mutants and disable it or find one that's already injured."

Chris turned Steel Samurai 2.0 in a westward direction. "There are a lot of big drainage tunnels that come in and out of the river. The cats will often hunt down there for things like rats and mice. If we leave a pile of bones in front of one of the openings, we can usually draw out one of the cats pretty quickly."

A few minutes later, Steel Samurai 2.0 was standing above a pile of bones, in front of a drain tunnel, with its sword drawn.

Emily had her hand on the controls of the sword. The young woman was ready to stab any mutant creature that emerged from the tunnel as she spoke to her father about their prey. "Why did the cats only reach a height of like twenty meters or so? Why didn't they grow closer to fifty meters like most of the kaiju?"

"I don't know. I specialize in fighting radioactive mutants, not determining their growth patterns. We don't really talk about him all that much, because it disturbs your mom, but I guess it's kinda like Ogre. I mean, as far as we can tell, he was a human at some point and the effects of radiation only caused him to grow to like fifteen meters tall. On the other hand, we know Yokozuna was a human and he grew to that fifty-meter or so mark. I guess different things just mutate differently depending on the type and amount of radiation they're exposed to."

As Chris finished his thought a mutant cat suddenly darted out from the drain tunnel.

"Sorry. I kinda thought they'd sneak out rather than dart out of the tunnel at full speed."

"They usually do, and they never run past the remains like that."

Chris looked down the tunnel below him to see a half dozen more cats come bursting out of the tunnel. The fleeing cats were accompanied by some force that was shaking the ground beneath Steel Samurai 2.0. The moment that he felt the ground shaking, Chris grabbed the controls to the mech. He tried to have it take off but before the robot could liftoff, the tunnel entrance exploded beneath them.

As the ground it was standing on gave way, Steel Samurai 2.0 fell onto its back as the remains of the drain tunnel covered its legs from its knees to its feet. Chris and Emily found themselves looking through the eyes of the downed war machine as a nine-headed rat, standing nearly sixty meters tall, rose out from under the ground. The beast climbed out of the tunnel and stood above the mech. In unison, all of its heads looked down at Steel Samurai 2.0 and hissed.

Chris's mind immediately went into battle mode. His instinct to protect his daughter weighed heavily on his mind as he tried to assess the best way to keep her safe while still operating the mech alone, in light of Emily's lack of experience with the machine.

He was about to override her control of the sword and switch it to his panel when Steel Samurai 2.0's weapon slashed the multi-headed rodent across the chest. A stream of blood trailed behind the sword as Emily grabbed the controls for Steel Samurai's left arm and used it to strike several of the beast's heads in the face. The blows from Emily's quick thinking caused the monster to take several steps back.

"Dad, you control our movements! I'll handle the weapons!"

Chris smiled as he began getting the robot back on its feet. "You're definitely your mother's daughter."

Steel Samurai 2.0 had just returned to a standing position when the writhing heads of the giant mammal once more lunged toward them. Emily used the sword to slice the creature across the shoulder, drawing blood for a second time and forcing the beast back.

She looked at the horrid beast in disgust. "Rats. Why is it always rats? It was pretty much the same time last year when those mutant rats attacked me and Sean and Ramrod had to save us. Those rats were way smaller than this though and they only had one head. What's the deal with that thing?"

Chris shrugged as he lifted Steel Samurai 2.0 into the air. "I don't know. There are just some pretty weird monsters made by radiation. It doesn't matter to us where it came from. What matters is if we want to take out a giant leech, and use it as bait to lure the elephant seals down here, we need to get away from it."

The mech was floating above the kaiju as its heads continued to hiss at the metal giant. Chris shrugged. "No need to engage that thing if we don't have to. I'm just going to fly away from it and double back to a spot where we can catch a cat."

Chris started flying back toward the outskirts of the city to regroup but as soon as the mech started moving, the rat creature dropped to all fours and started following it. Chris shifted the mech's direction a second time only for the nine-headed horror to change course and continue its pursuit. When Chris went to shift direction a third time, the rat actually climbed on top of a building and leaped at the robot. The former pilot cursed and avoided the rat's attack by flying higher into the air.

The war veteran watched the mutant as it crashed back down to the ground. The moment the vermin landed on city streets, it stood up and ran back in the direction of Steel Samurai 2.0. When the rodent was under the mech it started walking in a tight circle and hissing at its elusive opponent.

Chris sighed. "I think we're going to have to kill that thing if we have any hope of injuring and capturing one of the cats."

"I think we can use the rat itself. It's already injured so it might be easier than trying to bait a cat. Do you think you can keep us close enough for me to slice off its legs and a few of its heads without letting that thing pin us to the ground?"

"We'd have to work in pretty close tandem. To pull off something like that your movements with the arms are going to have to be in near-perfect sync with my foot movements."

"We can do it, Dad!"

"Okay, I'm going to dive straight at it. As we're flying past it, you use the sword to cut off several of the heads on the right side of the body. The second we hit the ground, I'm going to spin us around, while you switch wrist positions and then swipe low to cut the monster's right foot off. If we can ground and cripple it, then cutting it up the rest of the way should be relatively easy."

Emily nodded. "I'm ready."

Chris sent Steel Samurai 2.0 streaking toward the hideous beast. When the monster was within striking distance of the mech's sword, Emily used the weapon to decapitate four of the beast's heads. Chris then spun the robot around as Emily flawlessly matched his timing with the swing of her sword, cutting off the rat's right leg at the ankle.

Blood was gushing out of the rat's necks where its heads had been lopped off and from its severed foot. The rodent was writhing on the ground in pain and trying to stand on its remaining three legs when Chris yelled out. "Take out the other back leg. Once we do that this fight is pretty much over!"

He moved the mech a step forward as Emily used the blade to amputate the monster's other back leg. With the maimed creature losing blood from multiple wounds, Chris lifted the mech into the sky just above his injured opponent. "I'm going to use the thrusters on the Steel Samurai 2.0's feet to cauterize the neck wounds. We can't have that thing bleed to death if we're going to use it for live bait. Burning its wounds closed will probably cause it to try and roll away from us. When it rolls, its left leg will be right in front of us, be ready to cut that off too as soon as you see it."

Emily nodded with a grim determination in reply to her father's directions. Chris then maneuvered the mech directly over the still bleeding necks. The heat from the thrusters instantly cauterized the badly bleeding wounds and caused the monster to react exactly as Chris had predicted.

When the beast completed its roll Emily cut off its left front leg causing its shoulder to crash into the ground. Chris did not need to give Emily any further directions. The young woman sliced the rat creature's final foot off causing it to fall helplessly onto its back.

The helpless mutant squirmed as Chris used the mech's thrusters to cauterize its foot wounds as well. He then flew to the back of the rat, grabbed its tail, and took to the sky.

Steel Samurai 2.0 was flying back in the direction of the settlement and its nearby rivers as Emily looked over at her father. "How'd I do?"

Chris laughed. "Let's just say I think your mom's position as my co-pilot may be in jeopardy, based on what I saw today."

Emily laughed. "You don't want me to say that to her though, do you?"

Chris echoed his daughter's laughter. 'No. No I do not. But seriously, sweetheart, you did great. Now let's go use this ugly thing to kill some giant leeches and then make friends with those mutant elephant seals."

CHAPTER 13 -

Acapulco, Mexico

In the warm orange glow of the sunset, the hulking form of Manticore landed on shores of what was once Acapulco. Like many former cities across the world, this location too was ravaged by chaos and destruction. Various buildings that once housed both locals and tourists had long since crumbled to the ground. The bustling atmosphere that once made Acapulco Mexico's largest and busiest beach resort city was now only a memory in the survivors of Fortuna over a hundred miles away. However, despite the ruins of a bygone civilization littered across the land, the sandy beaches still appeared as serene as they were many years ago.

This quiet patch of land caught the African behemoth's attention once he began losing the scent of the unknown metal prey. He had chased after its scent of burning fuel throughout the day and not only did he no longer have a target to pursue, he was also beginning to tire from the long and seemingly endless journey. He scoured the area in search of a potential meal, hoping to find something as large as the mutant iguana he came across when he first stepped foot onto the western hemisphere.

With no such luck, his frustration grew to rival his hunger. Manticore thrusted his head back and roared into the air. Just then, his howl was abruptly silenced as hundreds of tiny sharp pieces of metal pelted against his face. They failed to cause much damage beyond bruising his hide, but a quick look into the direction of the projectiles revealed who had challenged him. To the beast's surprise, it was the tiny metal figure from before, standing atop the wreckage of a half sunken cruise ship nearby.

Deep within the mech's chassis, its pilot wore a devilish grin. He had hoped to meet the True Kaiju within this vicinity and had left his machine's engines turned off once he acquired a good hiding spot with a decent enough view of the whole area. Now was his chance to showcase the Red Menace's strength against Manticore before he set his sights on Bravura.

The winged lion lifted himself off the ground and prepared to grab the mech off its post, only for it to dodge at the last second, causing the monster to crash into the rusted remains of the ship. Ivanov aimed Red Menace's arm mounted chain guns at a spot of the cruise liner where he had previously left numerous landmines and ignited the entire vessel ablaze, enveloping Manticore in the process. The pilot cackled as he reveled in the excitement, something he had not felt in quite some time. He hoped that his duel with his arch rivals would provide an even greater challenge than this predictable brute.

His rival quickly dove into the shallow waters to douse the searing heat from his skin. By the time he made it back to shore, Manticore was once again met with a barrage of bullets from his irritating quarry, now stationed just beyond his reach. The monstrosity pounced on its enemy with no hesitation, only to miss as Red Menace took to the sky and zipped past him. As it did so, Ivanov had his mech whip out its massive knife-like blade and impaled it in the creature's snout, sliding it up to just below his eye before removing his weapon. Ivanov could've easily blinded the leviathan, but he still needed his opponent in top shape if it was to fight either of his true enemies.

Manticore snarled as he felt the sharp stinging pain that was emanating from his facial wound. At the same time, his nose caught the familiar scent of the machine's jet fuel, further confirming that this thing was indeed his target. As it faced his opponent, currently hovering in the air, the beast caught another scent. It smelled like a mutant, several of them in fact. They were not the iguanas from before, but whatever they were they were quickly approaching this location. At that moment, the egotistical Ivanov could not help but to gloat, even if Manticore would have no means of understanding him.

"Ha! You simple brute," Ivanov's voice echoed from Red Menace's external speakers. "You're nowhere near the tenacity and raw fury of Atomic Rex. Even with all that strength, you're nothing more than a pawn. Still, your strength is of great use to me. In that regard, you did not disappoint."

Just then, a pack of mutant Pitbulls exited the mountains of Sierra Madre del Sur and approached the two intruders. They had picked up the noise of Manticore and Red Menace's scuffle and were anxious to deal with their unwelcomed and dangerous guests. Each of the canines, all dwarfed by the sheer size of Manticore, were covered in tooth and claw marks.

Prior to arriving at Acapulco, the Pitbulls had gone into disarray in the aftermath of Bravura's battle with their two leading hounds. Their alpha male was slain at the hands of their mysterious foe, and once his hunting partner returned, wounded and frail, the rest of the pack left him to die as they fought each other for dominance.

Ivanov smiled. "Hmph, just in time. I'll leave these guys to you, Manticore!"

At last, he was ready to enter the next phase of his plan. He placed his blood-soaked blade into a sheath within his mech's leg and flew off in the direction of Fortuna. Manticore wanted to pursue his metal enemy, but his attention was too preoccupied with the eighteen hounds that had surrounded him. He was starving and his brief skirmish with his opponent only further famished him. He needed nourishment and these mammalian adversaries would have to suffice.

Manticore bellowed a massive roar at his new contenders, awaiting their next move. In disorganized fashion, every one of the Pitbulls dashed towards the wyvern-like creature at different times with no sense of coordination. With one swipe of his arachnid tail, the True Kaiju incapacitated two of the giant dogs, swatting them away as if they were mere flies. One canine immediately bit down on the membrane of his right wing while another attacked his left leg.

The foreign behemoth used his immense power to swing his arm to toss the first Pitbull away while lifting his leg and crushing the second one into a bloody pulp. The dogs retaliated by attacking in unison upon witnessing their first casualty. Each terrier tore into the flesh of each of his limbs and pulled the appendages away from his body in all directions. Several tried to bite down on the armored carapace of Manticore's scorpion-like tail, which proved to be a fatal mistake when said tail swung violently in all directions, smashing several dogs into the ground.

Irritated by these nuisances, the True Kaiju summoned every ounce of his strength and thrashed his body across the beach, shattering his enemies' bones and rupturing their organs in the process. Once he could sense that they were no longer attacking him, Manticore went in for the kill. He found ten Pitbulls still alive and proceeded to sink his teeth into each of their spines to finish the job. He avoided using his tail as he did not want to poison his meals. By the time he was done slaying his incapacitated challengers, the pack was down to less than half of their initial size. Several began to retreat, with the more stubborn canines standing their ground. One snarl from Manticore was all it took to make the remaining dogs flee for their lives.

While normally, the winged terror would not allow a potential meal to escape, he decided he had more than enough as he was running dangerously low on energy after his clash with the Pitbulls. He needed to eat and regain his strength if he wished to continue his pursuit of the relentless machine.

*****

It was now late into the evening and the pilot that had previously fought off the giant Pitbulls was hard at work fixing the radio device within Joaquín's humble abode. Spread across the living quarters were various electronic materials and tools, many of which the man had collected and stored over the years within his mech's cockpit.

Prior to the fall of human civilization, the pilot was never proficient with machines beyond what was necessary to fight on the battlefield. Yet, with the world in ruins, he had all the time in the world to learn the ins and outs of the very machine that kept him alive. While the emergency device he was working on had a very different system of wires and transceivers, he had studied Bravura enough to know the basic fundamentals of radio devices that he could tell what parts were necessary to repair the device and hopefully call for help.

Originally, he had planned to abandon the village once he learned of the possibility of the dreaded Atomic Rex arriving at the shores of this city. Ever since that fateful day when the towering reptile first unleashed his wrath upon the world, he had long tried to suppress those memories. Only in times of great stress would he hear the screams of countless soldiers and the ungodly ear-shattering bellows of the beast ringing in his ears. Yet, as much as he wanted to run away from the nuclear behemoth, another ghost from the past had changed everything.

Upon hearing from Lupe of the possibility of a crimson robot stalking the village everything started to make sense. There was no doubt that someone had been manipulating things from the very start. How was it that just as he stumbled across this village's people did the Pitbulls show up, the very same animals that regularly encountered the one and only Atomic Rex? Only a mind as deranged as the man who took joy in the horrors of war could orchestrate such a plan.

In the years since the fall of humanity, Bravura's pilot confirmed the rumors and surviving military records of the unknown enemy pilot and his machine, the one simply referred to as the "Red Menace." His reported behavior of relishing in the slaughter of his victims matched his own personal recollection of the events. While the pilot's name was never uncovered, it had been reported that as the war on that island went on, he had laid a trail of blood everywhere he went, leaving no survivors in his wake, all except for one: himself. What exactly would drive a man to find delight in such chaos and destruction? thought Bravura's pilot. What was there to benefit from holding such a grudge from a war long since forgotten? This, the pilot could never understand.

However, what he did know was that this was someone who was sure to follow him to the ends of the Earth and would stop at nothing until he was dead. If he was to live another day, then he needed the help of Steel Samurai, a machine developed shortly after the Colossi were discontinued in favor of larger machines capable of confronting Atomic Rex and the rest of the True Kaiju. While these new mechs would fall in battle, Steel Samurai miraculously managed to succeed in taking care of the majority of the True Kaiju. At least, these were the rumors the pilot managed to pick up. If he could get Bravura's successor to protect this village, maybe then he would have the chance to evade another war.

Just then, a spark from the radio shocked the distracted man's right hand.

"Ah, Jesus Christ!" he blurted out.

"Is everything ok, Señor?" Joaquín asked as he suddenly appeared from around the corner of the living room.

"I'm good," the tired and frustrated man responded. "Have you been standing there the entire time?"

"I'm sorry, but Lupe and I were getting worried about you. You haven't eaten anything since you started."

"I told you, I'm fine," said the pilot in an annoyed tone. "I'll take a break once this radio's fixed."

Just then he could hear small childish giggles coming from outside the house. He looked in the direction of the windows where he witnessed

Joaquín's children with their similarly aged friends staring at him. Upon noticing this, Joaquín opened the door and told the kids to stay at their neighbor's house and not to disturb their guest. As they conversed in Spanish, the pilot overheard one of the kids stating they only wanted to see "El Cazador," before being escorted out by Lupe.

"El Cazador?" asked the curious man.

"It means 'the hunter,' it's something the village has been calling you since you killed two monsters now, both the spider and that dog."

"Hmph, is that so?" The man now known to the villagers as "the Hunter" chucked. "It wouldn't be the first time I've been called that. Seems that's all I do these days."

Joaquín was shocked to hear him open up, if only slightly. He did not know how to respond to the stoic figure, though the man quickly returned to work. Joaquín figured there was more to this man than the hard exterior he kept around him at all times. He could now piece together that he lived a life of constant violence. He wondered just how much longer could this soldier keep on fighting before either his age or the elements got the best of him.

Just then Lupe came back screaming hysterically.

"Another monster is here!"

"No!" gasped Joaquín.

"Atomic Rex is already here?" asked the Hunter.

"No, Señor. It's another kaiju." She ran to her guest and clutched his tattered uniform in her hands as she wept. "Please, help us! You're the only one who can save my children!"

The pilot hesitated. Mutants like the spider and the Pitbulls were manageable, but if this new creature was anywhere near as bad as the Atomic Rex, he would not stand a chance. However, if he did not respond to this threat, he and everyone else would die. Sure, he could run away, but his inner soldier would never forgive himself.

The Hunter got up and ran outside, where he found the massive form of a winged giant circling the area like a vulture stalking its prey.

"You gotta be kidding me!" the pilot spoke. He figured the beast could land any second, thus he had to get on board Bravura as soon as he could. With a grim determination, the Hunter dashed in the direction of his hidden mech. As he entered his mech's cockpit, and sat at the controls, his hands began to shake. He was afraid, afraid of that day repeating all over again. Then, his deceased captain's final words echoed in his mind.

"Never stop fighting."

These words were what kept him going all this time, no matter how hellish the world around him became. He never fully understood why his superior gave him this last request, but he knew he would be soiling her memory if he turned back now. At last, he forced himself to activate Bravura's machine as the monstrous Kaiju landed on all four of its limbs.

The creature immediately noticed the humanoid machine rising up and snarled, as if it somehow recognized it as an enemy. Little did the Hunter know, the goliath monstrosity known as "Manticore" believed Bravura to be in league with the machine that lured him all the way from Africa and caused him much grief. For the winged feline, it was finally time for him to enact his revenge.

The beast towered over the mech and roared in furious anger, causing the machine's cloak to billow. Still, both man and machine stood in defiance as Bravura unclipped and extended its bo staff. By gripping the pole tighter than before, the weapon surged with visible crackles of electricity at both ends. At the same time, Bravura's shield unfolded once more. Next, the Hunter was ready to activate a function he had not used in quite some time. He grabbed two levers and slid them down across the control panel. A familiar helmet lowered and latched over the pilot's head. Outside, Bravura's helmet shifted down to form a mask before two red eyes fiercely shined through. The Hunter knew that if he was going to take down the True Kaiju, he was going to have to resort to every weapon at his disposal, including the Eagle Eye.

"Come and get some, freak!" shouted the pilot through Bravura's external speakers.

Manticore aimed his arthropod-like stinger at the small figure and threw down his appendage with amazing speed. Yet, as fast as the monster was, so too was the robot. Bravura slid past the tail as it came crashing down at the last minute. With the Eagle Eye system, the mech could zero in on one single target and predict where it would appear, allowing the pilot to act in advance. Still, this system was developed for similarly sized opponents, not a creature as gargantuan as Manticore. In order for him to successfully fend off his enemy, the Hunter had to carefully choose where to strike, turning one massive target into multiple smaller ones. For now, he had to take care of the tail.

With the monster's main form of attack stuck in the ground, the pilot flipped a switch and activated the machine's long dormant jetpack. It was not his Colossus's original attachment, but one acquired after his first backpack was damaged beyond repair. Bravura launched into the air, soaring over Manticore's head. The mech's eyes zeroed in on the base of the tail. With another burst of propulsion, the Colossus sped towards it and jammed its electric pole into the lower end of the True Kaiju's spine. Manticore winced from pain as it threw its head back and yelled an unnaturally high-pitched scream, prying its tails in the process. It rolled over in an attempt to crush its small prey. Luckily, Bravura flew away at the last minute.

Manticore took sight of the robot floating in the air, and took to the sky.

Good, thought the Hunter as he allowed the beast to chase after him and moved away from the village in the process. Once he landed on the other side of the mountain range, he had Bravura once again zero in on a new target, Manticore's right wing. He commanded his metal avatar to charge at the creature, this time aiming with his razor-sharp shield at the monster's right wing. The robot ducked underneath the front limb and aimed up to tear a massive bloody hole through the wing's membrane, the weakest and thinnest part of Manticore's body. The pilot then proceeded to repeat the same process, this time attacking the left wing from above.

Once Bravura pierced through the True Kaiju's remaining wing, the behemoth found itself unable to stay airborne and tumbled into the sharp rocks below. The mountains were not where Manticore was at his most comfortable as it had lived all its life on the flat savannah plains. The winged beast rolled down the side of the craggy terrain as it attempted to gain some kind of stable footing, only to find its claws were too weak and its body too heavy to stop its fall several thousand meters down the sharp incline.

Under the crushing weight of his own mass, Manticore landed at the foot of the mountain, bruised, battered, and broken. It struggled to get back up on its shaking four limbs, only for a shocking pain to erupt from its back left foot. It was Bravura, slamming its voltaic weapon repeatedly at the tendons above the paw before severing them with his bladed shield.

Manticore attempted to turn around and sink his teeth in the target, only to lose sight of the enemy. Further pain was brought upon the creature's other leg. He tried to move its stinger in an attempt to swipe away the infernal machine, yet the lion could no longer pick up any sensation from his appendage.

Once the pain subsided and his back legs were proven useless, Manticore witnessed the tiny Bravura land right in front of him, its red eyes staring down the grounded mutant. Rage boiled within the leviathan. He would not allow his life to end at the hands of this pathetic thing. With every ounce of his being, Manticore dug his front limbs into the ground to pull himself forward while baring his fangs. At the very last possible second, Bravura jumped back before thrusting his electric staff into the snout of the lion, frying every sensitive nerve connected to his nose and whiskers.

Manticore was helpless against the mech's assault as all five appendages were rendered useless. Its vision started to blur with all other senses incapacitated save for its hearing. The groaning beast picked up the sound of a furious human scream coming from above. His eyes peered up, only to find Bravura jamming its staff right between his eyes. At this point it was no longer able to sense any sort of pain. Sounds and sights slowly faded, as too did the creature's mind as the once mighty predator's consciousness faded into oblivion.

At last the beast was dead. Bravura's face reverted back into its default setup. Once the Hunter inside the mech took off his own helmet, he gasped and coughed. It had been a long time since he had used the Eagle Eye system for such a duration. He figured the last time he used the system for that long, he was a youth running simulations. The pilot struggled to keep himself from falling into unconsciousness from the massive physical toll the mech had placed on him. As sweat poured down his face, all he could think of was the radio, the villagers, Atomic Rex, and the Red Menace. At last, he grabbed a hold of the controls and launched Bravura back up the mountains.

Several minutes later, Bravura arrived back at Fortuna, greeted once more by waves of supporters, more so than before. The exhausted pilot exited his machine where he came face-to-face with Joaquin.

"Señor, are you alright?" he urgently asked as everyone around him chanted "El Cazador."

"I still got it," the Hunter responded with a faint smile before it faded from his face. "Now, let's get back to work."

CHAPTER 14

The Settlement

It was a sweltering hot night in California as Kyle Myers sat in a room with his friends, Rondel Herd and Gil Heinz, as well as his mother Kate Myers. Kyle had shown his friends how to use what was left of the internet to access still functioning satellites. He then instructed them on how to use said satellites to track Atomic Rex and other large mutants. For the majority of the past year, Atomic Rex had stayed in the southern hemisphere or the Eastern US. As the leader of the settlement, Kate had felt that tracking Atomic Rex and knowing his location at all times should be a top priority. At first, Kyle was the only person in the settlement who had figured out how to utilize what little technology still existed to successfully perform that task. Kate had instructed her son to work with friends of his, whom he thought could grasp how to utilize computers, and teach them how to track the monster.

Initially, Kyle had voiced the concern that people closer to his mother's age who had grown up using computers would be better suited for utilizing computers as they grew up with the technology. His mother responded that while people of her generation may be better predisposed to learning the skill, it was more important people of his age learned how to do it so they could pass on the knowledge of how to locate the monster to future generations.

Kyle could still remember his mother's exact words. "It's likely Atomic Rex will outlive you and I. With that in mind, we need to make sure there are people who can teach these skills to those we leave behind."

Kyle's body shook at his mother's declaration. He had never considered Atomic Rex's life span, or that the beast could be a problem long after he was gone. At seventeen years old, his own mortality was the last thing on his mind, but his mom had a point. For all they knew, Atomic Rex could be immortal. The monster could live forever and be a constant threat to humanity from now until man's final days.

Once the young man's mind had fully processed the concept of what Atomic Rex meant to humanity as a whole, he agreed to train two of his friends in how to utilize the tracking technology he had stumbled upon. Kyle had been teaching his friends over the past two weeks on how to log onto the internet and then utilize several different satellites such as Google's to locate Atomic Rex.

Kyle showed his friends how he looked for a variety of indicators as to the kaiju's location. The young prodigy taught his students how to find actual live images of Atomic Rex when he was on land. He also instructed them on how to look for drastic spikes in ocean temperature as well. It was this skill that allowed them to get a rough approximation of the monster's location when he was in the ocean.

Currently, Kate had come to see how the boys were progressing in their ability to track Atomic Rex. Each young man sat in front of a computer as the leader of the settlement stood behind them overseeing their progress.

Kate could see that her son had already determined Atomic Rex's location as his two pupils were still looking at various maps of both land and sea to try and find the kaiju.

Kate walked over and placed her hand on Rondel's shoulder. A shiver ran through the sixteen-year-old's body as the attractive middle-aged woman rested her hand on him. He took a deep breath and tried to maintain what he thought was his cool demeanor as he worked to find the infamous reptilian's location.

"Boys, I know you're working hard and that I asked you for this demonstration today, but we need to move a bit faster. The energy used to power these three computers puts a significant strain on the electrical supply. Some of the older people in the settlement are going without their fans in this heat so you guys have enough energy to complete this search. We need to locate Atomic Rex as quickly as possible and then get off these computers so we can divert power back to other needs."

Rondel could hear Gil typing away behind him and from the corner of his eye, he could see Kyle sitting in his chair watching him. Rondel knew that Kyle had already found Atomic Rex and that Gil was likely close to locating the beast as well. Not wanting to seem inadequate or uncool in the eyes of not only the settlement leader, but a woman he had a crush on, Rondel tried to focus on what he had accomplished.

"Sorry, Mrs. Myers. I thought I found Atomic Rex." Rondel switched his computer to show a picture of Steel Samurai 2.0 outside of Los Angeles. "But it looks like I found Captain Myers and Steel Samurai 2.0 instead." Rondel laughed nervously. "I thought it took both you and Captain Myers to fly the robot?"

Kate leaned forward to take a closer look at the screen. As she did so, Rondel forced himself to look forward as well. The last thing he wanted was for Kyle to see him looking at his mom's breasts, or even worse for Kate herself to catch him looking.

Kate shook her head. "Chris can fly the mech by himself but it works better with a co-pilot. Today, Emily is there with him learning how to operate Steel Samurai 2.0, just like you guys are working to find Atomic Rex."

Kate moved away from Rondel and he sighed at the thought of Kyle's sister Emily. In Rondel's mind, if Kate was attractive, Emily was out of this world hot.

Kate walked over to Kyle's other student. "What about you, Gil? Any luck finding Atomic Rex?"

"I was able to find several bursts of extreme heat in the Pacific Ocean off the coast of El Salvador. I'm pretty sure that's Atomic Rex. My guess is he's hunting some giant mutant or got into a fight with something."

Kate looked over at her son. "Kyle, is that what you think too?"

"Yeah, I found the same thing. Hot spots in the Pacific off the coast of El Salvador. I mean really hot spots. Like the water around the area in question was definitely boiling for a few seconds. I agree with Gil. For temperatures to be as hot as they are, Atomic Rex is doing that whole energy dome thing that he does."

Kate sighed. "His Atomic Wave?"

"Yeah, his Atomic Wave or whatever." Kyle shrugged "The main thing is, it looks like he might be moving north based on the dispersion of the hot spots and the time in between them. I'll bet he's heading for the place off the coast of Mexico that we've seen him stop at before. I've taken a bit of a closer look there and I've seen what looks like a population of giant mutant dogs in the area from what little satellite imagery I've been able to find. My guess is that Atomic Rex is hunting the dogs and he's regularly stopping there to eat as he swims up and down the coast."

Kate turned toward Rondel and smiled. "Rondel, sweetie, I know how hard you're working, but would you mind if Kyle walked you through how to use ocean temperatures to find Atomic Rex one more time? I just want to be sure you fully understand how to do this. That way, when it's your turn to track the monster, we know that you are fully capable of being able to do so."

Rondel did his best to seem both confident and easy going with Kyle holding his digital hand once again to show him how to use the computer. "Yeah, of course. I mean, you know, I wanna learn how to do this for you... and you know... for everyone in the settlement."

The young man was sweating bullets as he thought he had just clued in Kate about his crush on her. He was already embarrassed by not being able to find Atomic Rex. Now he was sure his awkwardness had made him look even more like a fool.

Kate was fully aware that Rondel had a crush on her. She did not want the young man to feel embarrassed. The settlement leader smiled warmly at the young man. "Thanks, Rondel. The fact that you're so willing to learn how to do this shows your commitment to the settlement's safety and security. Again, I can't tell you how proud I am of you and how much I appreciate your efforts."

She then turned to her son. "Kyle, if you could please?"

"Sure, it's super easy."

As Kyle was moving his chair over toward Rondel's computer. Gil returned to a website he had stumbled upon during one of his searches for Atomic Rex. Gil clicked on the link he had created to see the image of a Black and White mask. One side comedy, the other tragedy. Over the eerie face was a purple top hat with horns and a ring of pumpkins with faces. Gil took a brief look over at the other people in the room. Once he was sure they were all occupied in watching what Kyle was doing, he clicked on the link and turned down the volume on his computer. The young man then leaned as close to his computer's speakers as he could without looking too conspicuous and listened to the eerie voice and disturbing instructions coming through them.

Kyle was doing his best to speak slowly and show Rondel step by step exactly how he used ocean temperatures to track Atomic Rex. "Okay, the first thing you do is go to Google and type in 'Sea Surface Temperature-Google Earth.'" A link came up which he clicked on. "This will take you to the Google Earth Sea Surface Temperature site." A web page appeared with the Earth against a black surface with a key in the corner showing a human, a target, a 3D sign, and a globe.

Kyle pointed to the screen. "The red parts you see are the bodies of water and the blue parts are land masses. Anything dark red means the water is hot." He placed his hand finger on the mouse's wheel. "When I see a really dark red spot on the map, I use the wheel in the middle of the mouse to zoom in by spinning it forward." As he was giving Rondel instructions, he performed the action and caused the map to zoom into the west coast of South America.

The young man pointed to a very dark red spot on the globe with smaller and lighter red dots behind it. "See this spot with the other not as dark spots trailing it?"

Rondel nodded. "Yes."

"That's usually an indicator of Atomic Rex having moved through the area and let off an Atomic Wave. The little red dots are sort of like the after effect of the wave coming off his body as it spreads out. He's moved a bit since letting that blast go, but we know he was there pretty recently. Even if he doesn't give off a radiation blast, we can still find him in the ocean because his body still runs pretty hot. Tracking him this way can be a bit more difficult. If he's way south or way up north, he'll stick out a bit more because the ocean water is much colder than our monstrous friend. If he's closer to the Equator it can become really tough to track him unless he gives off an Atomic Wave. The waters are warmer there so the difference in the color scheme between Atomic Rex and the ocean temperature can be difficult to discern."

Kyle shrugged. "Plus, I'm pretty sure this system was made up to just sort of check ocean temperatures in general and not to track radioactive dinosaurs. Still, it's a better system than just waiting until we can see Atomic Rex standing outside the settlement, because you know, by then it's too late."

"Anyway, I'll write all of those steps down for you. That way not only will you have them but you can show them to someone else. Don't worry about not getting this on your first few tries. It took me months of fooling around online to figure these things out. Just keep practicing and you'll get it."

Kate patted her son on the head. While she had no desire to embarrass Rondel, embarrassing her own son was her right as a mother. Plus, it was fun. "Excellent explaining, Kyle. You definitely get that skill from me and not from your dad."

She turned back to Rondel as Kyle ran his fingers through his hair to reset it to the position he wanted.

Kate snickered. "You don't like me to mess up your hair anymore?"

Rondel grinned. "He probably wants to make sure it looks good for Jackie Carlson. You know, in case she decides to stop by and see what's up."

Kate smiled and gave her son a sly look. "Jackie Carlson, huh? She's pretty and smart. She's helping to set up the new hospital we're trying to retrofit from the old Patient First. You could certainly do worse."

Kyle glared at Rondel for putting him on the spot with his mother. "Yeah well, Rondel, is talking about who we all have crushes on really something you want to discuss right now? I mean, I've seen you giving two women in particular a look over on several occasions."

Kate fought back the urge to laugh and forced herself not to grin as she turned in the young man's direction. "Come on now, Rondel. Who are these lucky ladies you have your eye on?"

Rondel's face lost all its color at Kyle's suggestion. He once again tried to play off any hint of his crush on Kate or her daughter. "Well, you know it's…it's just a couple of girls in the settlement…" The teenager was desperately trying to find something to change the subject. He looked over at Gil's computer to see the image of a blue-haired catgirl with a jack-o-lantern eye patch on the screen. Behind the catgirl was a suited figure with a large hat on. His face was split in two like some kind of twisted demon.

Seeing a chance to not only take the focus of the conversation off himself but to possibly catch his friend in a compromising situation he blurted out, "Gil, what in the heck are you looking at? Is that some kind of a crazy dating site or something?"

Gil's body went rigid when he realized people had discovered his secret. He quickly shut down his screen and turned around. "That? I'm not sure what that was. It seems like you just, you know, stumble across some strange things on the internet sometimes. That thing was so weird it just sort of caught my attention."

Gil was almost shaking with apprehension at the thought of being caught visiting the site. He inwardly scolded himself for opting to try and look at it now with other people in the room. For the past several weeks, he had been sneaking back at night to access the computers and visit the site, where he could hear the entrancing messages that came from it.

Whatever happened next, Gil knew that he could not have the site taken away from him. A plan began to fester in his mind about how he could still access the computer if he was denied access to the internet. The plan would be difficult to carry out but he was sure he could do it. He was sure the voice would help him. The voice did not want to lose him any more than he wanted to lose it. The voice promised Gil everything he wanted for a price.

All three people were still staring at him when something came over Kyle's computer that drew everyone's attention to it.

"Come in, this is the pilot of an Atlus-class Colossus: Codename Bravura. I am addressing the pilot of Steel Samurai. I am with a group of people in a settlement in Mexico near Acapulco called Fortuna. Until now, they've been unable to contact the outside world and have remained undetected for the last 30 years. We are in need of assistance. We are under attack by a group of marauders, several mutants, and possibly a rogue mech. We fear Atomic Rex may soon be on his way as well." The message was then followed by a Spanish translation before being repeated again in English.

Kyle looked at his mother. "A settlement we don't know about, another mech, mutants, and whatever a Colossus is? Could it be real? I mean, I'm pretty sure the message is real but a mech other than Steel Samurai? Something like that would be a real game-changer for us, right? Plus, Atomic Rex does seem to be heading back to that spot in Mexico where I saw the giant dogs before. Could there really be people living with those mutants? Maybe they're using the dogs like we use Ramrod?"

The always cautious Kate was hesitant to make any declarations. "See if you can find anything from the satellites that can verify if there's a mech moving around Mexico. In the meantime, get me your dad. I have to discuss this with him."

As Kyle started to carry out his mother's instructions, Gil turned back to his computer and thought about sneaking into the house later at night to return to the site of the Crooked Man and his Crooked Catgirl. If what the Crooked Man had told him was true, then Atomic Rex would soon no longer be a problem.

CHAPTER 15

California near the Settlement

The multi-headed and crippled rat that Steel Samurai 2.0 was carrying by its tail struggled in vain to break the mech's iron grip. As the metal giant was flying over the forest below them, Chris looked down at the majestic trees and shook his head.

Emily saw her father's gesture and was puzzled by it. "Why are you shaking your head like that? The landscape below us is amazing."

"I know, sweetheart. It is amazing. Not just because of how beautiful it all looks, but because of how much of it there is. When I was a kid, we still had plenty of large forests around but to see how far they've spread in only one generation since the kaiju conquered the world is astounding. I flew over this forest dozens of times in Steel Samurai when we first started the settlement. The tree line was much farther back than it is now. I'd estimate that this forest alone is about fifty percent larger than it was twenty-five years ago."

"Huh, I never thought of you as someone who appreciates nature. I knew you were more than capable of taking care of yourself in the woods or whatever. I just always thought taking the time to appreciate something like a forest wasn't something you'd do."

"Really? What makes you think that?"

Emily shrugged. "Well, you're always so focused on taking out monsters and protecting people. Don't get me wrong, it's great how you're helping people all the time and saving everyone on a regular basis. It's just I always thought you were sort of hyper-focused on that task only. It seemed like you didn't have time to focus on anything else. I kinda worried it was hard for you to be happy. I'm sure when you were my age, you had different plans about how your future would turn out. Something that didn't involve living in a tiny settlement and trying to rebuild humanity."

Chris shrugged. "When I was your age, I was a pilot who loved his job and had two really good friends. I honestly thought I would stay in the

US Air Force for the rest of my career and sort of move up the ranks. That was literally the only plan I had. Shortly after that, the kaiju came and I was picked for the mech project. I couldn't believe it. I mean, you'd hear about some hotshot guy here or there who claimed to have stumbled across giant robots in the field on some kind of dark mission or something, but you could tell it was just them talking out their ass."

"How did you know they weren't telling the truth?"

"Well, pilots, in particular, were always talking about seeing some high-tech project, like a saucer-shaped craft, triangular shaped wings, and such, but no one ever had any proof of them. All they had were stories. At the time, giant robots seemed like something out of a comic book. If any pilot claimed they saw them, they were clearly trying to look cool. And as usual, no one was ever able to show any kind of proof. So, I always just brushed off reports of mechs or UFOs as guys just bullshitting."

"Anyway, back to the point, that all changed when Atomic Rex hit the US You know the story: my friends and I arrived in our mechs to fight him and he crushed us. Jeremy and Laura were like family to me. They gave their lives to give me a chance to escape. When they died, when civilization fell, I felt like a failure to my friends and to the human race. When I went out to try and clear out North America from the kaiju, I honestly thought I wasn't coming back. There was a big part of me that didn't want to come back. I wanted to be with my friends again. I wanted to honor what they did by going out the same way they did, fighting the kaiju."

"Then things changed when I met your mom. She had been through a situation far worse than I had and she prevailed. I'm still amazed at her strength. She not only gave me a reason to hope again, but she also gave me a reason to live. Your mother even helped me to find a way to honor my friends by incorporating parts from their mechs into, at the time, a badly damaged Steel Samurai."

He tapped the inner haul of the legendary metallic warrior. "Jeremy and Laura's mechs are a part of Steel Samurai 2.0, and knowing that helps me to feel like they are here fighting with me every time I go into battle."

Chris laughed a little. "As if your mom's love, strength, and idea to honor my friends weren't amazing enough, she gave me the greatest gift in the world. She gave me you. She made me a father. Before the kaiju, I never pictured myself as a husband and definitely not as a father. I didn't think I was disciplined enough to be any good at those roles."

"Then I saw you for the first time. When I held you, I discovered a happiness I had never known before. Happiness I didn't even know could be real even before the kaiju came. There you were, this little baby that needed me to be her dad. That needed me to protect her in a world where monsters still roamed the Earth. Where Atomic Rex still lived. When I was holding you for the first time, I told you that no matter what happened, I was going to do all I could to make this world a better place for you. A couple of years later, I had that same feeling when Kyle was born, and I made him that same promise."

He looked back at the woods below him. "That's why I fight so hard. Yes, I want to protect people. That's why I became a pilot in the first place, but I need to protect you and your brother. I need to keep my promise to you. I need to make the world a better place for you than it was for me. When I look down at a forest that is flourishing, it lets me know that I am keeping that promise. That is what truly makes me happy."

Chris looked back at his daughter to see tears in her eyes and a huge smile on her face. "Dad, the rest of the world may love you for being the tough guy hero, but I love you for the softy you really are."

She grabbed his hand. "I'm glad you're happy. I also think you've more than kept your promise. I mean, what other father is teaching his daughter how to operate a giant mech?"

Chris shrugged. "Probably, the same amount of daughters who are out there showing their dad how to use giant rams and elephant seals to protect their homes."

Emily laughed. "Well look at us, each teaching the other a skill to accomplish the same goal from different angles."

"Giant animal guardians wouldn't have been my first choice, but they have proven themselves effective in protecting you and the others. If I'm going to keep my promise to you, I need to be open to anything to help me accomplish that goal. Even if it's something I don't agree with at first glance."

Emily grinned. "I understand that overwhelming desire to help and protect others. It runs pretty deep in me too. I think it's a value I learned from my dad."

Chris smiled and then pointed to the river below them. "There's the river we want below us. Let's drop Splinter here into the water and go fishing, or leeching, I suppose."

Emily had a confused look on her face. "Splinter?"

Chris laughed. "A mutant rat from one of the shows that did make me happy when I was a kid. Maybe Kyle can find a clip for you on the internet when we get back. Right now, we have to finish off your plan to protect our western shore."

Chris brought Steel Samurai 2.0 to a hover over the water. The rat's tail was still in Steel Samurai's hand and the creature had its back arched as it tried to use its remaining heads to bite the hand holding it.

Chris ignored the mutant's futile attempts to free itself, and lowered the rat so that its back was in the river but its remaining heads were not submerged. "We need the thing to splash around a little without letting it drown. Like I said, the leeches prefer live prey."

Emily sighed. "I get why you have to use live bait. It also helps that the rat is a pretty vile thing, but I'm not sure I could do this with one of the cats you and mom usually use. I can't see myself mutilating a cat and then all but drowning it. It just seems so cruel."

Chris shrugged. "I knew doing this would be hard for you. It's an ugly task, but again it's better than having the leeches attack our people. Look, babe, I don't want this to come across the wrong way, but what do you think is eventually going to happen to Ramrod or the giant elephant seals if this plan works?"

"We'll keep feeding them and they'll keep protecting us."

"Until something comes that's stronger than they are. Something like Atomic Rex for instance. They'll be wounded in battle and then, just like this rat, or those giant cats, they'll die protecting their territory and us."

"No, Ramrod would run away if Atomic Rex came. I'll bet the seals will too." Emily cast her worried eyes down on the flailing rat mutant as its remaining heads screeched in a mixture of fear and pain. The mutant was experiencing a terrifying death all so her friends and family would be safe.

"Sweetheart, I've been around mutants and kaiju for a long time. One thing I've learned is that if they have a steady food source, they'll never turn and run. They'd rather die fighting to protect their access to food than slowly starve to death. Now that he's used to being fed on a regular basis, Ramrod will never leave our southern border alive."

Emily began to tear up. "What does that make me? Ramrod saved my life and Sean's life. In return, I've set him up in a situation where he's going to die trying to save us, just like that thing and the cats you've killed? That's not what I wanted. I wanted Ramrod, the elephant seals, and other mutants to benefit from us and us from them. I didn't want them to be bait or chained to a life where they're doomed to die."

"Dad, I... I knew that I was putting Ramrod in a position where he would need to battle threats. It's just I always told myself he could escape if he wanted to. I never wanted him to be a prisoner. I never wanted to use his own instincts to permanently tie him to the area around us. I wanted us to live in a mutually beneficial relationship with him. In reality, I'm exploiting him."

Chris spoke in as reassuring a tone as he could. "That makes you the person who gave Ramrod a better life than he ever would've had on his own, constantly foraging for food. It makes you the person who solved the problem for those elephant seals to stop having to swim deeper into the territory of Atomic Rex to find something to eat. It will make you the person who injured a giant rat that would have died in a fight with another mutant anyway, and used his death to save the lives of others."

"Learning how to fly the mech, how to cull the leeches, all of those things are secondary to what you're learning right now. People are already looking to you to be a leader, Emily. That's a tough role, especially if you never really wanted it. It's a role that requires you to make difficult decisions. Decisions where ugly things need to happen to prevent the worst from happening. Your mother and I know how kind-hearted you are. We know going forward, these types of decisions will weigh on you. Hell, they weigh on us now, but you need to be ready for them. You need to be ready to make the tough calls and live with them because the people of the settlement aren't going to give you another choice."

"The decisions you've made with Ramrod have benefitted both him and us. Last year, he saved your life and countless others by killing those giant rats." He looked down to see several gargantuan leeches attached to the back of the still squealing multi-headed vermin he was using as bait. "Look, we've managed to catch the leeches. Now, this thing has helped us save who knows how many more people from dying via a giant leech sucking out all its blood. These are tough choices, ugly choices, choices that make you think about their outcomes and your motivations. In the end, they're choices where you need to look at yourself in the mirror and ask if you made the best choice you could for those closest to you, for the people under your care."

He shrugged. "Honestly, I wasn't planning on having this conversation with you today. I was planning on just getting you some practice in piloting Steel Samurai 2.0, but then you had what I think is a good idea with those elephant seals. So, I made a hard decision to talk to you about a subject I planned to ease you into." He gestured to the dying mutant below them. "That monster has several leeches attached to it. Now it's your turn to make a decision. Do we just kill the leeches and protect some of our people? Or do we kill the leeches and see if we can use them as bait to set up another level of protection on the shore with those mutant seals even though we know one day they will die defending us because of the situation we are creating? The choice is yours. I'll back you either way."

Emily wiped the tears from her eyes. "There's hardly a choice is there? This process ends in death no matter what. It's just maximizing the benefit that comes from that eventually painful death, isn't it?"

Chris shrugged. "I'm not a wise enough man to know for sure, but that's the reasoning I use when I look in the mirror and rationalize my actions."

Emily shrugged and smiled. "I guess if that reasoning is good enough for the savior of the human race, it's good enough for me."

"Okay. Let's pull that rat out of the water. I can see at least three leeches on it. We'll cut through the leeches and kill the rat in a few strokes. No need to prolong the rat's death."

As Steel Samurai 2.0 pulled the mutant out of the water, Emily could see five leeches at least thirty meters long, each attached to the crippled vermin. Chris placed the mutants on the shoreline. Emily could see the multi-headed rat's remaining eyes filled with terror as the vampiric slugs drew the very blood from his helpless body. She felt as if the beast was looking right through the mech's eyes at her and begging her to end the suffering she had brought upon it.

Chris was reaching for the controls to the mech's sword when Emily stopped him. "No, I need to do this."

Chris nodded and sat back in his chair as Emily armed the mech and then lifted its sword over its head. The sun beat down on the metal giant as it stood next to the majestic river. The landscape seemed totally oblivious to the carnage that was taking place upon it. For a brief moment, Emily envied nature itself for being unaffected by the horror of the creatures that inhabited it. The young woman pushed the thought aside and brought the sword crashing down on the rat and leeches. The sword cut through three worms and cleaved the mutant rodent in two.

The halved mammal's body writhed when its spine was shattered, cutting off all input to its nerves and muscles. As the rat's heads swerved in all directions, Emily cut through the remaining two leeches. She then watched in silence as the rat and the worms squirmed until the blood drained from their bodies.

When the horrific monsters finally expired, Chris spoke up. "What now?"

The tears on Emily's face had dried up as she put the mech's sword back into its holding compartment. "Now, we gather up the remains of those damn worms. Then, we fly to the coast and see if we can help out those seals by giving them the food they need and a permanent home while also protecting the settlement from an attack from the ocean."

"Okay." He then grabbed the controls and put the mutilated bloodsuckers into the holding bays near the mech's torso. An hour later, Chris and Emily had flown back over the ocean and found the elephant seal they had encountered earlier still eating the fish off the wreck site.

Emily grabbed the controls to the mech and used them to drop parts of the deceased blood-suckers in front of the mutant seal. The gargantuan mammal circled the bloody body parts several times, before sinking his teeth into the side of one of the dead worms. The beast devoured the remains of the slain leech as Emily dropped another piece closer to shore.

She looked over at her father. "We'll lead him back to land where we'll leave the remainder of the leech parts. It may take a few months of dropping leech parts along the shoreline south of the main colony of mutant elephant seals, but we should be able to lure them south and give them enough food to limit their impact on the fish population."

Chris was about to congratulate his daughter when his son's voice came over the radio. "Dad, come in. It's Kyle! I'm here with Mom! There's something you need to hear!"

Kyle patched in the message he had received asking for help. Chris listened to it and replied in an unsure voice. "A mech being attacked by another mech as well as a group of marauders and mutants? Do we have anything to support this claim or did someone find an old Mad Max video and is doing some kind of joke?"

Kate's voice came over the radio. "I had Kyle check some of the satellite feeds. He was able to see a few images of what could be a relatively small object moving at high speeds in the area. Honestly, though, it's hard to say for sure if they're mechs or not. The only thing we can say for sure is that someone is sending out the message."

Chris bit his lower lip as he thought a moment before responding. "They also listed Steel Samurai by name and indicated Atomic Rex may be an incoming threat. Can we confirm if there is a settlement or village in the area? Or this group of marauders?"

"Dad, I was able to find images of a group of giant mutant Pitbulls in the area. I'm not so sure people could live near them. They seem to be pretty feral and violent. Also, I'm sure that Atomic Rex stops by to feed on the Pitbulls so, again, maybe not a good idea to live near them."

Emily grabbed the radio. "Maybe it makes perfect sense. Maybe the people are living in a cooperative relationship with the Pitbulls the same way we do with Ramrod or the elephant seals we are trying to lure to our shoreline."

Chris nodded at his daughter and then continued the conversation over the radio. "What about the marauders? Can we confirm them?"

There was a silence before Kate's voice came back over the radio with a tinge of fear in it. "Kyle was able to find at least one picture of what could be a mutated human similar in height to..." Kate took a deep breath. "Similar in height to Ogre. He appears to be carrying a large sack on his back."

Everyone was silent for a moment as they were fully aware of the years Kate had spent as a prisoner of Ogre. She had lived in constant fear as the mutated human kept her and several other women locked in a warehouse. She had watched all of the other women who were with her die under Ogre's rule. Kate herself was only saved when Chris brought Steel Samurai to engage the monster and draw him into another True Kaiju's territory.

The settlement leader spoke directly to her husband. "Chris, we didn't handle our first meeting with another settlement all that well. We need to do better this time. If there are people there that this thing is rounding up like Ogre did...then we have to at least look into it. Come back here and pick me up so we can see what's going on."

Emily looked at her father for a brief moment and then she replied to her mother. "Mom, it's a waste of time for us to come back and switch out. Dad and I have already fought a mutant together today. I can do this."

Kate responded with the passion of a mother wanting to protect her child from dangers she did not yet fathom. "Emily, if this mutant is anything like Ogre, you don't know what you're going into. Ogre wasn't like the other True Kaiju. He was evil. He wasn't a force of nature like Atomic Rex, he was a demon. That's something you're not ready for."

"Mom, Dad and I have been talking all day about how Kyle, Sean, and I are going to have to start making tough decisions as we move into leadership roles in the settlement. This is one of those tough decisions and I'm making it now. We're losing time and potentially lives the more we debate what to do next. Also, if I'm being honest, you are biased against anything that reminds you of Ogre. This mutated person may not be a monster, he may be a victim. Maybe with the right approach, he could be helpful to us and anyone we find in Mexico."

Kate screamed at her daughter with a mixture of fear and anger in her voice. "You're damn right I hate anything like Ogre! And if you knew what he put me through, what this monster could put you, my daughter, through, you'd be pretty fucking biased too! Now come home and let me go with your dad to investigate this!"

Emily glared over at her father. "Dad, what do you say about this?"

Chris sighed and threw his head back. "From the look on your face and the sound of your mom's voice, I think I can't win no matter what I say."

Chris spoke as calmly as he could. "Kate, Emily is right. We'd be wasting time to come back and get you. You're going to hate me for this but I think Emily's ready for something like this. I promise you, I won't let anything happen to her."

Chris could actually hear his wife fighting back tears as she responded. "Damn it, Chris. This is different from hunting feral cats and giant leeches. This is an Ogre-like monster and possibly Atomic Rex! Two creatures you've barely survived encounters with!"

Kyle spoke up. "Actually, Atomic Rex isn't there yet. I figure we can give them plenty of warning before he shows up."

Chris shook his head as he knew the scolding Kate would give their son when the conversation was over.

Emily decided the conversation had reached an impasse. "Mom, I love you. I'm going to be fine, this is the world I'm going to have to live in. If you really think I'm going to be an important leader in the settlement going forward, it would make sense for me to show a potential new village that I'm capable of helping them."

"Fine, Chris, you bring our daughter back home safely. Do you hear me?"

"I do and I will. I'm also sleeping on the couch for a while, aren't I?"

"Couch? Your ass better drop off Emily and then spend a few weeks at the bottom of the ocean by yourself in your mech before you even think about sleeping on my couch!"

Chris looked over at his daughter. "I can stay at your place, right?"

Emily grinned and shrugged.

Chris nodded. "Right, twenty-something newlyweds, never mind. The bottom of the ocean sounds great." He then grabbed the controls and took off in the direction of the call for help.

CHAPTER 16

El Salvador

Red Menace stood roughly a mile from a beehive that was the size of a baseball stadium. Inside the machine, Ivanov watched the twenty-meter-long mutant Africanized bees making their way in and out of the structure. The huge insects had adapted to their size by learning how to brush their massive bodies against flowering plants in order to collect the pollen necessary to maintain their colony.

The colony of flying mutants worked tirelessly to provide for their queen. Day and night, they scoured the surrounding area to find the pollen needed for the queen to feed the new larvae that she had created.

Ivanov had suspected that Atomic Rex would survive the mutated box jellyfish that he used to attack the nuclear theropod. With that in mind, he had determined several locations where he could draft similar mutants into his cause when the True Kaiju came ashore. The beach near the giant beehive was one of his more highly preferred locations. While Atomic Rex's body was still fighting off the effects of the box jellyfish's venom, he could also add a debilitating dose of bee venom into the monster's system as well.

Ivanov checked his bearing to see that Atomic Rex was roughly ten kilometers from the location of the hive. It was a distance well within the range he had determined he could draw the leviathan into from the beach. Red Menace leaped into the sky and then flew in the direction of the most powerful monster on the planet.

Atomic Rex's amazing regenerative abilities had made significant progress on healing his wound from his past two battles. He was still resting when his keen olfactory senses detected the presence of the small mech that had been near him with increased frequency over the past couple of days. At first, the saurian beast thought nothing of the annoying yet seemingly harmless mech.

Atomic Rex opened his eyes to see the metal figure flying toward him. He took a quick look at the relatively small robot carrying something in its arms and then closed his eyes to continue to let his body recover. The moment that the monster closed his eyes, he felt his snout being struck with a barrage of high-powered rounds.

The enraged titan opened his eyes to see Red Menace firing at him. A wave of rage coursed through Atomic Rex's mind as he realized that the metallic warrior was attacking him. The nuclear theropod rose to his feet, threw out his arms, and roared at his attacker. Despite his warning, Red Menace continued to fire a stream of bullets directly into the beast's gaping maw. Furious at the flying object's attack on him, Atomic Rex charged his hovering tormentor.

The moment that Ivanov saw the kaiju running toward Red Menace, he did two things. The first was to turn and start flying in the direction of the beehive. The second was to open the airtight compartment that held what remaining blood of Manticore's he did not use to coat his bullets. Ivanov had no sooner opened the compartment with droplets of blood than Atomic Rex stopped moving and sniffed the air. Upon picking up the scent of a rival kaiju and immediately tasting the metal bullets that were lodged in his mouth, Atomic Rex unleashed an anger-filled roar and ran toward the colossus at a full sprint.

Even though he had clocked Atomic Rex's running speed on several occasions, Ivanov was still amazed at how fast the leviathan could run and how quickly he could change directions.

Still, as fast and agile as Atomic Rex was, he was not able to catch up to Red Menace. Ivanov's main concern was keeping at least two kilometers between his mech and the monster so that he was clear of the blast radius of the kaiju's Atomic Wave attack. The robot continued to fly backward so that he could see Atomic Rex and fire the occasional salvo at the monster in order to ensure that his enemy continued his pursuit of him. Roughly five minutes into the chase, Ivanov saw the first few giant bees fly past him. Two minutes later, he saw a constant stream of the winged insects moving around the air.

When the mountainous beehive was finally in sight, Red Menace fired another round at Atomic Rex's face. The high-powered bullets bounced off the monster's thick hide and while the bullets did not injure the nuclear theropod, they did annoy him.

In response to the robot's attack, Atomic Rex once more bellowed at the flying machine, offering a challenge for the metal monster to engage him in combat. There was such fury in Atomic Rex's roar that it shook not only the ground but the colossal beehive as well.

Ivanov heard a dramatic increase in the buzzing behind him. He quickly glanced at the beehive to find numerous agitated bees hovering around outside of it. He then looked back to see Atomic Rex charging towards him once again. With the True Kaiju finally maneuvered into the position he desired, Red Menace aimed his rocket launcher and fired its only missile at the giant beehive. As the missile was streaking toward the insects' palace, Red Menace flew into the atmosphere at top speed. He was a kilometer above the ground when his missile struck the colossal beehive and blew a massive hole in the side of it.

After being agitated by Atomic Rex's roar and then sent into a frenzy by the attack on their hive, the swarm of mutant Africanized bees emerged from their decimated home to see Atomic Rex charging toward them. The legion of giant bees flew toward the reptilian horror with the intent of slaying the beast.

Atomic Rex had his eyes fixed on the ascending Red Menace when the first wave of killer bees reached him. The second that they were within striking distance of their target, the huge bees landed on the nuclear theropod and drove their stingers into him. Atomic Rex's body was covered by five of the giant insects as they attacked him. The initial sensation of the stinger entering the monster's body was painful enough, but the agony Atomic Rex was experiencing increased exponentially as the bees implemented the second phase of their attack.

With their stingers firmly implanted in their prey, the mammoth insects began to contort their bodies in an effort to both drive their stingers deeper into Atomic Rex and to pump as much of their venom into the saurian creature as possible. The bee venom passing through Atomic Rex's system caused a similar sensation of near debilitating pain that he experienced earlier in the day during his battle with the box jellyfish.

Atomic Rex opened his powerful jaws to bite down on a mutant that was attacking his chest, but to his surprise, when he went to close his jaws on his attacker, the bee tore his body off his stinger and then fell to the ground at his feet. The nuclear theropod stomped on the dying bee and crushed it under his foot. The moment he felt the insides of his crushed opponent sliding between his clawed toes, another bee drove its stinger into his chest.

Across the breadth of Atomic Rex's body, this action repeated itself over and over again. With each stinger that was driven into his body, the monster felt a wave of pain and an increased sense of fatigue. When the second bee to rip itself free from its stinger fell off his chest, the True Kaiju let it fall to the ground in front of him. Rather than actively trying to crush his dying opponent, the saurian beast lashed out at the third bee flying in to attack his torso. Atomic Rex's claw slashed the bee that was flying toward his chest in half.

As a spray of ichor, wings, and legs flew into the air, a fourth insect flew through the remains of his fellow soldier and stung the invading kaiju.

This process was repeated on Atomic Rex's legs, back, head, and tail in rapid succession. The mighty reptile briefly fell to one knee and had to use his arms to catch himself as the weight of the bees and their accumulating venom took their toll on his system.

In the sky above the fray, Ivanov looked down on the carnage he had created. For the briefest moment, he thought that the swarm of giant killer bees was going to slay Atomic Rex. While the death of the monster was one of his goals, he needed the True Kaiju weakened by this encounter, not slain, for his plan to reach its fruition.

When he saw Atomic Rex fall to one knee, Ivanov lowered his mech several meters to see if he had underestimated the hated kaiju's endurance. He peered at Atomic Rex's eye and was sure that the monster was looking back at him. To further enrage the monster, Ivanov fired more blood-coated bullets into the ground below. The action caused Manticore's scent to once more waft into Atomic Rex's nasal cavity.

Ivanov knew the exact moment the monster caught the scent of a rival beast. He saw Atomic Rex's pupils grow wider and the warrior in him knew that the dilation was not the result of the venom coursing through his body, rather it was the recognition of a hated enemy that caused the change in the radioactive reptile.

Atomic Rex was starting to blackout when he saw Red Menace hovering above him and smelled Manticore's odor. The pain that the monster was in was blocked out by the increasing fury he felt over the mech confronting him and then leading him here to be attacked by the swarm of insects. This anger was exacerbated by the odor of the rival kaiju that he knew had invaded his domain.

With five twenty-meter-long killer bees attached to his body, the saurian creature willed himself back into a standing position. He then lifted his head into the sky and roared at the watching Red Menace. The reptilian horror then lifted his foot off the ground and as he did so his body began to give off a light blue hue.

The True Kaiju roared as he slammed his foot to the ground and sent the dome of energy known as the Atomic Wave cascading out of his body. The blast of pure radiation immediately vaporized the bees that were stuck to his body. The other insects that were caught in the blast were either set ablaze or scorched and sent hurtling across the sky before crashing to the ground.

Atomic Rex looked at the damaged beehive to see a new wave of soldiers flying over the smoking bodies of their brethren to renew their collective assault. The newest round of attack bees was only a few meters away from their target when Atomic Rex unleashed a second Atomic Wave that instantly slew the mutant insects. Scores of burning mutant bees fell to the ground as the leviathan glared at the hive that had caused him so much pain.

The radioactive horror roared at the damaged hive and the newest round of defenders came out of it, as he continued to move toward the structure. The nuclear theropod had taken three steps closer to the hive when he utilized a third Atomic Wave to slay another horde of bees. Atomic Rex repeated this process five more times before he reached the hive itself. With a field of burning giant bees in his wake, the True Kaiju approached the hive itself. When he reached the bees' stronghold, the monster knew that there were no more soldiers to attack him. Despite the lack of attacking bees, Atomic Rex was still able to sense another threat waiting inside the crumbling structure.

The green-scaled demon roared at the hive and then he ripped open the side of it to reveal the queen bee. The moment that the queen saw the saurian creature, she lunged out at him with her stinger. With his reflexes dulled by the massive amount of bee venom coursing through his veins, Atomic Rex was unable to dodge the queen's attack. The queen drove her stinger into Atomic Rex's abdomen. The True Kaiju's eyes went wide from the pain he was in, then to his surprise, he felt the queen remove her stinger from his stomach and then drive it into his leg.

Like most queen bees, the mutant queen's stinger was smooth and not barbed like those of her soldiers. This unique attribute allowed her to sting opponents multiple times and inject a larger amount of venom into her victims than her solider bees could. She was pulling her stinger out of Atomic Rex to attack him a third time when the scaled horror grabbed onto her body and held her closer to him. The decreased distance prevented the queen from pulling her stinger out of the nuclear theropod 's leg.

The scaled leviathan unleashed a ferocious roar into the queen's face and then he closed his massive jaws around the top half of her body. The mammoth insect's body was reduced to a mushy pulp that the injured monster swallowed. Atomic Rex reached down and pulled the giant stinger out of his leg. The kaiju then tried to use his Atomic Wave to destroy what remained of the beehive, but for the first time since he had absorbed the phoenix, he was unable to call the power stored within his cells. The monster could not comprehend that the queen's venom attacking his central nervous system was blocking his ability to unleash the nuclear energy stored within him.

Atomic Rex then slowly turned around and stared at the mech that had attacked him and carried the scent of the beast that had invaded his domain. His vision was blurred and his balance was tenuous as his already taxed healing factor was now working to fight off the latest toxins that had been introduced into his system. The nuclear theropod knew that despite the anger he felt, his body needed to rest before he could continue his pursuit of the red machine and his search for the invading kaiju. A wave of vertigo caused Atomic Rex to stumble and fall back into the decimated beehive.

Atomic Rex had almost passed out when Red Menace flew down to the hive. Close to the outer perimeter of the insectoid structure was the same device Ivanov used in El Salvador. He had planted it in this location in preparation for Atomic Rex's battle with the hive. Each time the tall thin machine was left near Atomic Rex, it had slowly absorbed his radioactive energy. The Atomic Waves from the True Kaiju's most recent fight expelled just enough energy for the dual meters on each side of the device to indicate that it had reached full capacity. With the gadget reacquired by the Red Menace, it flew above the dinosaur and fired another salvo of bullets at both his mouth and nostrils so that Manticore's odor and taste would continue to antagonize Atomic Rex.

The attack and then the scent of his enemy aroused the nearly exhausted kaiju. Atomic Rex's fighting spirit forced him to rise to his feet and pursue the crimson robot that had vexed him. The leviathan roared and then took a slow groggy step in the direction of the fleeing mech as his body fought to counteract the poisons he had been exposed to.

CHAPTER 17

The Ruins of Acapulco

After an entire day of following the path Alexander Ivanov laid out for them, the Hounds of Hades were finally within reach of the village they long sought after, Fortuna. To Lopez and his men's surprise, their new ally was right about the Pitbulls' weakened power. The mutant canines were too busy fighting amongst themselves to notice their caravans' approach towards the beaches of the once popular resort town. By the time they arrived, more than half of the dogs that survived Manticore's onslaught were either killed or brutally mauled as the strongest of the diminished pack fought for the position of the new alpha. El Silbón, the wolves, and Lopez's army were more than enough to finish off the rest of the adult dogs and capture what few pups remained in the hopes of training them as they had done with their own canines.

As the team regrouped and took their short rest, Lopez's men picked up a signal that seemingly came from Fortuna. It was the pilot of the machine Ivanov told them about, who was asking for the assistance of the US's Steel Samurai. He was not sure if the US would come to their aid, but if they were he and his men would have to act quickly. They needed to get in and out before Chris Myers could arrive on the scene.

Once more he approached El Silbón, who had since become his most trusted confidant. This was mostly due to the fact that the former human did not care for frivolous things such as leadership and power like many of the Hounds did. Therefore, the pair had reached a silent agreement; as long as Lopez was still in charge, he gave the mutant whatever accommodations he needed for him and the wolves to be comfortable.

"Are you ready for this?" the Hound's leader asked his teammate, who was washing off Pitbull blood using the ocean's saltwater nearby the resting wolves.

"Yes, I've recovered enough," he responded in a blunt manner.

"That's not what I mean. This is going to be our biggest invasion yet, Silbón. I need to know if you're mentally prepared for what we're about to do."

"What do you mean?" the soaked giant asked suspiciously as he stepped away from the water. *"We've attacked plenty of targets before."*

"Yes, but this will be our largest invasion yet. We've raided small settlements and travelers before, but this village in particular is on the scale of a small town with plenty of men, women, and children. Many will die, and those that survive our raid will be given the chance to join us or perish if they don't comply. Are you willing to do this to your own kind?"

El Silbón began laughing, a haunting sound Lopez had not heard before. It was unlike any real human laugh as it sounded more like wheezing and choking. Only his ally's smile could clue him in as to what was happening.

"You fool," El Silbón retorted. *"You should know by now that I stopped considering myself 'human' long ago. I feel no sympathy towards mankind, especially when I was abandoned by my own village and left for dead. Besides, this is a matter of survival."*

Before Lopez could respond, his gigantic associate spoke once more.

"If anyone should be uncomfortable, it should be you, an actual human."

"You're right," responded Lopez as he turned to face the moonlit ocean. *"But like you said, it's a matter of survival. Sympathy only gets you killed. I learned that the hard way when my family died from a mutant attack in Mexico City. I was picked up by the Hounds soon afterwards when I offered to help them fight off the local mutants and loot some houses in order to join their ranks. I killed three families that day."*

El Silbón chuckled. *"Then let's get down to business."*

The mutant whistled to his pets as Lopez gave his men the order to begin their ascent up the mountains in their heavily armored vans towards their largest bounty yet.

*****

It had been an hour since the Hunter had broadcast his message to all frequencies in ten-minute intervals. He had to take a break, his first since fighting off the flying lion, otherwise he would have lost his voice. Little did he know, his brief retreat would be disturbed by the sound of a now-very familiar alarm. By the time he was getting Bravura ready for battle, Joaquín approached him with the latest news.

"This is it; the Hounds of Hades are here!"

"What do they have?"

"Several armored vehicles, no doubt armed with all sorts of weapons. They also have five mutant wolves and," he paused, unsure of how to properly describe the last creature, "a giant man," was all he could utter.

A giant man? This left the Hunter puzzled, that was until he remembered reports decades prior of two of the True Kaiju, Yokozuna and Ogre, as well as rumors of human experiments down in South America.

"How big are these mutants?"

"Our men said they were about twenty meters in height with the man at thirty meters."

On one hand, the Hunter breathed a sigh of relief at the thought that he would not be up against another leviathan like the lion. However, these smaller creatures were not going to be pushovers if they were under the control of the Hounds of Hades. At a stature of twenty-five meters, Bravura stood in the middle of the Hounds' abominations. He previously had his hands full with the two similarly sized Pitbulls, so going up against six targets was not going to be easy in the slightest. Still, the former soldier had no choice if he wanted to protect Joaquín, his family, and the rest of Fortuna.

"Set a barrier along the perimeter of Fortuna. I'll lead the defense while you and a squadron of your most trusted men stay back and guard the rest of the villagers."

"You can't be serious!" protested Joaquín. "You need all the help you can get out there."

"Do you want your family to survive this?" the pilot aggressively asked his associate, who responded with bewildered stammering.

"O-of course I do!"

"Then what good are you to them if you're dead? Look, if this situation goes south, they're gonna need your help to escape. Now, is there a way out of this area?"

"Y-yeah, there's a rocky path to the west of here."

"Then hide out there. If I give the signal, you and everyone else get the hell out of here."

At that moment, Joaquín realized what he was tasked to do. If he was to continue leading his village towards prosperity, he needed to be the one to keep watch over them at all costs. It was his responsibility to protect the people of Fortuna just as his father had done years ago. Now was the time to prove he was capable of handling such a burden.

"Alright, be safe out there," Joaquín said as he held out his hand.

Without hesitation, the Hunter accepted his brother-in-arm's handshake. The last thing he wanted was to see another man be separated from his family. So, he took comfort in knowing that his caretakers would be as far away from the battlefield as possible.

Just then, Joaquín's ten-year-old sons, Nicolás and Carlos, ran over to them with their mother frantically trailing behind.

"*My brother and I made this while you were resting,*" Nicolás explained in Spanish as he held out a Mexican Huichol beaded bracelet, adorned with a lavish red, blue, green, yellow, and orange diamond pattern.

"*It's a good luck charm we made for you,*" Carlos added.

"I'm very sorry. I told them to wait until we were safe to give it to you as thanks for protecting us. It's something my family used to make and sell in Acapulco."

The foreigner grabbed the handcrafted gift from the child and stared at it. He was struck with a feeling he had not felt in some time, gratitude.

"Thanks," was the only word that could escape his lips before his mind drew back to the approaching danger.

"You all stay back, and remember my signal. Have the radio by you at all times, Joaquín. I've set it and Bravura to a private frequency. Have everyone's communication devices tuned in as well. We can't allow the enemy to drop in on us in case they have radios of their own. No doubt they already heard us recruiting Steel Samurai."

Without waiting for a reply from any of the family, the Hunter entered his cockpit and readied himself for battle. Joaquín and his family watched as their mechanical guardian marched towards the front lines.

A few moments later and the pilot was standing in front of the remaining men who all aimed to protect their beloved settlement. Each villager carried one of many weapons Joaquín and his men collected over the years ranging from shotguns, to handguns, to sniper rifles, to hunting bows and arrows. They would be greatly effective against a rowdy gang of thieves, but would have little to no effect against a militia like the Hounds of Hades. The Hunter readied his fold out shield and one of his bo staffs. He was hesitant to use his mech's Eagle Eye mode as his body was still sore from its extended use last time. He needed to hold out for as long as possible without it.

At long last, the Hounds had arrived. Leading the charge were armored trucks and tanks, each armed with mounted missile launchers. Exiting from these vehicles were numerous men wearing padded bulletproof gear and wielding bazookas, grenades, high power rifles, and shotguns. At the back of the caravan was a flatbed truck with a giant cage attached to it. Inside the cage were the captured Pitbull pups. The hungry and orphaned infants let out a mixture of barks, whines, and howls as they called for their slain mothers.

Leaping over the men were five wolves, as reported by Joaquín's men. Each one carried varying degrees of mangy scab-ridden skin. All five let out blood curdling growls, indicating that they were itching at the chance to tear the pilot's machine apart limb by limb.

Stepping between the vehicles and men was the alleged giant carrying a massive leathery sack, a surreal sight by the Hunter's standards despite witnessing untold horrors throughout the apocalyptic wasteland. Even knowing the reports of past human mutations, seeing one in person was a chilling sight. This being carried the visage of a man with its ragged clothes and hat. Yet every other feature was the stuff of nightmares from his hunched over posture to his dry greenish brown skin to his sunken eyes and emaciated build. The former soldier began to wonder how much of this being was still human on a cognitive level.

He would get his answer immediately when the figure raised his sack before him and dropped it. The clattering noise it made indicated that there were multiple smaller objects inside. Tools perhaps, thought the Hunter. Immediately afterwards the wolves backed down and laid on the ground. This appeared to have caught the Hound soldiers by surprise too as they all began asking each other what was going on. At that moment, a lone human approached the humanoid giant. Thankfully, Bravura's audio sensors could pick up what they were saying as they conversed in Spanish.

"*What are you doing, Silbón?*" the man demanded.

"*I wish to fight this thing alone. Long have I heard of these machines that fell to the mutants and True Kaiju. I'm curious which of us is the superior fighter.*"

"*Are you insane?*" Lopez argued. "*That thing will blow you apart.*"

"*Are you saying I am weak, Lopez?*" the mutant responded as he raised a crooked brow.

"*Of course not! But look around, the True Kaiju Ivanov mentioned is nowhere in sight, meaning that mech must've brought it down!*"

"*Then he must be a great soldier. Grant me this one selfish request, especially after all I've done for you. If I win, that's one less obstacle in your way. If I lose, I'll have weakened him enough for your men and the wolves to finish the job.*"

In reality his reason for facing off against the mech was more than a simple test of strength. Indeed, for many years, he had listened to stories of mankind creating awe-inspiring mechanical avatars. Inventions that were said to have been capable of taking down the True Kaiju and saving humanity. Of course, history had proven that these metal goliaths succumbed to the beasts' wrath. The failure of these robots led to El Silbón's village resorting to experimenting on human test subjects. It was these very trials that turned him into his current deformed self.

Had the machines not failed, perhaps he would have a normal life. If the mechs were defeated by the True Kaiju of the past, then he would take it upon himself to do the same onto this man-made relic of the past. The age of mankind was over, for in his eyes this world truly belonged to Earth's atomic children.

"*Our ally, El Silbón, wishes to face you in one-on-one combat!*" Lopez announced to Bravura's pilot.

El Silbón raised a pointed finger at the machine's staff.

"*No weapons!*" the giant added in his gravely hoarse voice.

All around him, the pilot could pick up chatter from the villagers.

"*Did he say, 'El Silbón?'*"

"*As in the demon that collects bones?*"

"*Of course, it's him, that bag must be where he carries his victims!*"

"*Dear God. I never thought he'd be real!*"

The Hunter quickly weighed his options. Would he adhere to the mutant's demands and entire a gladiatorial match? Such a match up would allow for many to come out of this battle alive. On the other hand, he was unsure of the creature's limits, nor was he confident in Bravura's own hand-to-hand capabilities. Yet, despite the fact that his mech was originally designed for ranged combat, he managed to adapt to the ever-changing landscape and fully accustom himself to fighting with handheld weaponry. Now came the time to adapt once more and rely on Bravura's steel hands and his fighting prowess.

He finally did as he was told. He had his staff retract to its portable form and attached it to Bravura's forearm compartment. With another press of a button, the shield on his mech's left forearm folded back up. The Hunter manipulated his humanoid weapon to step forward and approached El Silbón, just as the mutant approached him.

"This will be your end!" the former human bellowed as he rushed towards his opponent.

Bravura's arms raised, covering its chest and face before being tackled to the ground with an earth-shaking thud. It was clear that despite his lanky appearance, El Silbón carried a ferocious amount of strength. The mutated humanoid proceeded to tirelessly pummel his foe with strike after strike from his fists. Each impact dented and chipped away at the robot's armor. The Hunter knew he had to act soon or else he would fail not only himself, but everyone in Fortuna that placed their faith in him.

With precise timing, the pilot launched his machine's hands to capture El Silbón's. With both titans struggling to overpower each other, the Hunter activated Bravura's jetpack, its thrusters aimed at the ground below. The propulsion lifted the pair up into the air. As it was still holding onto El Silbón's hands, Bravura thrust its leg into El Silbón's chest, kicking the mutant down to the ground. While the mech was hovering above the ground, the Hunter wondered if he could take their fight to the sky, where he would have a real advantage. Yet, as he pondered, he realized that moving away from the village would place everyone in danger as that would give the Hounds the perfect opportunity to strike once he was out of sight.

Back on the ground, El Silbón groaned and clenched his ribs. He stared up at Bravura as it landed back on the ground. He could tell this machine, despite not wielding its weapons, still had many tricks up its metal sleeves. Yet, it appeared it was holding back. Was the pilot taking pity on him or everyone around them? Whatever foolish reason it was, El Silbón sought to prove what a grave mistake that was.

"Very well!" he shouted as he got back on his feet. *"We shall use weapons. I want to see you at your full strength!"*

He quickly scrambled to his bag and rummaged through it until he pulled out two boney weapons, possibly the shoulder blades of a massive creature he had previously slain. Each tool was as long as El Silbón's arms and sharpened into the shape of two serrated blades.

"Fine by me," the pilot told himself as he once more extracted his trusty bo staff.

Once more, the slender giant went on the offensive and slashed at Bravura as it defended itself. The Hunter was surprised at the durability of El Silbón's weapons. Whatever creature those blades came from, it must have been a powerful creature as its bones refused to break when struck against the metal rod.

Finally, the soldier activated his staff's electrical capabilities and aimed one end at one of El Silbón's blades. He knocked it away and stabbed his weapon into his opponent's chest. Yet, despite being surged with electricity, the mutant was still standing, his weapons still gripped tightly in his hands. Was it that his leathery skin and bone blades offered some protection against his attack?

A smile crept along the giant's face before he went back on the offensive.

While the two giants resumed their fight to the death, one of Lopez's panicked men addressed him.

"Why is Silbón going against his own rules? Has he gone crazy?"

"It's possible," Lopez said, *"that this fight is more personal to him than he lets on. Whatever the case, have everyone prepared to attack once I give the signal."*

With the Hounds preparing a preemptive assault, the Hunter found himself running low on steam as he kept up with El Silbón's constant flurry of attacks. His enemy meanwhile showed no signs of tiring out. It was possible that if he did not change tactics soon, he would be done for. Being a trained fighter, the Hunter did the only thing he could do, he studied his enemy's movements and began to notice a pattern. It was always two swipes from above followed by two from the sides. He had to dodge and parry at the right moment in order to utilize his shield that he was unable to focus on.

With quick thinking, he dodged the first vertical attack while retracting his pole. Then, as El Silbón readied his second strike, Bravura extended the pole into his enemy's blade, knocking it out of his hand. As predicted, El Silbón responded with a horizontal swipe, which the Hunter was ready for. He blocked the attack with the pole in Bravura's right hand as he activated the shield in its left arm.

The mutant backed away as he did not know what the pilot was thinking nor what he was planning to do with both of his machine's weapons. As he stood back, Bravura raised its left hand and curled up its index finger. Regardless of language barriers, it was a universal sign that the pilot inside the machine was daring El Silbón to attack. This enraged the giant to the point where he did not care what became of the village or the Hounds of Hades. He would make sure that this foolish human would pay with his life for mocking him.

By now, the Hunter had seen enough of the mutant's fighting to guess what would happen next. At the moment El Silbón raised his bone sword, now clutched with both hands, Bravura thrust its razor-sharp shield into the blade. With his weapon wedged firmly into the bone, Bravura pulled his opponent closer. The pilot forced his machine to drop its staff in order to punch El Silbón directly in the face enough times until he dropped his weapon. Dazed and unarmed, Bravura wrapped its arms around his body and forced the mutant to the ground. With his enemy pinned beneath him, the soldier proceeded to bash his mechanical fists into the humanoid's skull until he was left a bloody mess.

As much as he wanted to finish him off, something prevented the Hunter from performing the deed. Despite El Silbón's appearance, he still saw the mutant as human, a survivor like himself. He decided that he would offer his opponent this chance to walk away from it all. He had Bravura stand up, walk past his bested foe, towards the Hounds of Hades, all of whom were stunned at the defeat of their most reliable mutant. He found the man who previously addressed the giant, figuring he was the Hounds' leader, and addressed him.

"Be lucky I didn't kill your guy. I'm giving you and your men a chance to get the hell outta here or I swear to God you're all gonna get it worse than him."

Lopez stared down the mech unfazed. The men closest to Lopez looked to him for guidance.

"*Not until I give the signal,*" he reiterated.

Without giving it away, he knew his trusted ally was regaining consciousness and didn't want his eyesight to betray him.

Bloodied and enraged, El Silbón grew ever furious. How dare this man make a mockery out of him. Mutants have proven themselves superior to humans in every way. If he could not take down this machine, what did that make him? Noticing Bravura's staff, he grabbed a hold of the weapon, got back up and launched another assault at the robot, all while uttering a horrific guttural scream.

Bravura turned and stabbed its bladed shield directly into the giant's chest. El Silbón, his eyes widened and gasping for breath, dropped the staff and used the last of his strength to push his body away from the mech. The shield slid back and out poured a fountain of the mutant's irradiated blood. The moment he collapsed on the ground he could hear Lopez uttering one word.

"*Fire!*"

The Hounds all opened fire onto the machine that had killed their comrade with everything they had at their disposal, meanwhile, the wolves cautiously stood back from the loud explosives. The Hunter tried his best to maneuver his machine so as to draw the militia's aim away from the rest of the village as the brave men of Fortuna began their counterattack on the Hounds. Distracted by the arrival of his allies, the Hunter was blindsided by several rockets aimed at Bravura, knocking him off his feet.

Before he could decide how to fend off against the Hounds and protect the men with what little strength he had left, a blaring sound echoed across the entire area like a thousand jets tearing through the horizon. The Hunter looked up and gazed in awe at the appearance of a towering humanoid figure far larger than Bravura descending from the sky, decorated in silver, gold, and red armor. Was this the fabled mech known as Steel Samurai? Unfortunately, he no longer had the strength to stay conscious, let alone figure out who this mysterious new arrival was.

At that instance, Lopez commanded all his men to fall back, leaving El Silbón behind. The mutant meanwhile laid on the ground face up and losing gallons of blood by the second. His fading consciousness was no longer paying attention to his surroundings, rather he began looking over everything that led him to this exact point. Just then, his mutant senses detected the presence of another atomic being, an ability shared by all irradiated creations on Earth.

This was not the supposed winged-lion that the human, Alexander Ivanov, talked about. This was a familiar aura belonging to one creature El Silbón had spent all his life avoiding through this ability he had. It was none other than the one and only Atomic Rex, the reigning king of the True Kaiju. Suddenly, it all made sense. Ivanov had not only brought about the African monster and the Hounds of Hades to enact his revenge against the mech pilot, but the dreaded dinosaur as well to wipe out all survivors in one fell swoop.

As he lay dying, El Silbón began laughing as he decided to keep this information to himself. His suspicions of humanity had been confirmed after all, the sheer irony that no matter how dire things got, humanity would always find new means of betraying one another. With one last haunting cackle, he wished death upon every single human left on the planet as he left them to face their eventual doom.

CHAPTER 18

Fortuna Village

The Hunter was enveloped in an unfamiliar sensation of comfort as his confused mind attempted to piece together what occurred within the last several hours. He remembered clashing with a mutant that fought with blades carved from bones. He then recalled defeating him shortly before he was caught in a chaotic whirlwind of gunfire, rockets, and explosives. The last things he remembered were the giant mech and the coughing sounds from his slain foe. Realizing that Fortuna might very likely still be in danger, the Hunter ripped his eyes open.

He looked all around him and found that he was in a bed, back in the shack he previously rested in earlier in the day. He then noticed that beside him were three people. One of them was Joaquín, but the other two were unfamiliar to him. It was a man and woman. The man appeared to be roughly the same age as him, either in his late 40s or early 50s. The woman was significantly younger, possibly in her 20s. All three looked relieved that he was still alive. If they were with Joaquín, then they most likely were not a threat.

The Hunter heard a faint barking sound outside and he immediately thought that the mutant Pitbulls had returned. He tried to jump out of bed when Joaquín held out his hands to stop him.

"It's okay, the barking you hear is only the captured pups. We're perfectly safe." He helped the Hunter back into a sitting position. "Are you okay, Señor?"

"I'm fine," responded the Hunter as he rubbed his eyes. "What happened after I blacked out?"

"It was incredible! After you killed that mutant man, Steel Samurai arrived and drove the Hounds of Hades away. This is Captain Chris Myers and his daughter Emily, the pilots of the robot."

"It's a pleasure to meet you, sir," said Chris. "Thanks for reaching out to us. We tried to get here as fast as we could."

Emily meanwhile stood quiet, unsure how to address someone like the man before her. She figured it was best to let her father take over diplomatic duties.

"Sure," the Hunter said hesitantly before shifting his attention back towards Joaquín.

"How long was I out?"

"About two hours, Señor. Don't worry about Bravura, Chris and Emily placed it right where you usually leave it."

"When you have the time, I'd really like to ask you about your machine," said Chris. "I've never seen anything like it. Joaquín told me how you single handedly took down a True Kaiju with that thing."

"Figures," replied the injured pilot as he partially ignored his comments. "The Colossi were never meant to be public knowledge. Not even to other branches of the US military."

"You used that word before in your message, Colossus. I'm intrigued to know what they were. Are there any like yours still around?"

"Yeah, I've encountered a few survivors here and there from the war, though we got one extremely dangerous one whose pilot has his eyes on this village."

"Say no more," said Chris. While he was alarmed and confused by the "war" the pilot was alluding to, he knew there were more important matters to attend to.

"My daughter and I will do everything in our power to help you and everyone else here," affirmed the experienced Kaiju slayer. "However, that's not all you have to worry about."

"Explain," the Hunter firmly asked.

"Reports from my settlement state that Atomic Rex is approaching the area. He should arrive at Acapulco in a few hours."

Sweat began pouring from the Hunter's forehead. Was this the Red Menace's doing as well?

"You don't have to think about it now," Emily finally spoke up as she attempted to assure the nervous and exhausted man. "Please take as much rest as you can and you can meet us later to develop a battle plan."

All three individuals soon left the Hunter to be alone with his thoughts. Was he seriously going to go up against not one, but two ghosts from the past? Even with the aid of Steel Samurai 2.0, would he be capable of fending them off? For the next half hour, the soldier lay in bed, unable to fall back asleep with so much on his mind between the Hounds, the Red Menace, and Atomic Rex. He knew running away was not an option. On top of leaving everyone in a more vulnerable state, he was sure the Red Menace would most likely continue to chase him down for as long as both of them were still alive.

Realizing that sleep was pointless, the Hunter got dressed in his old uniform and walked outside. He was greeted with the sight of Chris Myers sitting by a bonfire, as if he was waiting for him. In the distance he saw Joaquín introducing Chris's daughter to his family. He turned to find Bravura laid where the Myers said they placed it, beside it was the gargantuan frame of Steel Samurai 2.0.

"Hope you don't mind," Chris said, "but when we escorted you out of your mech I took a look inside in case it needed any repairs. I was surprised to find a lot of the mechanisms being very similar to what my comrades and I used for our machines."

"I wouldn't be surprised," the Hunter chuckled, "if it turns out the Colossi served as the bases for your mechs. In a way, Bravura could be Steel Samurai's older brother unit."

"Okay, you got to explain to me what the Colossi were and that war you mentioned."

"They really did keep all of you in the dark about that, huh?" questioned the Hunter.

"Believe me, as far as I know, no mechs were ever developed prior to the invasion of the True Kaiju and mutants."

The Hunter sat opposite from Chris at the bonfire as he prepared to explain his story for the first time in ages. Chris offered a quesadilla made by Lupe, to which the fellow pilot accepted.

"I'm sure you at least know of the island where all those dinosaurs showed up, right?"

"Of course, the US was testing an atomic bomb and that's what mutated all the wildlife into monsters."

"That's where you're wrong. See, that explanation you were given? It was all a cover up. What really happened was that every major nation not only knew of that island's existence prior, they all wanted a piece of it. They called it "Eden." There was no telling what scientific discoveries could be made from the soil, the plants, or even the animals themselves, be it for medicinal or military purposes. That's when war broke out for control of Eden, and from that war, the US was the first to invent a man-piloted giant humanoid robot that came to be a Colossus. Eventually, word got out about our Colossus and pretty soon every country was developing their own Colossus. Well, as we continued to lay waste to everything on that island, our fight escalated into nuclear warfare. I think you can guess what happened from there."

Chris was shocked as he took all this information in. As far as he knew, the creation of the True Kaiju was the result of reckless nuclear testing brought on by his nation's arrogance. Now he was being told that it was no accident, but an act of warfare. How many lives had been lost as a result of this private war, a pointless confrontation that ultimately doomed all of civilization? Though, the more he thought about the truth, the more he realized that nothing had changed.

"I guess at the end of the day, the world still ended as a result of a handful of idiots at the top. Only now, I know there was a higher body count prior."

"Exactly."

Emily smiled at Joaquín's wife and children as she did her best to address them in their native language. *"Hello it is meet for me to nice you. My name is Emily."* Joaquín's wife smiled at Emily and addressed her in English. "It is nice for us to meet you as well, Señorita. If you prefer, we can speak in English."

The American smiled. "I would appreciate that. I have learned a little Spanish from some of the bilingual people in the settlement, but I would be lying if I said I thought I could carry out an entire conversation."

Joaquín nodded. "It's okay, you've already shown that you can speak more Spanish than most of the Americans we met before the Kaiju appeared."

Emily nodded. "You've all been here since before the time of the Kaiju?"

"Not all of us. My father founded this village along with the surviving residents of Acapulco. Some of the villagers found their way here as they wandered through our destroyed country." Joaquín smiled at his children. "Of course, the younger ones were born here."

Emily gestured toward the resting form of Bravura. "You say that the mech only came here recently?"

"Sí, Bravura arrived shortly before you."

"The only two groups of survivors we've met before have had some form of protection. Our settlement has Steel Samurai 2.0 and the people in Peru had a mutant protector they had created. What protected you from the kaiju and the mutants?"

Joaquín shrugged. "I wouldn't say we have been protected so much as a small part of the greater food chain." He gestured toward the cage of giant pups. "The pack those pups come from has long roamed this territory. Sometimes the dogs will attack our town and devour some of us. We have learned to always be vigilant. We look for the dogs and when we see them coming, we hide as best we can."

The town leader sighed. "While the pack has killed many of us, they are the lesser of two evils. The dogs keep away most other mutants. The only thing that seems to be able to kill them is Atomic Rex. He stops near here occasionally to feed on the dogs. We've heard him challenge the dogs and then we hear a ferocious battle. Over the years, we have stumbled across the remains of dead Pitbulls. As far as we can tell, the alpha dog will answer Atomic Rex's challenge. After the monster kills the alpha, he eats it and then leaves without pushing farther inland towards us."

"The pack kills some of us and we live in fear of them, but their presence keeps away much more dangerous threats."

Emily nodded. "They're kind of like Ramrod, just without the mutually beneficial relationship established."

Joaquín shook his head. "I'm sorry. What is Ramrod?"

"He's a giant mutant ram that's become a guard for our settlement."

"A mutant protects your home? How did this happen?"

"He was a danger at first. Not to the extent the dogs are to you, but a danger. Like the dogs did with your community he sort of settled near ours. When I noticed he was staying there I started leaving food in the area. Each time I left food I would move a little closer to him. After a while I could almost walk right up to him. Not too long ago, when some mutant rats tried to attack me, Ramrod jumped to my defense and saved me. I think he sees me and the rest of the settlement as part of his family. We feed him and in return he protects his food source by protecting us."

As Emily finished her story, Joaquín looked over at the yapping mutant Pitbull pups in the cage. His eyes went wide as he realized the implications of Emily's relationship with Ramrod.

He pointed at the caged animals. "We could never forge a friendship with the adults, but the perritos! If we could care for them, train them, perhaps they could protect us as this Ramrod protects you!"

As his mind continued to process the implications of what he was saying his enthusiasm dwindled. "No, training the perritos is a dream. We have to scavenge to find enough food to feed ourselves. We couldn't possibly find enough food to feed the perritos as they grew." He looked solemnly at the cage. "The best thing we can do is kill the animals now before they grow into adults and hunt us. Besides, none of this matters. Without the large dogs to feed Atomic Rex, the next time he comes he will not find the prey he desires. He will make his way inland and crush this town beneath his feet. Our only hope is to flee and find a new way to survive."

Emily put her hands on Joaquín's shoulders. "It's not the only way." She looked over at her father. "I've learned a lot from my father lately and I think he's learned a few things from me. Let's go over and talk to him. I think between the three of us we can work out the details for a plan that will have long term benefits to our settlement, your town community, and the survivors in Peru."

Joaquín looked over at his family. As he stared at his sons, he said, "Long term benefits. Benefits that would help to ensure my children live long enough to become adults?"

"I can't make any specific promises, but I think it will greatly improve their chances, if you're willing to make friends out of former enemies and share some of what you have?"

"Señorita, there is nothing I wouldn't do to help my children survive. Come, let's speak with your father."

Back at the bonfire, Chris continued to consider the information given to him by the mysterious pilot. If what he said was true and that there may be other mechs in the world, this also meant that this technology could help them rebuild civilization or eradicate what's left of it if it were to fall into the wrong hands. The fact that one such pilot had been aiding these marauders while another had been protecting this village was proof of that.

"So, what have you been doing all these years?" asked Chris. "I could've used someone like you while I was out there fighting off the True Kaiju and mutants."

"What have I been doing?" the offended pilot reacted. "Surviving, that's what I've been doing! After I lost my team, I had no one to rely on but myself. Heck, I was lucky enough to have escaped that island with Bravura in one piece!"

Chris could detect the anguish and regret the pilot carried in his words, the same feelings he felt years ago when he lost his best friends on Coney Island. If this man was suffering as much as he had, then he was in no position to judge him for not partaking in the reconstruction.

"Your teammates, they meant a lot to you, didn't they?"

The Hunter stood silent, thinking back at the good times he shared with his squadmates, all the times they laughed, cried, and everything in between.

"Yeah," was all he could muster.

"You know, I lost my teammates as well, to Atomic Rex in fact."

The Hunter's eyes widened. "You serious?" As much as he wanted to share that his teammates also fell prey to the True Kaiju, he was still hesitant to share that much personal information with the fellow mech pilot.

"Yup, I felt like a failure, like I left them there to die. I don't blame you if you wanted to get as far away from all that. In fact, shortly after the True Kaiju took over, I felt like giving up as well."

"What kept you going?" the curious Hunter asked.

"It was my hope for a better tomorrow. Though trust me, I was barely hanging by a thread at that point. Eventually, I met Kate and started a family. At that point, my family became my motivation."

"Heh, lucky you. I never had much of one myself," the soldier responded. Though, contrary to his statement, he realized that his squad was the closest he had to one, with Captain Garcia as their matriarch. "You know, my captain told me something just before she died. 'Never stop fighting,' which was part of a mantra she used to tell each of us. 'Never stop fighting... to protect the ones you love.'"

"Sounds like she was a true soldier."

"You bet she was. Wish I could say the same for myself."

As he reflected on her words, possibly for the first time since she last uttered them, did he realize how much he'd failed to live up to them. For decades he spent so long fighting just to stay alive that he had forgotten what his purpose was as a soldier. He could remember when she first shared this mantra. It was the same day he and the rest of his team were given the same alpha-omega hybrid tattoos on their right shoulders. It was to symbolize that they were to represent the first and last line of defense against any threats to their country.

"Well, if it's anything," Chris replied, "it's not too late to find that thing to protect."

The Hunter looked back at Joaquín's family with Emily and saw how happy they all were as they enjoyed their all too brief calm before the storm. Was hope possible in an age of monsters and mad men? The Myers and the people of Fortuna seemed to believe so.

"You might be onto something."

Emily and Joaquín walked over to Chris and the Hunter. The young woman then explained her plan to her father and asked for his input as well as Joaquín's in regards to certain matters. The future leader of the settlement explained her idea about Joaquín's people establishing a relationship with the dogs similar to the one she had with Ramrod. She then told Joaquín about how Chris had shown her how he hunted down less dangerous mutants to bait more dire threats into situations where he could slay them.

She then suggested using this same process to provide food for the pups as well as to leave some dead mutants to placate Atomic Rex when he came ashore. Chris, the Hunter, and Joaquín all thought the plan sounded good for the people in Mexico, but it was Joaquín who questioned how this would help Emily and her people.

The town leader suggested that if his people could train this first set of dogs, and then breed them, they could create a steady supply of trained mutant protectors. These animals could be dispersed between the people in America, Mexico, and Peru. In return for receiving the trained giant Pitbulls, the American settlement would provide the aforementioned mutants for Atomic Rex and the pups.

Emily then explained that the acquisition of a new guardian to the people in South America would provide them a chance to expand their fishing operation.

From there her plan called for a north-south trade route with Steel Samurai carrying crops and mutant meat from near the settlement, Joaquín's people providing the valuable asset of guardian mutants, and the Peruvians providing not only food in the form of fish but fertilizer for the crops in California.

Joaquín and the Hunter were both impressed by Emily and Joaquín's ideas. The father and pilot of Steel Samurai 2.0 shook his head and then began to smile.

Emily looked at her father. "Dad, are you okay?"

Chris smiled as he walked over and hugged Emily. "I'm… just so proud of you. A parent always hopes that their children will learn from both their success and their failures and you've done both. Your mother and I more or less forgot about the people in Peru. We thought that becoming too involved with them would stretch us too thin. Now, in only one outing with Steel Samurai 2.0 and learning some of the things I use him for, you've worked with Joaquín to put together a plan that benefits every person who we know to still be alive on the planet."

As he let go of his daughter, he looked her in the eye and said, "Just so you know, when we get home, I'm telling your mother this was all my idea."

They both laughed as Joaquín stood up and walked over to them. "Señor, you have raised a wonderful daughter." He looked at Emily. "Señorita, I will be happy to work with my people on carrying out my part of the plan. What about the people in Peru? Do you think they will go along with it?"

Chris shrugged. "We'll have to find out, but I think we're offering them a pretty good deal."

CHAPTER 19

The Ruins of Acapulco

The sun rose on the eve of a new battle as the Hounds of Hades were licking their wounds within the heart of the devastated remains of Acapulco, having been caught off guard by the sudden appearance of Steel Samurai 2.0. As soon as the metal titan arrived on the scene, it managed to annihilate a third of their forces and forced them to leave behind both El Silbón and the Pitbull pups. Their wolves, however, were still alive and well, having only been grazed by a few stray bullets from the mech's machine guns. Though without their mutant master, controlling them had been more difficult than before.

At the center of it was Lopez, who not only lost his most trusted enforcer, but was also the receiver of a lot of the ire from his men. He had to think fast, otherwise he would quickly lose the trust of his men and potentially his life. While his men continued to rest from the failed assault on the village, their leader attempted to contact their mysterious ally.

"Lopez to Ivanov, come in, Ivanov."

After a few seconds of static, he received a response.

"This is Ivanov. What's the status of the invasion? Has Bravura been terminated?"

"That's a negative; we were stopped by Steel Samurai. Fortuna must've been able to get in contact with the US settlement. We also spotted no visuals of Manticore. We presume he was killed in action prior to our arrival."

"I see. Any casualties on your end?"

"We lost sixteen of our men plus El Silbón."

"What's the status of your inventory?"

"We have all five of our wolves, five armored trucks, ten missile launchers, seven bazookas, sixty grenades, twenty high power rifles, and a dozen shotguns."

"Good," the mech-piloting consultant said confidently. "Then we shall continue the invasion."

"I take it you'll be joining us this time?" Lopez asked cautiously as he doubted his forces were enough to take on both mechs.

"Of course, I shall be there momentarily."

"Where are you currently?"

"I'm just along the coast. I've got a trump card that'll take care of all our problems. It's a little thing I've been working on for quite some time."

"Should we wait for you?"

"No, go on the offensive. I've seen Steel Samurai in action, you must take advantage of its size and fight around it. Keep it and Bravura busy with the wolves and go for their ground forces. I'll ambush the larger targets once I'm there."

Looking over his ally's plan, Lopez saw no issue with enacting it if all went well. However, there came the matter of Ivanov's skills, Red Menace's strength, and his secret weapon. There were too many unknown factors to rely on. Could he trust him? He had been right before up to this point, but never factored in Steel Samurai. Even still, he did not skip a beat nor stammer at the reveal of the mech's involvement, almost like he expected it to show up. Was he really that confident that he'd show up?

Lopez had to make a decision quickly, and unfortunately for him he no longer had El Silbón there to give his input. He then thought about what would happen if he turned back now. His men would surely be enraged at leaving everything behind and doubt his abilities as a leader. No, this entire venture could not be all for naught.

"Alright, we'll head there now. Contact me once you've arrived."

Lopez then ordered all his men to regroup and prepare a second assault, having told them of Ivanov's plan. As tired as his men were, they were itching at the chance to avenge their fallen brethren, to which Lopez used to his advantage as he rallied his men. By the time they entered the outskirts of the beachside city, they all heard a very familiar sound of rocket propulsion.

"*¡Maldita sea!*"

Lopez cursed himself under his breath, having never considered that his enemy would take offensive measures themselves.

*****

"Do you have the targets in sight, Captain Myers?" questioned the reputable mutant killer within the armored chassis of Bravura.

"Targets confirmed," replied Chris Myers as he and his daughter flew alongside the Hunter within their respective mechs. "By the way, you can call me 'Chris.'"

"Got it, I'll head down there."

"Roger, over and out."

As Bravura descended, weapons in hand, Steel Samurai 2.0 began unloading round after round at the unsuspecting militia with its chain guns while avoiding its partner.

Within the Japanese-themed mech, Emily's conscience grew concerned, having not fought any humans at all throughout her life. The young woman knew she and her father had to protect the people of Fortuna from these men from the very beginning. The previous night, the Bravura's pilot, who went by no name, suggested taking the fight to the Hounds of Hades. The idea was that they would inspect the surrounding area, starting with the wasteland that used to be Acapulco. If they caught sight of the Hounds, then they would strike first. According to the former soldier, if the enemy was still around, it meant they had not given up on the village. Having caught them heading towards Fortuna, it was all the more reason to strike. Still, something in the pit of her stomach did not sit well with her about what they were doing. Killing mutants was one thing, but attacking her fellow man, no matter how vile they may be, was something else entirely.

Emily took a deep breath and looked over her father. "Dad, we're about to kill people. Not mutants or kaiju, but human beings. I... I'm not sure I can do this. How do you prepare yourself for something like this?"

Chris spoke in as steady a voice as possible. "In the previous world, before you were born and before the time of the kaiju, we didn't engage in wars with monsters, we fought each other. I was in the United States Air Force where they trained me to kill other people. They taught me to focus on the mission first and not the ramifications of what it took to make the mission successful. I repeated combat drills over and over again until they were almost reflexive in nature. If I was in a battle, I could deliver a killing shot or blow without even thinking about it. My mind and my body just reacted by accessing the training it had done so many times."

"And did all that training and all that practice prepare you to kill people?"

Chris sighed. "No, it didn't. The truth is nothing can prepare you for taking another human's life. Killing someone changes you forever. Once you take another human's life it's something you can never give back. From that moment on, you'll go through the rest of your life knowing that you ended someone else's existence. Over the course of my career as a fighter pilot, I shot down five other planes and bombed numerous sites. I never really saw anyone I killed but I remember each and every target I hit, because I know there were people in them."

He quickly looked over at his daughter. "One reason your mother and I wanted to stay away from the people in Peru is that we know when people are desperate, they can be as dangerous as any kaiju." He gestured to the gathered Hounds of Hades. "Desperate people become ruthless and right now those people are desperate. In a world where things like food, water, and security are scarce, people will do anything to get it. A long time ago I started to wrap my mind around the idea that I might have to kill other humans again someday. Showing you how we deal with the giant leeches by catching the mutant cats and killing them was a dark aspect of what your mother and I have to do to keep the people of the settlement safe. I knew that would be hard for you, but I thought you were ready for it. What we're about to do, though, attacking humans is a whole other thing."

Emily looked down at the controls in front of her and her hands were shaking as she tried to reach for them. "I know we have to fight off the Hounds to protect the people of Fortuna, it's just I'm not sure I can do it." Her eyes began to fill with tears. "Dad, I ... don't think I'm ready."

"Honey, I'd like to tell you that you'll never have to take another human's life to save your own life or those of the people you love, but in the world we live in, there's a good chance you will have to one day. You can take that step with me now or you can sit back and help me by keeping an eye on the radar. I can't operate the robot's weapons as well on my own as I can with a copilot, but I understand if you can't do this."

Emily was speechless as she looked at the controls in front of her and once more at her shaking hands. She shook her head. "Dad, I...can't do it...I'm sorry. I just can't do it."

Chris reached over and grabbed his daughter's hand. "It's okay, Emily. You've met every challenge that was presented to you, not just today but in life. Your ability to rise to the moment is why the people of the settlement love you so much. You're a remarkable young woman, but you're also human. There will be some challenges you can't overcome at the time you meet them. That doesn't mean you won't be able to overcome them later, but sometimes you'll come up against something you can't at that time."

She wiped a tear from her eye. "Okay, I'll work the radar. What else can I do?"

"Keep an eye on our ammunition supply. We don't have much left and we need to save some in case we run up against Atomic Rex or another True Kaiju. We want to end this quickly, so I am going to hit them with a volley of our long-range weapons to hopefully thin them out and disperse them. Then I'll use our close-range weapons to finish the job."

Emily nodded. "Dad, I'm sorry I'm not ready for this. I feel like I'm letting you and everyone else down."

The loving father shook his head. "You're not letting me down. You're learning how to be a leader and part of being a leader is knowing your limits. When that happens it's better to look to others for help rather than letting the challenge overcome you or others because you were too insecure to admit your shortcomings. I'm proud of you, honey. I wish to God I could hug you right now but we're about to engage the enemy and I need to focus on that. You keep me posted on the radar if anything unexpected is coming our way and keep me aware of ammunition supplies."

The tearful Emily nodded and then followed her father's orders.

As bullets rained from above, the Hounds of Hades all scrambled to hide in and around the run down and battered buildings that still remained standing after all these years. As the massive shells obliterated the rooftops, rubble crumbled down to the broken pavement below. Several slabs of concrete toppled over and crushed one of the armored trucks as another was blown up by a direct hit from Steel Samurai 2.0.

Once the Hounds found themselves situated in their hiding spots, their leader ordered them to open fire at the massive flying robot. Between the barrage of missiles flying up and down, Bravura swerved between the multitude of projectiles before sliding down on the cracked asphalt that formerly made up the roads of a four-way intersection.

Inside, the Hunter had Bravura shield itself from the oncoming fire from a nearby armored truck. Shortly after, his mech's audio sensors picked up the sound of loud growls and barks. His radar detected several massive objects closing in on him.

"Right on time," he jested to himself as he had Bravura remove a second staff from its right forearm compartment. Now dual wielding both of his bo staffs, the pilot commanded his mech to begin spinning its weapons in an intimidating display as each artificial wrist rotated each metal bar. Normally, an Atlus unit would only carry a second retractable staff in the event it were to lose its first primary weapon. To utilize both tools simultaneously was a talent only ever mastered by one other pilot. That person was Captain Garcia, who taught Bravura's pilot shortly after his promotion to becoming the second-in-command of their squad.

The furious circulation of electrified steel kept the wolves at bay, all save for one. The one-eyed, three-legged canine Tucker was unfazed by his prey's tactic as it was too impatient and frenzied to feel any sense of fear. Just as he was the first to attack, so too was he the first to fall as he was struck in the chest by one of Bravura's staffs.

Distracted, the mech was ambushed from behind by the brutish Thor. The Hunter anticipated this attack and swung his second staff into the beast's maw, the electricity searing from his sensitive mouth throughout his body. Up next was the nimble Baldwyn as it ran literal circles around Bravura. The Hunter kept the gaunt lupin at bay with his staffs until he heard a bark from above. He had been preoccupied with the wolves on the ground, and he did not notice that two of them, Elise and Ada, had climbed a nearby building and got the literal drop on the mech. Ada latched onto Bravura's cloak while the pack leader bit down on the great automaton's helmet that would normally serve to convert into its Eagle Eye mask.

As the wolves pressed down on the machine, Baldwyn finally struck as it found an opening and attacked Bravura's chest, knocking the entire machine over on the ground. The pilot tried activating his metal goliath's rocket boosters, but the combined weight of the three canines kept the metal warrior grounded.

That's when he realized Bravura still had his leg rockets. He set them to full blast, which propelled the machine to slide across the streets, dragging the three dogs with him. Baldwyn and Elise let go, but the blind Ada was too entangled in the mech's cloak to make such an escape. Finally, Bravura crashed into a nearby hotel, simultaneously crushing the mange-covered wolf and causing all twenty stories to collapse on the pair. For a robotic soldier capable of storming through a battlefield, a tumbling building was nothing, but for the already injured Ada, the hotel remains would serve as her grave as she was buried alive in a shower of steel, masonry, and concrete.

"Sorry, pooch," said the pilot as he remorsefully addressed the muffled howls and whimpers from the slowly dying mutant.

Surrounded by dust and debris, the Hunter had no choice but to rely on his radar and found the four remaining wolves approaching him. He sighed in exhaustion as he readied his staffs, though he doubted the intimidation display could work a second time. That was when the gigantic Steel Samurai 2.0 landed with enough force to blow away the enormous cloud of dust. The metal goliath opened fire on the wolves, causing them all to scurry in different directions.

"Got you covered!" shouted the elder Myers.

"How many of the Hounds are left?"

"We managed to get most of them. Once they began retreating, I thought you could use some help."

"Thanks. How about you take out two of these damn mutts and get back to finishing off the Hounds."

"You sure about that?" asked a concerned Chris.

"Believe me, these things are too quick for you. Plus, one of us has to keep Fortuna safe."

"Gotcha." Understanding what Bravura's pilot was trying to do, he readied Steel Samurai 2.0's thrusters until he picked up one more message from his fellow mech pilot.

Meanwhile, a smile formed on the Hunter's face. For only a brief moment, he felt like he was back in his prime fighting alongside his old squadmates.

"I recommend going after One-Eye over there especially," the veteran said to his new teammates.

Ahead of them was Tucker, more enraged than ever before. The mammalian creature refused to back down, even from an opponent as large as Steel Samurai 2.0.

"With pleasure," Chris said as he was readying his mech's blade. As he charged at Tucker, Thor leaped off a building and bit down on the machine's right arm. Tucker then attacked the metal giant's left leg.

"Chris!" Just as the Hunter was about to assist his compatriot, he was blocked off by both Baldwyn and Elise. He figured they must have been aggravated about the stunt he pulled before.

"You two don't give up, do ya? Well, you're asking for it."

As Steel Samurai 2.0 wrestled with the two larger wolves, Bravura gripped each staff as its pilot set each pole's electrical setting to its max. Both weapons now crackled with constant sparks with enough energy to blind the wolves. Utilizing this opportunity, the Hunter threw one of his rods at Baldwyn, the quickest of the two animals. As he guessed, the dog leapt out of the way, giving Bravura the perfect chance to ready its shield and go for the kill. The mechanical soldier held its remaining shining staff to further blind the wolf as it swung its shield into the monster's spine. The canine tried to escape, but it was too late as the shield's edges sliced through his fragile body, severing his spinal cord in two. Bravura then finished the mutant off by stomping on its head, ending its misery.

Chris yelled, "Emily, I'm going to need your help. These things are too damned fast for me to fight off alone!"

Emily could hear the sound of metal tearing and she felt the mech she was sitting in being pulled to the ground. Not just her hands but her entire body was shaking. Chris immediately recognized that his daughter was lost in the heat of the battle and unsure of what to do.

Acting with the speed of thought, Chris swung the arm with Tucker on it down toward Thor who had already caused significant damage to Steel Samurai 2.0's leg. When Tucker crashed into his brethren it sent both predators tumbling away from the man-made titan.

The moment the dogs stopped tumbling they regained their feet and snarled at the mechanized warrior. Chris knew the beasts were about to pounce. He looked over at his daughter and did his best to channel the voice of his old drill sergeant. "Emily, arm the sword! Now!"

The surprise of hearing her father's normally supportive voice in such a harsh tone snapped Emily out of the semi state of shock she was in. She grabbed the controls and immediately had the robot arm itself. She had no sooner deployed the sword then Tucker crashed into the mech's chest and drove his exposed and sharpened bone into the metallic warrior's shoulder. Tucker's impact knocked the Steel Samurai 2.0 off balance and caused it to stumble backwards.

Chris was trying his best to steady the robot, when the massive Thor sank his teeth and claws into the robot's right hip. The combined weight of both mutants caused Steel Samurai 2.0 to fall onto its back. With their opponent down, the two wolves once again began tearing into the giant warrior's frame.

Chris yelled at his daughter. "Use the left hand to get the wolf off our chest! I'll work the legs and try to free us from that big bastard!"

Emily immediately followed her father's orders and delivered a blow to Tucker's face. When the first strike did not force the monster off of the downed machine, she rapidly delivered blow after blow. With her fifth punch she knocked out several of Tucker's teeth and sent the canine rolling off the mech's chest.

As Emily was repeatedly striking Tucker, Chris hit the husky Thor with multiple strikes from the mechanical titan's right knee to no effect. Chris cursed as the cockpit continued to shake from the damage being inflicted on it. "You're one strong mutt, aren't you?" Realizing that he would not be able to break free from Thor with brute strength alone the veteran pilot switched tactics. He opened the storage compartment on Steel Samurai 2.0's legs that he used to fill with water when moving on the ocean floor.

The moment the compartment opened, Thor's right front paw slid into it and caused the mutant to lose his balance. When Chris saw the wolf lean to its side, he quickly closed the storage compartment. The bulky Thor howled in pain as the closing door slammed into his leg and cut it to the bone. Chris then opened the door and let the monster pull its leg out and limp away.

With Steel Samurai 2.0 free from both wolves, Chris got the robot back up to its feet.

Emily moved the sword in front of the titan as she yelled, "Dad, what do we do..." Before she could finish her sentence, the speedy wolves had pounced at them once again. Emily had managed to back hand Tucker as he was mid-leap and sent the mutant crashing to the ground. Thor however took advantage of his brother's distraction and jumped up at the mechanized titan. The powerful Thor put his paws on the robot's shoulders as his teeth closed around the area where Steel Samurai 2.0's neck would have been were it an actual human. Emily tried to angle the sword to stab the huge wolf, but the creature was too close for her to effectively utilize the weapon. She was able to use the mech's free hand to grab the beast by its throat, but she quickly realized the mechanical warrior lacked the strength needed to throw back the heavily muscled Thor.

She screamed over the sound of metal being torn to shreds. "I can't push him off!!"

"I know, he's too strong. We're going to have to use his strength and weight against him! I'm going to shift our right leg back as you grab him and use his own momentum to help throw him to the ground! As soon as you toss him, hold the sword out directly in front of us! Go now!"

Chris then had Steel Samurai 2.0 slide his right leg back and toward its left leg as Emily used the mech's arms to grab the beast and throw it to the ground. When Emily finished her move, she positioned the sword in front of the mech as her father suggested. As Emily was moving the sword, Chris had the mech fall down flat on its back. The quick fall shook the entire robot and jarred its occupants. Emily suddenly found herself looking through the metal giant's eyes at a blue sky that was immediately blocked out by the form of Thor leaping at her. Emily closed her eyes for the impact when she suddenly felt the mech shaking and heard a terrible yelping sound.

She opened her eyes to see Thor impaled on the sword she had positioned in front of Steel Samurai 2.0's body. The massive canine was in agony as its body weight forced it farther onto the mech's sword. Blood streamed out of the creature's chest and back as well as its flailing mouth. The young woman was transfixed by the geysers of blood pouring out of the dying canine until Chris yelled at her, "Emily, roll to the side and release the sword!"

Emily grabbed the controls and forced the mech to roll to its side. As the mech was rolling over she saw the ferocious Tucker leaping toward her with his bone shiv pointed directly at the mech's eyes. Steel Samurai

2.0 completed its roll and positioned itself between the dying Thor and the attacking Tucker a moment before the latter reached its target. Rather than driving its shiv-like exposed bone into the mech's face, Tucker's make-shift weapon punctured the back of Thor's skull and plunged into his brain.

As Tucker tried to pull his damaged leg from his brother's head, Chris activated Steel Samurai 2.0's thrusters. The mech skidded along the ground and then took to the sky. He steadied the man-made titan in the air and said to his daughter, "Activate the crossbow."

Emily used the mech's left hand to pull the weapon off its back. She then loaded a bolt into the crossbow and aimed it at Tucker who had pulled his bone leg out of Thor's head. The beast quickly licked some of his brother's gray matter off his exposed bone and then he looked at the hovering colossus.

Chris looked at his daughter. "Three legged dogs aren't as agile as four legged dogs. Think you can hit him?"

Emily's response was to fire a bolt that struck Tucker in the chest. The animal's body briefly went rigid as blood seeped out of his mouth. The wolf swayed side to side for a moment before he regained his footing. The canine refused to submit to his critical injury for it survived too to be swatted away like a fly. Long had Tucker fought to become the alpha of his pack, only to be defeated time and time again by both Elise and El Silbón. With the humanoid mutant dead and Elise possibly on death's door, he knew this was finally his chance. He mustered his strength and sprinted towards a nearby buildings as it did last time to leap at the towering titan. Further shots fired from the mech, only for them to miss as the wolf climbed up the structure. Finally, Tucker leapt towards the mech, his jaws wide open. With her target launching towards her and having no means of escape, Emily landed the killing shot right in the monster's forehead. In an all-too brief and sudden moment of recklessness, the wolf's corpse tumbled down until it smashed into the pavement. Tucker died how he lived. He attempted to reach the top time and time again, only to fail miserably as a result of his vicious and short-sighted nature.

Back in Steel Samurai's cockpit, Emily looked over at Chris. "Yeah I think I can hit him." There was a brief moment of silence as Chris nodded at his daughter before the radar sprang to life. The young woman looked at her dad. "There's something heading this way. Something big."

Chris's heart skipped a beat as somehow, he knew what the threat was. For the first time Emily saw her father shaking as she was only moments before. "Dad, what is it?"

He shook his head. "We need to kill that other wolf and then get the people of Fortuna out of here, fast."

At last, all that was left was Elise, the matriarch of the pack. With both her clan and her master dead, the logical choice would be to abandon this fight and run away as far as she could. However, the emotions her mammalian mind felt would not allow her to do such a thing. She witnessed the metal figure in front of her murder those she deeply respected and looked after. She would at least avenge her family by taking down the smaller of the two targets.

As she approached Bravura, Steel Samurai 2.0 readied its crossbow once more before the smaller metal humanoid raised its arm.

"I got this one," was all the Hunter needed to say as he held his remaining staff in both arms.

This time, Bravura came in swinging, with Elise leaping out of the way. With each attack missed, sparks of electricity burned her fur and skin. However, Elise did not care as she bore the pain and continued circling around her prey. Finally, one more swing and she found her opportunity. She leapt onto the machine and was ready to bite down on the glowing blue visor that adorned Bravura's face.

Mere seconds before her teeth came into contact with the machine, a mask slid down and replaced the visor with two burning red eyes. Her teeth clamped down on this new face, though she was unable to pierce through this armor. Still, she attempted to claw at the mech's body; the only thing stopping her was the shield it raised in front of itself.

While she struggled, the pilot inside the machine had his weapon retract and extend directly into the wolf's chest. Hundreds of volts surged into her body until her chest exploded, taking her life with it. Still, her undying resolve refused to allow her jaws to let go of Bravura's armored head. The blood-covered mech had to pry her jaws off, causing her teeth to shatter in the process. As the pilot dropped the corpse, he stared at the burnt remains of his enemy and acknowledged her fierce and enduring loyalty to her pack.

The Hunter turned his machine around to stare up at Steel Samurai 2.0. He seemed almost glad that it was all over. Unfortunately, this moment of glory would be cut short as a haunting ear-shattering roar boomed across the city, shattering every remaining glass window around the two metal warriors. Both pilots were regrettably all too familiar with the source of this primal declaration of war.

CHAPTER 20

Lopez was at a loss for words when he and his team caught sight of the horrific Atomic Rex bursting from the ocean and bellowing a challenge into the sky. His forces had dwindled down to only one last armored truck and a dozen men after Steel Samurai 2.0 had eliminated his forces like they were sitting ducks. Now, just as he and his men were about to make their escape near the shore, they were confronted with a threat no one on either side of the conflict was prepared for.

The ruler of the kaiju lifted himself out of the water and onto the sandy beach. As he peered at the landscape he was led to, he found his senses still dulled due to the lingering effects of both the mutant wasps and jellyfish's venom. While he no longer felt any pain, his entire body moved much slower, his nostrils could not pick up much beyond what was directly in front of him, and his vision was slightly blurry. Yet, despite his weakened state, he searched for the flying contraption that brought him to this area. Scurrying along the ground was a small metal box, whatever it was, the theropod knew it was definitely human in nature.

"*He sees us! Drive faster, you idiot!*" screamed Lopez as he witnessed Atomic Rex lumbering towards their direction.

"*This is as fast as it goes, sir!*" his subordinate replied back.

"*Damn it! Well, radio the others and tell them to get the rockets ready.*"

"*But sir,*" the driver protested, "*we're down to our last batch. We used the rest on the US mech.*"

"*I don't care!*" Lopez then grabbed the driver's radio out of his hand and made the order himself.

"*Attention all men, get the rockets and whatever you have left aimed at the monster!*"

Just as soon as he gave the order, two of the marauders appeared out of two canopy doors, each of them armed with rocket launchers. As they fired on the approaching Atomic Rex, Lopez used his personal radio to contact the elusive Alexander Ivanov.

"Ivanov, where the hell are you? You sent Atomic Rex here, didn't you?"

"Sorry I'm late," replied the jovial voice of who Lopez previously thought was his ally.

"Bringing the big guy here was more troublesome than I thought he'd be. He can be so easily distracted, much like he is right now."

As the two spoke, several rockets landed on the snout of the behemoth. They were no more effective than a mosquito's bite was at bringing down a human being. Additionally, Atomic Rex was so dazed that he was incapable of even feeling whatever miniscule pain the rockets inflicted. His attention was directly on the truck. He let out a low grumbling sound as he grew ever closer.

"Get it off our tail, you bastard!"

"Oh, now why would I do that? He's awfully tired from all that swimming. He could use a snack before the main course."

"You son of a bitch," Lopez was angry at Ivanov's betrayal more than he was afraid for his own life. "Were you always planning this?"

"Not exactly like this, though I was going to have all of you taken care of eventually."

Just then, the ominous form of the Red Menace landed before the armored truck. It lifted its foot and stepped on the hood of the vehicle, causing it to come to an abrupt and violent stop. The rocket launcher-wielding men were flung from the roof of the truck and died on impact as soon as their craniums came in contact with the ground.

Lopez quickly regained consciousness, only to find his face full of glass and the driver next to him dead from the impact. He called his men within the truck, but heard no replies. He shambled his way out of the truck and found himself standing between the deadly frame of the Red Menace and the towering figure of Atomic Rex. As he stared at the mech, Lopez could see a massive object held in its arms. Behind him, he could hear the dinosaur's guttural vocalizations grow ever louder from the sudden appearance of his pesky metal escort. Before Lopez could form any coherent thoughts, the pilot spoke from his mech's external speakers.

"Don't get to upset. It's nothing personal, you were only ever a means to an end."

Red Menace then raised its right arm and aimed its twin machine guns at the mountainous beast. In response, the mutant reptile opened its gargantuan maw and prepared to chomp down at the ground where they all stood.

"Farewell, Sebastián Lopez!"

The machine took off into the sky, narrowly avoiding the serrated incisors. The leader of the now decimated Hounds of Hell yelled in sheer terror as his life was extinguished in an instant.

Off in the distance, Bravura and Steel Samurai 2.0 flew as quickly as they could toward the coastline where they witnessed Atomic Rex tearing out a chunk of the street with its jaws before spitting out the asphalt, and scrap metal it contained. As soon as his eyes noticed the two hovering machines, the beast let out another blaring roar at the pair.

"Is it me, or is that thing a helluva lot bigger than before?" asked the smaller mech's pilot as he rubbed the sweat from his forehead.

"I take it you two had history?"

"He's the one that took my squad, and my eye."

"I'm sorry to hear that. Well, to answer your question, no, he's certainly grown since you last saw him. But don't worry. Together we can lead him away from here. Just follow my lead!"

As soon as Steel Samurai 2.0 began swerving to the Atomic Rex's left side, the metal warrior was hit with a concentrated blast of light blue energy that fired from the ground below them. With its chest scorched and its balance thrown off, the Myers's machine was sent tumbling into a nearby building, demolishing it to the ground.

"Are you guys alright?" Bravura's pilot asked frantically before another beam of energy shot from the ground.

He barely avoided the beam as it burned the edge of his mech's cloak. Suddenly a massive red and black blur rammed itself into Bravura. The object pushed the Hunter far away from both Steel Samurai 2.0 and Atomic Rex before crashing into several buildings.

The radar was blaring as Chris shook his head and looked out the great automaton's eye to see rubble obscuring his view. He could see a few cracks of sunlight sneaking through the tons of concrete his mech was buried under. Chris first looked over at Emily. "Are you okay?"

"I think so, but that was him, wasn't it? That was Atomic Rex. right?"

Chris confirmed the monster's identity, then he tried to contact the Hunter to determine his status. "Bravura, come in, Bravura. This is Steel Samurai 2.0, are you there?"

When the pilot did not receive a reply, he grabbed a hold of his controls to start digging himself out of the rubble when he felt an impact tremor shake the ground. The tremor was followed by the all too familiar roar of the monster that had been Chris's nemesis for his entire adult life.

He looked back at Emily and the thought of his daughter dying at the claws of Atomic Rex sent a surge of adrenaline coursing through his body. He quickly activated the metallic warrior's thrusters and sent Steel Samurai 2.0 bursting out of the rubble it was buried under. The instant that the mechanical goliath escaped rubble, Atomic Rex's foot came crashing down and crushed the debris that Steel Samurai had been buried under into dust.

Steel Samurai was flying low to the ground and scraping its already damaged hull against the ground when Chris pulled up hard and sent the machine flying into the sky. When the mech was far enough away from the True Kaiju, he commanded the mech to hover in the air facing the monster.

Chris took a deep breath and then looked at his daughter. Emily's mouth was hanging open and her body was rigid. She had never seen Atomic Rex in person before and the sight of the True Kaiju was both awe inspiring and terrifying to her at the same time. Chris called out to his daughter but she was so transfixed by the nuclear therapod that she did not hear her father's voice.

The already angered Atomic Rex was enraged when he saw the form of Steel Samurai 2.0 hovering in the air before him. For over two decades, the metal warrior had vexed the saurian horror by attacking him and then fleeing. The True Kaiju was determined to finally put an end to the annoying mech's existence. The radioactive dinosaur threw his arms out to his side and unleashed a challenge that echoed across the sky at his long time enemy.

Atomic Rex's roar shook Steel Samurai's frame and caused Emily to snap out of the trance she had fallen into. She quickly aimed the mechanical giant's crossbow at the raging kaiju. "I can hit him. I can hit him right in the chest from here."

Chris held out his hand to stay his daughter's action. "I've hit him with the crossbow before. His healing abilities will quickly counteract any serious damage from the bolt. If you hit him, all it would do is piss him off."

The nuclear therapod roared again and moved closer to his hated rival. Chris had the mech fly back as Atomic Rex advanced to ensure he was out of range of the monster's Atomic Wave. After taking a few steps, Atomic Rex stopped and waited for the metal being to accept his challenge.

As Chris looked down at his lifelong enemy he was faced with an impossible choice. He could stay, fight Atomic Rex, and possibly buy the people of Fortuna enough time to escape the monster's wrath. If he chose that option there was a decent chance he would die in the struggle. His own death did not bother him, but the thought of Emily dying was more than he could bear.

His other option was to fly away from Atomic Rex at top speed. Doing so would guarantee Emily's safety but leave Bravura and Fortuna to fend for themselves against the radioactive reptile.

Chris looked over at Emily. "Strap in. We're going to fly away from here at top speed."

"What? Dad, we can't do that! We're the only chance the people of Fortuna have of living to see another day!"

"I hope they do make it. I really do, but I've barely survived multiple encounters with Atomic Rex, and can tell with the damage already done to our hull, all it will take is one blast from his Atomic Wave and the interior of the ship will be filled with so much radiation that he won't even need to lay a hand on us to kill, because we'll have been exposed to a lethal dose of radiation."

As if in response to Chris's fears, Atomic Rex roared again and took several more steps toward the floating giant. Chris went to flee when Emily fired a bolt from the crossbow that embedded itself on Atomic Rex's left shoulder and caused him to unleash a pain-filled roar.

While Atomic Rex was trying to pull the bolt out from his shoulder, Emily looked over at her father. "Dad, I love you and appreciate your concern. Yes, you will save me if we run, but it will likely mean the deaths of everyone on Fortuna. What you said before about killing someone, about how it changes you forever, about how it weighs you down; if we leave now we will be condemning the people of Fortuna to death. We will be responsible for all of them. If what you said before is true, if killing someone else really does taint your life, would you rather live out the rest of my life knowing I did nothing to save all those people, or would you prefer that if I die, I do so trying to save as many lives as possible?"

Chris first looked at his daughter and then at Atomic Rex. He was surprised to see the monster was struggling to remove the bolt from his shoulder. He shook his head. "I've seen that bastard rip out bolts I shot into his hide almost instantly. Why is he struggling to do so now?"

As Chris finished his sentence, Atomic Rex pulled the projectile out of his shoulder and tossed it to the ground. Once again, he roared at the mech and started moving forward. Chris slowly backed up Steel Samurai some more as he armed the machine gun and fired a volley at the True Kaiju. The bullets bounced off the saurian beast but they stopped his forward progress. When Chris saw the monster stop moving, he grabbed a hold of Steel Samurai 2.0's controls and flew straight up, increasing the mech's altitude by over a thousand feet. Once he reached his desired height he looked down at the monster and waited for the creature to respond.

Chris watched as Atomic Rex lifted his foot into the air and then brought it crashing back down. The hardened kaiju fighter shook his head in disbelief as he said, "No Atomic Wave."

"What do you mean 'no Atomic Wave?'"

"When he stomps his foot like that, it's usually to unleash his Atomic Wave. There should be a dome of pure radiation expanding out of him, but look, there's nothing. It also took him a really long time to get that bolt out of his shoulder. There's something wrong with him. He's hurt or sick or something."

"Dad, if he doesn't have his Atomic Wave, is there a chance we can defeat him?"

"Maybe not defeat him but survive and hold him off long enough for the villagers to escape maybe."

"Alright then! Let's save those people."

Chris took a deep breath. "Okay, but if he gets the upper hand, we're outta here." Chris flew Steel Samurai 2.0 directly toward the monster as he shouted, "Put away the crossbow and grab the sword!"

The mech flew past Atomic Rex and as it did so Emily swiped at the mutated dinosaur with her sword. The glancing blow left a gash along the right side of Atomic Rex's body. The monster ignored the pain and spun around to attack the robot only to have the mech deliver a punch to its face that staggered him. The creature was still reeling from the punch when Steel Samurai 2.0 kicked him in the chest and sent him stumbling backwards. The monster's tail kept him from falling on his back, but he was off balance when the metallic warrior lifted his sword over its head and slashed the saurian horror across his chest. The blow caused Atomic Rex to list down and to his left.

When Emily saw Atomic Rex's neck exposed in front of her, she thought she had a killing blow. Steel Samurai 2.0 lifted its sword above its head with Atomic Rex's blood still flying off its blade. As Emily prepared to strike, the more seasoned Chris shifted the robot's legs so that he was falling to his right.

The reason for Chris's maneuver became clear as Atomic Rex used the direction his body was going in to swing his tail around and strike Steel Samurai in the side. Had the mech not been falling to its side the True Kaiju's tail would have cut the metal giant in half. Chris and Emily were rocked inside the cockpit as the mech tumbled across the terrain.

Chris managed to get Steel Samurai 2.0 back on its feet as Atomic Rex was charging toward it. When the elder Myers saw Atomic Rex's right claw raised above his head, he immediately threw a kick that struck the nuclear therapod in its sternum. While the kick did not halt Atomic Rex's progress it threw off the monster's claw so that it tore a chunk out of the mech's right hip rather than destroying the majority of its torso.

Before Atomic Rex could strike again, Emily delivered an uppercut to the saurian's mouth that snapped his jaw shut. Chris then had the mech ascend to a height out of the monster's reach.

As they were hovering above the radioactive dinosaur, Atomic Rex once again roared out a challenge at them.

Emily looked over at her dad. "You knew that tail strike was coming and you kept it from finishing us."

"Yeah, we've fought each other enough that we know each other's moves. He's weakened but he's still too strong for us to beat him. I don't think we've given enough time to the villagers to escape. We can't last much longer on our own. We need Bravura."

*****

As soon as the nameless pilot got his machine up from the rubble, he found a hulking silhouette matching that of the one and only Red Menace. Its once radiant crimson paint had dulled into a rust red. Despite the worn-out armor, the machine was armed with even further upgrades since he last saw the Colossus. Aside from the three harpoon launchers attached to each shoulder, each forearm was equipped with twin machine guns. Its feet now had claw-like attachments that tore into the ground as it walked. Attached to its hips was the same armored skirt that contained a new blade, this time a serrated hunting knife. In place of a standard jetpack that most Colossi carried from the war, two giant rockets sat in place. These engine thrusters were like miniaturized versions of the rocket boosters used on shuttles to make orbit.

The most alarming addition to the Red Menace's arsenal was a massive cannon, equal to the mech's height, held in the machine's hands in lieu of a rifle. This barrel-shaped weapon was restrained via two attachments that extended from the cannon and docked into the robot's torso. The whole device pulsated the same light blue energy it previously fired. The glow was familiar somehow, like he'd seen it at some point in time. Just then, the Red Menace's pilot exited his cockpit at the base of the mech's neck. From the speakers came a laughter he recognized immediately, one of devilish glee and delight.

"Miss me?" the stranger boastfully asked. "I mean, I'd hate for you to forget a familiar face."

There was no doubt about it, this man was indeed the very same soldier he had fought 30 years prior. His enemy then proceeded to take off his helmet.

"Then again," he stated, "this is the first time you've seen me in the flesh."

Beyond the helmet revealed a ghastly sight. His entire face was horribly burned and scarred. Random tufts of hair sprouted from his incinerated scalp. His nose was almost nonexistent to the point where his visage resembled more of a skull with lips and eyelids than a human face. His face was so disfigured it was almost impossible to tell what he would have looked like prior. The Hunter could only imagine what happened to this crazed killer. Did these scars come from before, during, or even after the apocalypse?

"Who the hell are you?" the Hunter demanded. "What do you even want?"

"What I want," the scorched man answered, "is to settle a score thirty years in the making!"

"You're kidding," the bewildered pilot retorted. "The war's over, what's even the point?"

"I never cared for the war. This is a matter of pride!" The Red Menace controller's voice raised to the point where he did not even need the speakers.

"I live only to kill and conquer. Before everything ended, I moved from country to country, whoever offered me the chance to thrive on the battlefield! I took pleasure in the fact that no one could ever survive an encounter with me. That was until that fateful day when you and that damn lizard destroyed my perfect streak! Since then, I've been watching you both, carefully biding my time until the moment was right. I even took a page from that foolish American and his ridiculous machine, having his enemies take care of each other and take out whoever is left."

"Look," the Hunter interrupted, "if you want to settle things one on one, that's fine. Just leave the Myers and Fortuna out of this. No one else has to die."

"Ah, but where's the fun in that?" cackled the scarred pilot. "I haven't had this much fun in decades! By the end of this conflict, I will take my spot as the greatest killer of them all. Not Atomic Rex, not Steel Samurai, and certainly not you!"

The mysterious pilot then entered his cockpit and activated his thrusters.

"Now, fight me! Prove your worthiness of the title 'Bravura'!"

The Hunter decided that he would not take any chances. He pulled the twin levers needed to activate Eagle Eye mode and within seconds, the mask came down over Bravura's face, as did the special helmet over the pilot's cranium. He activated his staff and shield just as the Red Menace lifted its massive cannon. It stomped the ground, ensuring its clawed feet would grip the broken road. All six harpoons shot down and pierced the asphalt, securely anchoring the mech in place. Finally, it charged its cannon as it held the weapon with both hands and fired a beam wider than the previous two instances.

Bravura dodged the beam, but the force of the blast knocked the metal giant back into a nearby neighborhood. The Hunter got back up and witnessed the stream of energy blast through several blocks, causing numerous buildings to fall in its wake. If this maniac keeps this up, he will surely level the entire city, thought Bravura's pilot.

"You like that? Over the last several days I've been siphoning Atomic Rex's energy and stored all of it in a weapon of my own design. I call it the Atomic Cannon! With this device, I'll finally be powerful enough to even take out Atomic Rex single handedly!"

Was this lunatic bragging in the middle of a fight? questioned the Hunter. He figured that his foe must have gone insane with the lack of any war to partake in. Then again, he was not one to talk when he had been spending all this time running away from imaginary ghosts.

The Red Menace then retracted his harpoons and repositioned itself so that it faced its humanoid target. The machine fired its harpoons to the ground once more and began charging another blast from its Atomic Cannon. The Hunter activated his Colossus's jetpack and flew in the air. His enemy, however, remained unfazed as he lifted his cannon and fired into the sky. Once more, the masked mech dodged as the beam raised higher and higher in the air. The pilot inside knew he couldn't stay airborne for long as his jetpack was not capable of flying for very long.

Just then, the Red Menace flew into the air, its cannon still attached to its torso. The mech held out its right arm and fired its machine guns. Bravura spun and swerved to avoid the maelstrom of bullets heading its way. For the cloaked Colossus's pilot, focusing on that many objects was beyond the Eagle Eye's capacity. He had his machine raise its shield and spin its staff as he attempted to hide within the various abandoned buildings in the city. The Hunter maneuvered Bravura into the shadow of a massive cathedral. As the Hunter hid, he could hear the Red Menace landing and slowly stomping its way around the block.

"You never changed, did you?" the crazed enemy continued to gloat. "All these years, and you still wish to run away like the coward that you are!"

What was Bravura's controller to do? He could not outrun a machine like the Red Menace. Nor could he attack the machine directly, unless he wished to risk blowing up a nuclear-powered contraption like the Atomic Cannon. That's when he realized that the Red Menace required those two docked attachments and the harpoons to keep the weapon stable, and needed both hands in order to operate it. If he could aim for those targets, then he might have a chance to take him down.

The enemy's steps grew louder as it approached the church before coming to a stop. That's when the Hunter heard the Atomic Cannon powering up a third time, yet he did not hear the harpoons launch. Bravura took to the air just as a smaller stream of atomic energy penetrated the holy structure. It was clear that the Red Menace did not need its harpoons when firing a smaller stream of energy.

This was it, the moment of truth. Bravura aimed its elongated bo staff and set its voltage to its maximum setting. With the form and skill of an Olympic javelin thrower, the steel rod was hurled towards the Red Menace. Thanks to the Eagle Eye's incredible accuracy, the projectile shattered the left harness. With his enemy caught off guard, Bravura took out its second electric lance and thrust it into the enemy's right shoulder. Its harpoons blew off as electricity surged down through the arm, leaving it twitching and unable to follow its pilot's commands.

"Ha! Well, what do you know? It's déjà vu all over again!"

The mastermind cackled giddily as he manipulated his machine to drop the Atomic Cannon, no longer able to use it, and fired another round of bullets from its still functioning left arm. Bravura took cover behind another building as it activated its last bo staff. Just then, the Hunter heard Chris Myers's voice over the radio as the Red Menace continued firing at the building, tearing each layer of brick and mortar to shreds.

"This is Chris Myers contacting Bravura, are you there?"

"It's me. You two alright?"

"Barely, we have Atomic Rex on our tail. We've kept him at bay, but we can't hold him back any longer. Where are you at?"

"I'll send you my coordinates, I'm about several miles south of where we last met. That Colossus I told you about fired a cannon at us earlier. It's not a problem for now, but the mech still is."

"What do you propose we do?"

The Hunter thought for a moment; how could they possibly take care of both uncontrollable forces? It was at that point, he remembered what the Red Menace's pilot said about getting his enemies to fight each other.

"Lure Atomic Rex to my location and I'll keep this Colossus busy."

"What about you?"

"Don't worry about me. Just do it!"

Bravura's pilot then forced his machine to reveal itself from its crumbling safe zone. The steel goliath raised its shield against the seemingly endless bullets and charged towards the Red Menace.

"At last, a real fight!" the mad man proclaimed as he had his mech take out its serrated knife.

The two automatons engaged in a battle for supremacy as Bravura swung its staff at its opponent, only to be countered with the Red Menace's blade each time and was able to nullify the rod's electricity thanks to its insulated handle. Even after all these years, the scarlet mech's pilot's reflexes were as sharp as ever.

Fortunately, the Hunter was able to pick up his enemy's limited movements as a result of only using one arm. Finally, the US soldier found an opening and thrust his lance at the left forearm just as it was about to plunge its weapon at Bravura's cockpit. Once the knife dropped from the Red Menace's twitching hand, Bravura maneuvered around the wide Colossus and sliced the right side of its opponent's rocket pack with its shield. The resulting explosion knocked Bravura off its feet.

The Hunter checked for any signs of critical damage done to his machine. He stopped struggling to get his mech to stand up until he heard the clanking sounds of the Red Menace coming his way.

"It'll take more than that little stun baton of yours to take me down!" the enraged pilot shouted. "I've lived too long to be defeated by you and your insipid toy!"

The Red Menace then fired its three working harpoons from its left shoulder at the smaller machine. Two of them pierced through the cloak Bravura wore, and another one went through its lower torso, any higher and it would have killed its pilot instantly. Inside, the Hunter tried to get his mech free of the iron cable, only for him to feel the weight of the Red Menace's foot latched upon his machine. Outside, he could hear his exhausted enemy speak once more.

"You know, I may not be able to eliminate that mindless beast today. But that's alright, I'll take pleasure killing just you."

All of a sudden, the Red Menace was attacked from above as Steel Samurai came to its ally's aid. Before the man who had called himself

Alexander Ivanov could react, the largest of the three mechs descended, freed the ensnared Bravura with its katana, and carried its partner off into the sky. Meanwhile, the scarred pilot turned his machine around and found a furious Atomic Rex.

The pilot began to feel a twinge of fear lurking at the bottom of his heart. He had always gone into battle expecting each battle to be his last, and he reveled every minute of such excitement. Yet, he did not feel any excitement at that moment, for he did not have any control over the situation. His weapons were either destroyed or out of reach. As for his means of escape, it had been rendered obsolete when his rival destroyed half of his rocket pack. With no means of getting out of this situation alive, the faceless man snapped. With whatever propulsion was left in its remaining rocket, the Red Menace launched itself towards the True Kaiju as its pilot laughed hysterically all the way. What he was thinking of in those last seconds, no one could imagine. As he blasted his way ever so closer toward his enemy, Atomic Rex countered by opening its jaws and ensnaring the contraption that had caused him so much pain and torment, crushing the mech in its jaws.

In the air, Bravura and Steel Samurai watched from above at the death of the Red Menace and its enigmatic pilot.

"Who was he?" asked Chris.

"It doesn't matter," the Hunter said as a feeling of relief swept through him. "What matters is that he's dead."

Suddenly he remembered that his mission to protect Fortuna was not finished. The Hunter got Bravura back into working order and had it escape Steel Samurai's grip and descend towards the Atomic Cannon. "Hey, where are you going?" a confused Chris Myers asked.

"We still have work to do. There's no telling what Atomic Rex will do. As far as we know it'll end up staying here and put everyone's lives at risk."

As soon as both mechs landed, Bravura picked up the incredibly heavy Atomic Cannon with both hands.

"Then there's the matter of this thing."

"Is that the weapon that fired at us?"

"Exactly, that maniac said this thing runs on Atomic Rex's energy. If you check the damage on your mech, you'll find signs of radiation."

"What exactly do you plan to do with it?" Emily asked, afraid of what the Hunter was about to say.

"I'm gonna kill two birds with one stone. That way, Atomic Rex will be driven away and this weapon will never fall into the wrong hands again."

"But how though?" Chris protested.

"Forget how! You guys have to evacuate everyone out of Fortuna. Your mech is the only one that can do it."

Chris paused for a second, until he overheard Atomic Rex beginning its trek across Acapulco towards the mountains. From what Joaquín told him, the True Kaiju periodically came to this land, only to be stopped by the Pitbulls. Now, nothing was stopping him from making this entire land his territory.

"Engage the thrusters," he told his daughter. "We're heading back."

"But we can't leave him!" Emily shouted.

"There's no other way," said the Hunter. "Though I gotta say, it's been nice knowing you two."

"Same to you, stranger," Chris said as his eyes began welling up, knowing he'd be losing a kindred spirit, another relic like him who would understand the struggles he had faced. He kept himself from saying it out loud but he suspected that part of the reason the Hunter was telling him to leave was because Emily was with him. Chris suspected that the Hunter was giving him a chance to save his daughter's life and that was something he would be eternally grateful to the enigmatic figure for. The former Air Force pilot quickly tapped out a thank you in morse code over the radio. In the same modality, he then asked the Hunter his name.

"It's Cota. Lieutenant Enrique Cota."

Bravura then launched itself, Atomic Cannon in hand, with Steel Samurai 2.0 lifting off in the opposite direction. By the time Steel Samurai 2.0 was no longer visible, the Hunter had flown past the mutated behemoth all the way to the beach, desperately holding onto the overbearing weight of the Atomic Cannon. At last, Bravura arrived at the beach and placed the weapon down before it managed to tear off its arms. Now free to use its upper limbs, the steel giant held out its lone bo staff and charged its electricity to its maximum setting once more. The metal warrior took to the sky once again and navigated around the lumbering mass that was Atomic Rex.

Without a moment to lose, Bravura struck the monster's nostrils. As the True Kaiju shook his snout back and forth, the Colossus went straight for the reptile's right eye, damaging the creature's most sensitive areas much like it did with the winged Manticore. With his attention drawn to this new unfamiliar machine, Atomic Rex began to give chase.

Once Bravura landed on the beach, its pilot noticed Atomic Rex marching towards him, though at a much slower pace than before. The creature had been coerced into fighting various enemies, had poison and venom injected into his veins, and had confronted several mechs all within a short span of time, its endurance was wearing thin. Still, the reptilian leviathan was not about to let this latest annoyance get away. He was determined to cease any mechanical machines from ever bothering him again. Just then, it detected the presence of nuclear energy. Atomic Rex saw through his undamaged eye that a mass of atomic energy was gathering where the mech was. With the perpetual energy he had absorbed from the phoenix temporarily stifled by the venom in his system, the saurian horror saw the radiation as the perfect chance to revitalize himself. The monster summoned whatever strength he had left to bellow out his war cry and reach the shores of Acapulco.

In that time, Bravura held the Atomic Cannon in its arms, as the energy winded up, its pilot made sure to hold onto the trigger, believing that the longer he held it, the larger its blast would be. The force of the growing energy kicked mounds of sand into the air and rocked the pilot in his seat. The servos and mechanics that allowed Bravura to function were pushed to their limits under the pressure of wielding such a weapon. The force eventually blew away the mech's brunt cloak and its only staff. The cannon was now charging up more energy than the pilot had previously witnessed and saw that it too had difficulty sustaining that much atomic power. Both the weapon and its wielder were on the verge of falling apart when the Hunter saw the theropod finally open its jaws for one final attack.

"Come on, you bastard! Give me your best shot!" shouted the pilot. No longer was he afraid of the behemoth that had taken everything away from him and had left him all alone in the world. No, he thought. He wasn't alone, not anymore. There were people, good people, and as his fellow pilot said, hope.

As soon as Atomic Rex reached down for the mech, Bravura aimed at the beast's literal blind spot and fired at the left portion of his skull. The blast destroyed the monster's eye and burned the skin off half of his face. In that instant, the Atomic Rex fought through the searing pain and dove his head into the cannon. The overloaded weapon exploded in a display of nuclear fire that scorched the True Kaiju's skin and covered the entire city in a blinding light.

Miles away, Steel Samurai had finished escorting the last of the residents of Fortuna. Through the shielded eyes of their mech, Chris and Emily witnessed the demise of Acapulco as the city erupted in flames. Deep down, they prayed to any god who would listen to them that it did not take the soldier that history forgot.

Emily looked over at her father. "That blast, is that what the Atomic Wave looks like?"

Chris sighed. "Yeah, it is. If Bravura was in the blast radius, there's no way Cota would have survived it."

Even though Chris was fairly certain that Cota had perished, he tapped a "Thank you, you saved my daughter's life," over the radio in Morse code. Then he flew in the direction of the fleeing people of Fortuna.

CHAPTER 21

Chris and Emily quickly found the people of Fortuna where they had relocated them, beyond the mountains of their village. After landing and briefly explaining to them the events of the battle that occurred with Atomic Rex and Bravura, they agreed to use Steel Samurai 2.0 to act as the villagers' protector until they could find a new place to call home as Fortuna was too dangerously close to the radioactive remains of Acapulco. As they were watching over the villagers, Emily radioed back home to inform their family of what they were doing. She had never been gladder to hear the voice of her mother, husband, and even her brother. Chris was a little less pleased to hear his wife's voice as she unleashed a tirade of curses at him for bringing their daughter into a conflict with Atomic Rex. Chris ended the conversation with an "I love you, honey." He then looked over at Emily and said, "I may have to sleep in the mech a few days, but she'll get over it pretty quickly."

The mech followed the people until they reached an abandoned city that was formerly in the possession of the Hounds of Hades. With Steel Samurai 2.0's help, the villagers were able to clear away the debris and dead mutant coyote corpses from a partially demolished supermarket. Within the abandoned store there was enough canned food to support the villagers until Chris could fly down food from the settlement for them.

After a brief sweep of the area turned up no immediate threats to the villagers, Steel Samurai 2.0 flew off in the direction of Bravura's battle with Atomic Rex. When the mech reached the beach, they saw that nearly a half-mile of sand had been turned to glass from the heat of the explosion they had seen. While they did not see Atomic Rex, they did find a trail of footprints soaked in blood leading into the ocean. Unfortunately, there was no sign of Bravura. The Myers spent the next twenty-four hours searching the ocean and the surrounding area but there was no trace of the brave Cota or his mech, all save for Bravura's tattered cloak and both bo staffs in the irradiated battlefield.

Chris and Emily returned to the villagers where they then took Joaquín and his family into Steel Samurai 2.0. Chris flew to the ruins of Fortuna. Chris made a makeshift flag out of the cloak and the staffs. He planted it in the middle of the irradiated town and then he looked to the sky. "I only knew Enrique Cota for a short time, but I feel that in that time we formed a bond. He was a man of honor and courage. A man who lost everything and yet still deep within himself harbored a great love for his fellow human beings," Chris sighed. "When faced with the horrors of this world he was willing to fight and give his life for others because he felt that the lives of others were worth saving." Chris looked over at Emily and at Joaquín and his family. "I know what it's like to be ready to give your life to save others. Thankfully, I never had to actually make that sacrifice and I was rewarded for my actions with a loving family that a man like me had no right to ask for. Enrique gave his life for families like ours and the best thing we can do to honor his sacrifice is to love and support each other. That's what he gave his life for and the least we can do is to live up to being the people he believed we could be."

Joaquín walked over to the flag as he said, "You saved not only my family, but my entire village. You performed a miracle and for that we will always remember you for the saint that you are." He then fell to his knees and prayed for Enrique Cota's soul.

After the memorial for the Hunter ended, the two families flew back to the relocated villagers. Joaquín thanked them for their help and informed them that they would call this new village "Nueva Fortuna." Emily loved the name and asked her father why their home was only called "The Settlement." He shrugged and replied that she could give IT a proper name if she was elected town leader.

Chris and Emily decided to stay in Mexico for a few days so Emily could teach Joaquín how to train the Pitbull pups. The canned food also provided an excellent opportunity for Emily to work with Joaquín and his wife on establishing a positively reinforced relationship with the pups. She showed them that by feeding them, approaching them in a non-threatening manner, the creatures would slowly become accustomed to them. After three days of working with the pups, Joaquín attempted to let them out of their cage. Chris and Emily were ready to react with Steel Samurai 2.0 if the dogs became aggressive, but their fears were alleviated when the first pup stumbled out of the cage and licked Joaquín, covering him with saliva. Joaquín's wife and sons got a good laugh at the expense of Joaquín as the pups began their journey toward becoming humanity's future protectors.

Emily assured Joaquín that she would work with her mother and the people of Peru to establish the trade system they had discussed, then after a heartfelt goodbye, Chris and Emily climbed into Steel Samurai 2.0 and flew home.

As Steel Samurai flew home, deep in the ocean off the coast of Mexico, near the Sea of Cortez, Atomic Rex slept on the ocean floor. His body had nearly rid itself of the venom that was limiting his abilities. The nuclear theropod's remaining eye snapped open when he sensed another kaiju entering his hunting grounds. He had a vague memory of battling strange things that were being controlled by a strange feline-like creature he could not comprehend.

Atomic Rex's reptilian mind quickly pushed the thought of the feline-creature aside. He then rose off the ocean floor as his body took on a light blue glow. With the power of phoenix once again unhindered from coursing through his body, the saurian horror lifted his leg off the ground. As his leg slammed back into the seafloor, an Atomic Wave cascaded out of his body and killed any sea life caught within its wake. Now that his strength had begun to return, Atomic Rex swam in the direction of the beast that dared to hunt in his waters.

CHAPTER 22

The Settlement

Chris and Emily landed Steel Samurai near Emily's house where Sean, Kate, and Kyle were waiting for them. Emily quickly ran over to Sean. The burly man wrapped his thick arms around his wife, lifted her off the ground and passionately kissed her.

Chris walked to his wife who he could tell was not thrilled with him. He smiled. "Kate, it wasn't my intention to get Emily wrapped up with Atomic Rex. It just sort of worked out that way."

Before Kate could say anything, Emily walked over to her mother. "Mom, Dad tried to run to protect me, but I told him to stay and fight. You're always saying that the people of the settlement, which needs a more proper name by the way, look at me as a future leader. What kind of leader would I be if I turned and ran from danger while other people put their lives on the line?"

Kate sighed. "You'd be a leader who was alive if you turned and ran."

Chris smiled. "But by staying and fighting, you proved yourself to be a brave and selfless leader who thinks of others before herself. Just like your mother does." He looked at his wife. "She's your daughter. Where do you think she gets that *I have to act heroically in moments of need* streak in her from?"

Kate softened her look and smiled at her husband. "From both her parents, I guess. Look, I'm sorry if I came across as mad, I'm proud of you both, I really am. This new trade system looks like it could really benefit everyone. It's just that I get scared when my kids are in danger." She turned her head toward Emily and Kyle. "I have to remind myself that one of you is an adult and the other a teenager, and I have to treat you both as such."

Chris walked over to Kyle. "Have you had any luck looking for Atomic Rex?"

"Nothing yet. We haven't seen him since the explosion. I've been working with Gil and Rondel on tracking him as well. They haven't found any sign of him either. It's like he was either blown to pieces or maybe

192

taken into one of those portals like he was when he fought that Gurral monster."

Chris sighed. "Either way I hope he's gone for good, but knowing our luck I somehow doubt it."

Emily whispered into Sean's ear and then the newlyweds bid her family goodbye. They walked back to their house and when they closed the door Emily threw herself at her husband. After a long kiss she pulled away from him and she looked into his eyes.

"In Mexico it really struck home how much I want a family. I saw people who were dedicated to saving lives, people dedicated to keeping towns functional, and people who were dedicated to their family. My dad was one of the people who did all three and I met another man and his wife who did the same." She took a deep breath. "It made me realize how badly I want a family of our own."

Sean smiled. "Baby, you know that nothing would make me happier than to be a dad."

Emily gave her husband a sly look. "We'll get there, but to put things in farmer talk, you can understand let's not put the cart before the horse. While I want us to have family, there's plenty of fun to be had in making one."

Sean grinned from ear to ear as he scooped up Emily and headed for their bedroom.

In the computer house, Gil sat in front of the computer. He swallowed hard as he typed in the question he had been working up the courage to ask. *If I was to ask you to permanently remove Atomic Rex from our world, is that something you have the power to do?*

The two-face figure on the screen nodded as half of his face smiled and his answer appeared on the monitor. "*Yes, that's something I can do, but using that kind of power requires a great sacrifice, and I'd have to be on your plane of existence to make it happen.*" He looked through the monitor into Gil's eyes. "*Is that something you really want? Because every deal comes with a price.*"

EPILOGUE
Fortuna

Days later, the sun set on the last day any person stepped foot in the village that was the original Fortuna. However, this was not just any man, but rather it was a man housed in a tall, charred, damaged, yet miraculously still functional machine known as "Bravura." Against all odds, prior to the explosion, the soldier's machine was thrown back, inches away from being swept into the maw of the True Kaiju, the moment he let go of his unstable weapon. When the device exploded, taking its technological secrets with it, the mech was buried in the sand and would be encased in a coffin of crystalized glass as the flames extended outward.

The pilot was lucky that his machine was built for nuclear warfare and was thus safe from the dangers of radiation poisoning. Unconscious within his mech, he unwillingly took his long deserved rest when everyone else was looking for him. Eventually, he had awoken and fought his way out of his makeshift grave. Afterwards, the Hunter, who until recently remained nameless, eventually made his way back to Fortuna. It was here he found his flag, built in his honor. It was a sure enough sign that wherever the Myers, Joaquín Muñoz, his family along with the rest of the villagers were, they were all right. No longer did they need his help, especially with Steel Samurai and potentially the Pitbulls now looking over them.

Having been reminded of the Muñoz family, he looked to his wrist, still wearing the beaded bracelet the children made for him. He removed it and wrapped it around one of the levers that activated Bravura's transformation. This way he'd always be reminded of his time in this village every time he took control of his machine.

Before he left, he did figure that one day, Chris Myers or some other relative would return to this spot for one reason or another. In which case, they would find their flag missing, with a message etched into one of the surrounding rocks with Bravura's broken shield. It served as a response to a message he received in Morse code when he was unconscious.

"Thanks. Now the score is settled."

With both staff re-equipped and his cloak draped over his Colossus once more, the man who was known to many as "the Hunter" exited the village and marched off into the sunset. While he was unsure of what he would find out in the unknown, what he was sure about was his resolve to move forward and to make due on a promise he made long ago.

Coming Soon: The nigh omnipotent being known as Augustine takes
Atomic Rex into a realm of pure horror in

Atomic Rex: There was a Crookedman

Art by Garayann

Atomic Rex vs Bravura
By Danny Gray

CHECK OUT OTHER GREAT KAIJU NOVELS

KAIJU SPAWN
by David Robbins
& Eric S Brown

Wally didn't believe it was really the end of the world until he saw the Kaiju with his own eyes. The great beasts rose from the Earth's oceans, laying waste to civilization. Now Wally must fight his way across the Kaiju ravaged wasteland of modern day America in search of his daughter. He is the only hope she has left . . . and the clock is ticking.

From authors David Robbins (Endworld) and Eric S Brown (Kaiju Apocalypse), Kaiju Spawn is an action packed, horror tale of desperate determination and the battle to overcome impossible odds.

KUA MAU
by Mark Onspaugh

The Spider Islands. A mysterious ship has completed a treacherous journey to this hidden island chain. Their mission: to capture the legendary monster, Kua'Mau. Thinking they are successful, they sail back to the United States, where the terrifying creature will be displayed at a new luxury casino in Las Vegas. But the crew has made a horrible mistake - they did not trap Kua'Mau, they took her offspring. Now hot on their heels comes a living nightmare, a two hundred foot, one hundred ton tentacled horror, Kua'Mau, Kaiju Mother of Wrath, who will stop at nothing to safeguard her young. As she tears across California heading towards Vegas, she leaves a monumental body-count in her wake, and not even the U.S. military or private black ops can stop this city-crushing, havoc-wreaking monstrous mother of all Kaiju as she seeks her revenge.

CHECK OUT OTHER GREAT KAIJU NOVELS

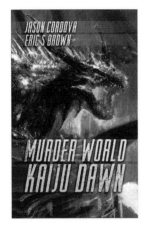

MURDER WORLD I KAIJU DAWN
by Jason Cordova
& Eric S Brown

Captain Vincente Huerta and the crew of the Fancy have been hired to retrieve a valuable item from a downed research vessel at the edge of the enemy's space.
It was going to be an easy payday.
But what Captain Huerta and the men, women and alien under his command didn't know was that they were being sent to the most dangerous planet in the galaxy.
Something large, ancient and most assuredly evil resides on the planet of Gorgon IV. Something so terrifying that man could barely fathom it with his puny mind. Captain Huerta must use every trick in the book, and possibly write an entirely new one, if he wants to escape Murder World.

KAIJU ARMAGEDDON
by Eric S. Brown

The attacks began without warning. Civilian and Military vessels alike simply vanished upon the waves. Crypto-zoologist Jerry Bryson found himself swept up into the chaos as the world discovered that the legendary beasts known as Kaiju are very real. Armies of the great beasts arose from the oceans and burrowed their way free of the Earth to declare war upon mankind. Now Dr. Bryson may be the human race's last hope in stopping the Kaiju from bringing civilization to its knees.
This is not some far distant future. This is not some alien world. This is the Earth, here and now, as we know it today, faced with the greatest threat its ever known. The Kaiju Armageddon has begun.

CHECK OUT OTHER GREAT KAIJU NOVELS

ATOMIC REX
by Matthew Dennion

The war is over, humanity has lost, and the Kaiju rule the earth.

Three years have passed since the US government attempted to use giant mechs to fight off an incursion of kaiju. The eight most powerful kaiju have carved up North America into their respective territories and their mutant offspring also roam the continent. The remnants of humanity are gathered in a remote settlement with Steel Samurai, the last of the remaining mechs, as their only protection. The mech is piloted by Captain Chris Myers who realizes that humanity will not survive if they stay at the settlement. In order to preserve the human race, he leaves the settlement unprotected as he engages on a desperate plan to draw the eight kaiju into each other's territories. His hope is that the kaiju will destroy each other. Chris will encounter horrors including the amorphous Amebos, Tortiraus the Giant turtle , and the nuclear powered mutant dinosaur Atomic Rex!

KAIJU DEADFALL
by JE Gurley

Death from space. The first meteor landed in the Pacific Ocean near San Francisco, causing an earthquake and a tsunami. The second wiped out a small Indiana city. The third struck the deserts of Nevada. When gigantic monsters- Ishom, Girra, and Nusku- emerge from the impact craters, the world faces a threat unlike any it had ever known - Kaiju . NASA catastrophist Gate Rutherford and Special Ops Captain Aiden Walker must find a way to stop the creatures before they destroy every major city in America..